A Christmas PROMISE

TIMELESS *Regency* COLLECTION

A Christmas PROMISE

Joanna Barker
Annette Lyon
Jennifer Moore

Mirror Press

Copyright © 2020 Mirror Press
Print edition
All rights reserved

No part of this book may be reproduced or distributed in any form whatsoever without prior written permission of the publisher, except in the case of brief passages embodied in critical reviews and articles. These novels are works of fiction. The characters, names, incidents, places, and dialog are products of the authors' imaginations and are not to be construed as real.

Interior Design by Cora Johnson
Edited by Kelsey Down, Jennie Stevens, and Lisa Shepherd
Cover design by Rachael Anderson
Cover Photo Credit: Stitch Stock Photo and Deposit Photos #91289936

Published by Mirror Press, LLC

A Christmas Promise is a Timeless Romance Anthology® book

Timeless Romance Anthology® is a registered trademark of Mirror Press, LLC

ISBN: 978-1-952611-02-5

TABLE OF CONTENTS

The Two Bells of Christmas by Joanna Barker _____ 1

Promise Me Again by Annette Lyon _____ 112

A Christmas Journey by Jennifer Moore _____ 205

TIMELESS REGENCY COLLECTIONS:

Autumn Masquerade
A Midwinter Ball
Spring in Hyde Park
Summer House Party
A Country Christmas
A Season in London
A Holiday in Bath
A Night in Grosvenor Square
Road to Gretna Green
Wedding Wagers
An Evening at Almack's
A Week in Brighton
To Love a Governess
Widows of Somerset
A Christmas Promise

One

CASSANDRA BELL LEANED her head against the cold window, staring out at the bleak and colorless December landscape outside their coach. Well, not colorless, exactly. But the bare trees and dead, dry grass did not inspire any great appreciation for nature at the moment.

A moan came from beside her, and Cassie winced as she turned to her sister. The constant bumping and swaying was enough to make anyone feel ill, but Vivian never traveled well to begin with. She slumped against the side of the coach, eyes glassy and unseeing.

"Are you certain you do not wish to stop?" Cassie asked yet again. Her twin sister's face was as green as the pea soup they'd eaten at the inn while their horses were changed. Though people often had difficulty telling the sisters apart, Cassie doubted anyone would have that trouble today.

Vivian only shook her head, gripping the bench beneath her so tightly that her hands turned white.

"You must know that stopping to rest an hour will hardly hurt your chances of marriage." Cassie attempted a bit of humor—she could always make Vivian smile.

But Vivian did not smile. She gulped a breath and shook her head once again. "No, we cannot stop. We must arrive early."

"Yes, of course," Cassie said dryly. "Because Roland Hastings will surely fall in love with you the moment he sees you looking like a sailor who hasn't yet found his sea legs."

Now Vivian shot her a scowl, though her inability to move without groaning made her infinitely less threatening. "I am certain I will feel better when we arrive at Hartfield Court. But I'll not stop now and lose any chance of spending time with Mr. Hastings before the other ladies arrive."

"Ladies? Tabbies might be the better word."

Vivian's lips twitched. "They certainly will be desperate to sink their claws into poor Mr. Hastings."

"I'm certain Mr. Hastings is many things," Cassie said, "but poor is not one of them." She did not bother to mention that Vivian was acting increasingly like a tabby herself. She was the one, after all, who insisted on arriving as early as possible for the Christmas house party at the Hastings estate, dragging Cassie with her. Now she was on her way to spend the holiday with a group of near strangers, when she would much rather be at home with Grandpapa.

Vivian sighed. "I only wish I knew what inspired the invitation. Was it solely from his mother, or did Mr. Hastings have a hand in it? I doubt he even remembers me at all." She pulled the coach blanket tighter around herself. The warm brick the coachman had laid at their feet had gone cold hours ago, and the winter chill had begun to creep inside.

"Of course he remembers you," Cassie insisted. "He danced with you twice at the Borlands' ball, and took you in to supper."

He would be more likely to remember Vivian than Cassie, at least. When Papa had introduced them to Mr. Hastings at the ball, Vivian had been ushered to the forefront, as was normal. Cassie had earned nothing more from the gentleman than a brief bow before he'd taken Vivian off to the dance floor. Her first—and only—impression of the man had not been terribly good.

Vivian had obviously not had the same impression, since she'd been pining after the gentleman since they'd returned from the Season months ago. When the invitation to the house party arrived, it had caused a celebration the likes of which had not been seen since Wellington's victory at Waterloo.

Vivian looked unconvinced. "I hope you are right, but I am still determined to do what I can to claim his attention. I'll not leave such a thing as love to chance."

Cassie raised an eyebrow. Did her sister's ambitions toward Mr. Hastings truly run so deep? "I think the poets might disagree with that sentiment."

Vivian flapped her hand feebly as she leaned back. "Oh, you know what I mean. I just think Mr. Hastings will need a bit of encouragement, and I should like to offer it first."

"You're more likely to frighten him off than encourage him, the way you're looking now."

Vivian sent her a mock glare. "Any slight about my looks is also against yours."

"Nonsense," Cassie said with a grin. "Everyone knows I'm the prettier twin."

Vivian gave a weak laugh, closing her eyes. "Today that is certainly true."

"Hush now." Cassie tucked her sister's blanket against her. "No more jesting. Try and rest."

Vivian nodded, already half asleep, and Cassie blew out a breath. The next fortnight would be a bore, no doubt, playing her sister's companion as Vivian attempted to entice a proposal from the ever-elusive Mr. Hastings. The invitation had been for Vivian and their mother, but since Mama had been forced to decline due to a younger sister being only weeks from childbirth, Cassie had been sent as a reluctant replacement.

"Do mind yourself," Mama had said reproachfully as Cassie bid her farewell yesterday morning. "Your sister's future depends on this house party, as does yours. If she can make such a conquest as Mr. Roland Hastings, surely you'll soon attract suitors of your own."

"Oh yes, because my foremost requirement for a husband is that he marry me for my family connections."

Mama had not found that particularly funny. "That tongue of yours is precisely why I am uneasy sending you. But as I have no choice, I shall have to hope—nay, pray—you realize behaving yourself is in Vivian's best interest."

Cassie had sighed and kissed her mother on the cheek. "I will bite my tongue, Mama. You needn't worry on my account."

After all, Cassie hardly planned on bringing any amount of attention to herself during the next fortnight. She would do as she always did during social events: hide when she could and keep her mouth shut when she couldn't. It wasn't that she did not like people, or that she was particularly shy. But experience had proven that if Cassie found something interesting or amusing, society generally thought the opposite, and she had learned it was better to keep her thoughts to herself.

Cassie jumped as Vivian suddenly sat up straight beside her, grasping the sides of the swaying coach.

"Viv?" Cassie watched her anxiously. "What is wrong?"

Vivian did not answer. She lurched forward and fumbled with the latch on the window, pulling it open and sticking her head out. Then she expelled the contents of her stomach onto the moving scenery outside.

Cassie moved quickly. She snatched her sister's curls back to keep them from blowing across her face, the only help she could offer as Vivian heaved again and again, the coach coming to a stop under the oppressive gray sky.

Lovely. They had yet to set one foot inside Hartfield Court, and already this house party was off to an excellent start.

Two

ROLAND HASTINGS LEANED forward in the coach as Hartfield finally came into view through the oak trees lining the drive. He didn't mind London, not really, but his last months there had drained his reserves of patience and energy.

Seeing now the comforting white stone and Grecian columns of his family home in Hampshire brought a relief he hadn't realized he'd been longing for. At last, some quiet and solitude. And surely Mother had a warm meal waiting for him, even if he had been delayed in London an extra day.

But as they approached the front doors, he spotted an unfamiliar coach already stopped before the steps. That was not surprising in and of itself—his mother was quite popular—though it was late in the day for visitors. What did surprise him was the flurry of activity surrounding the coach as servants unloaded trunks and carried them into the house.

Roland threw open the door and stepped down before the coachman brought the equipage to a complete halt. He scaled the steps and marched inside. "Mother?" he called, tugging off his gloves.

No response, but female voices came from down the corridor. He handed a footman his gloves, greatcoat, and hat, then strode to the sitting room, where he found his mother in deep conversation with the housekeeper. Mother's dark, graying hair was tucked up inside a mob cap, and she wore a black dress edged in lace. The sight of her made him pause in the doorway. He'd hoped while he'd been gone she might have allowed some gray or lavender back into her wardrobe. But it appeared that a year was still not long enough for her to grieve her husband.

He swallowed hard but stepped forward. "Might I enquire as to whose coach has taken up residence outside?"

Mother looked up, and her eyes brightened. "Roland, you're home!" She stood and embraced him, the smell of her perfume encircling him in a cloud of jasmine and memories.

He allowed her a moment before pulling back and fixing her with a stern look. "You may try and distract me, but I assure you it will not work."

"Hush, you've been gone for months." She tugged his jacket straight. "Allow me to fuss over you a bit."

"Mother..."

She stepped back with a sigh and gestured to the housekeeper, who scurried from the room. "Oh, all right. But it is entirely your fault, arriving home late. I'd planned on more time to tell you."

"Tell me *what?*"

"I've organized a little house party." She waved a hand, as if that would dismiss the sinking sensation in Roland's stomach. "Just a few friends to pass the time until Christmas."

"Until Christmas?" The disbelief in his voice could not begin to match the dismay inside him. "You mean to tell me I've come home anticipating a quiet holiday, and instead I must entertain guests for a fortnight?"

Mama raised her chin. "I've been lonely while you've been away. You cannot deny me some company."

"And you could not have had this company while I was gone?"

She swept back to her chair by the crackling fire. "I was certain you would not wish to miss it."

He gave a short laugh as he ran a hand through his hair. "I think you were certain of the opposite, which is why you did not tell me."

She offered a pained look. "It is hardly my fault you insisted on being a hermit for the last four months."

"I am busy. That does not make me a hermit."

She went on as if he hadn't spoken. "I am only trying to broaden your circle of acquaintances. You'll never meet any ladies of quality if you hole yourself up in your study for weeks on end."

"Ladies?" Roland raised a finger. "Please do not tell me you invited a horde of young women to this house party."

She huffed. "A horde? Do not be ridiculous. I only invited three or four, all accomplished and well-bred."

He nearly threw up his hands. What was she thinking, ambushing him like this? "I am leaving. Going back to London this instant."

His mother straightened, her severe gaze seizing Roland in a vicelike grip. "You most certainly are not," she hissed. "I have put up with your nonsense for long enough. First you carouse your way through the Season, and then you abandon me for months on end."

Roland stepped back. "I haven't abandoned you. You know I had to see to my investments."

"All I know is I have been more than patient, but it is high time you took your responsibilities seriously."

"I have," he insisted. What did she think he'd been doing all that time in London? "The estate is running smoothly, and if all goes well, the return on my new investments will be more than enough to—"

"Not your financial responsibility." Mother clasped her hands in her lap. "Your responsibility to provide an *heir*."

His mouth went dry. Of course. He exhaled and walked

to the window, the panes edged in frost. "I'm not yet thirty, Mother. I hardly see that as shirking my duties."

"*If* something does not happen to you." She leaned forward. "What if you suffered an accident and died? You would leave me alone and penniless, forced to relinquish Hartfield to that odious cousin of yours."

Roland sighed. "You would not be penniless, Mother. I know what Father left you."

"That is beside the point. You made a promise, and I intend to make you keep it."

Roland braced his hands against the windowsill as the memory stole back into his mind. His father lay in bed as Roland clasped his limp hand, his raspy voice insisting that Roland marry and continue the family line. Roland could do nothing but agree. In truth, he'd always known he would marry, so it had seemed an easy thing to promise. That is, until he'd actually made an attempt to find a bride.

"I will marry," Roland said now, still staring out the window. "I promised, and I will."

"Then why can't you see this house party for the opportunity it is?" Mother asked. "I made the invitations very carefully, and I do not think you will find your guests lacking."

He turned to face her. "Who have you invited?"

A triumphant smile leaped across her face. "Miss Tindale and her mother, of course, since you have always been friends."

Friends was perhaps a stretch, but it was true Roland did know the young lady better than most, since their fathers had been good friends in life. But he'd never given her more than a second thought as far as marriage was concerned.

"And?" he prompted, moving to the seat beside hers.

"The Marsdens will be attending, and I must tell you, Miss Marsden has grown quite pretty."

The Marsdens were nearby neighbors, but he couldn't begin to bring an image of Miss Marsden to mind. Was she the timid one with the brown hair? He likely hadn't seen her in over a year.

"And the Bell sisters have just arrived, though I admit I hesitated a bit over that invitation."

Roland looked up. "The Bells? Are they the twins?"

He'd met the Bell family in London last Season and had even danced with Miss Vivian Bell, if he remembered correctly. He had found nothing offensive about her, which was almost unfortunate. He'd hoped to critique his mother's choice in houseguests.

"Yes, the twins." Mother frowned. "I do like the elder Miss Bell, but I cannot say I entirely approve of the younger sister."

"How can you know she is younger? They look exactly the same." He'd had to look twice at the two sisters when he'd first seen them at a ball. Golden-blond hair, bright-blue eyes, and their pert features unnervingly identical.

"I *know*," his mother said coolly. "In any case, I was disappointed to learn that the mother would be unable to attend and that Miss Cassandra would come in her absence. But I assure you you'll find the other young ladies perfectly acceptable." She raised a finger. "And you will treat them well, no matter that you did not want them here."

A shrill meow came from behind him, and his mother's cat, Sir Chester, came slinking into the room. It leaped onto Mother's lap, and she stroked its back distractedly, still watching Roland closely.

Roland crossed his arms, not wanting to give in so easily, not when he knew she must have been planning this for months. "I won't be rude to our guests," he said. "I am civilized enough for that."

"I want more than civility, Roland." Mother's voice softened unexpectedly. "I want you to *try*."

He was half tempted to give a cheeky retort, but he stopped himself. She only wanted the best for him, even if he didn't at all agree with her methods.

"Let us make an arrangement," he said finally. "If I promise to allow this house party a chance, *you* must promise that if nothing comes of it, you'll let me be. You will not attempt to play matchmaker in the future."

Mother considered his offer, then nodded. "Very well. I accept your terms. But know I will be watching."

He groaned. "Yes, because nothing encourages romance like the watchful eye of a potential mother-in-law."

She picked up the paper she'd been perusing when he'd arrived, one hand still stroking Sir Chester's back. "You'll manage somehow, I am sure. Now go and dress for dinner. Our other guests will arrive shortly."

"All right," he said. "But come Christmas, I expect to have my house back."

Mother only gave a sly smile. "Hopefully with one new addition."

He blew out a frustrated breath as he left the room and started up the main staircase. Was there a worse way to spend Christmas than an entire fortnight with three young women determined to pry a proposal from him?

He would not come away unscathed.

Three

OF ONE THING Cassie was absolutely certain: her sister had gone mad.

Though Vivian had spent the last two hours of their journey alternatively moaning or sticking her head out the window, she now slumped weakly in an armchair as she and Jennings deliberated over dresses.

"No, not that one," she said, her voice faint. "Try the white."

Jennings set down the blue gown and rifled through the trunk.

Cassie rubbed her forehead. "You cannot be serious, Viv. Mama wouldn't let you attend dinner tonight in your condition, and neither shall I."

"I am just a bit queasy from the ride, that's all." Vivian clenched the arms of the chair in her shaking hands.

"This is more than a bit of queasiness," Cassie insisted. "I think you might be truly ill. Can't we send for a doctor?"

When the sisters had arrived at Hartfield Court a half hour ago, Vivian had said nothing of her illness. Instead, she'd plastered a smile on her face while greeting Mrs. Hastings. As soon as the housekeeper had shown them their rooms, she had collapsed in a chair and hadn't stood since.

"I cannot see a doctor." Vivian's voice had taken on a strange insistence. "I need to attend dinner tonight."

"You can barely stand." Cassie strode to Jennings and took the white-silk gown from her hands. "You certainly cannot endure an entire night, even in the name of love."

A knock came at the door, and the housekeeper peeked inside the room. "Pardon, Miss Cassandra, but your trunk has been brought to your room."

"Thank you." Cassie was desperate to change into something that did not smell like—well, like retch. She turned back to her sister. "Will you please lie down until I change, at least? Then I might stop planning your funeral."

Vivian sighed. "All right. For a few minutes."

After helping Vivian to the canopied bed and tucking her into the blankets, Cassie went to the room the housekeeper had shown her when they'd arrived and hurried to the trunk set at the foot of the bed. She undid the latches and propped open the lid—then stared. Her eyes were met not by petticoats and stockings, but by white-linen shirts, bold-colored waistcoats, and a stack of neatly pressed handkerchiefs.

She took up a handkerchief. What on earth? She stepped back and inspected the trunk. It looked like hers at first glance, but no, the leather was a darker color, and the buckles more gold than bronze. The footmen must have confused her trunk for someone else's—surely a gentleman arriving for the party.

Gentleman. Cassie's face heated, and she slammed shut the trunk before she saw anything scandalous. She hurried back into the corridor, intent on finding the housekeeper. But halfway to the stairs, a door flung open in front of her. She yelped and threw out her hands to stop it from smashing into her face.

"Blast," a masculine voice said, and a man stepped from behind the door. Dark hair, thick brows, and the deep-brown eyes that had entranced half of London during the Season. "I'm terribly sorry. Are you all right?"

Cassie shook out her hand, still stinging from slamming against the hard wood of the door. "I'd be better if you hadn't nearly broken my nose." Did Mr. Hastings always run around throwing open doors haphazardly?

He winced. "My apologies. Miss Bell, is it?" Then he squinted at her. "Or is it Miss Cassandra?"

She could hardly be annoyed with him for being unable to tell her and Vivian apart. But she wasn't yet reconciled to forgiveness.

"Cassandra," she said coolly, offering a brief curtsy. "A pleasure, Mr. Hastings, but I'm afraid there has been some mix-up and—"

His eyes wandered to her hand, where she still clutched the handkerchief from the trunk, and he nodded unexpectedly. "Ah, I think I've solved the mystery. Might I guess that your trunk does not contain your usual belongings? Mine was shockingly filled with ruffles and lace."

Cassie blanched. Had Mr. Hasting rifled through her things? "You didn't—"

He held up his hands. "I did not touch a thing, though that is more than you can say."

The handkerchief itched in her hand, as if accusing her. She held it out to him immediately. "I thought it might identify the owner."

He took it. "Success. Shall we correct this mistake?"

She expected him to call for a footman to switch the trunks, but he instead disappeared back through the doorway. Cassie reluctantly followed him down a short corridor to what she assumed was his room. She peered inside as he went to the trunk—*her* trunk—and hefted it into his arms. Rather easily, she admitted reluctantly.

"Now, which room is yours?" he said, carefully maneuvering through the doorway.

Cassie started down the corridor, and he followed with heavy footsteps. She glanced back to find him already watching her with narrowed eyes. She cleared her throat. "Pardon my asking, Mr. Hastings, but are you only now arriving?"

When they'd arrived earlier, she hadn't thought to wonder about his absence when Mrs. Hastings greeted them. She'd been far too concerned with helping a staggering Vivian to her room, barely avoiding a repeat performance of the incident in the coach.

Mr. Hastings frowned. "Yes, I was delayed in London, and I'm afraid a great many unexpected obstacles have made their way into my life today."

Did he mean their trunks? It seemed such a small thing to make him frown so. But Cassie refrained from saying anything more. If Vivian was successful in her endeavor, this man would be her future brother-in-law. She hardly wanted him thinking worse of her than he already did, considering he already assumed she'd ransacked his trunk.

"Here it is," she said as they stepped into her room. She gestured at the open trunk. "As you can see, I did not touch anything beside the handkerchief."

He sent her an odd look as he set her trunk on the floor. "I hope you know I was only joking about that."

"Oh." She cleared her throat. "Well, good. Thank you for your help, Mr. Hastings."

He raised an eyebrow at her dismissal but did not protest as he lifted his trunk. "Of course, Miss Cassandra."

He made his way back to the door, and she moved to her trunk, wanting to reassure herself that all was in order.

"By the way," Mr. Hastings called from the doorway. She looked up. "I am also quite fond of cherry comfits." He flashed a grin and vanished down the corridor, leaving her staring after him.

Then her eyes dropped to her trunk, and she opened it. She'd carefully packed her package from the apothecary, but apparently the wrapping had come loose during the journey, and the small sweets wrapped in twists of paper had spilled all over her trunk.

"Drat," she muttered. She began scooping up the comfits and depositing them on the nearby writing desk. Now Mr. Hastings thought her a snoop *and* a glutton. Mama would be so proud.

When her trunk was free of sweets, she changed quickly, used to dressing without help since Vivian often monopolized Jennings's time. Then she hurried back to her sister's room.

"I must tell you," she said, slipping inside. "I just had the strangest meeting—"

Cassie stopped. Vivian was not resting on the bed. Instead, her sister sat beside the chamber pot on the floor, leaning her head against the wall.

"Oh, Vivian." Cassie went to her and helped her sit on the edge of the bed. Where had Jennings gone? "You cannot still be thinking of going down to dinner."

"No," Vivian said, still pale. "I think it is very clear I cannot."

"Good." Finally she was seeing reason. "Now you must—"

"But you can," Vivian interrupted.

Cassie crossed her arms. "There is no point in me going down. *I* haven't set my cap for anyone, and I would rather stay with you." Truthfully, Cassie was relieved. Now she had the perfect excuse to miss the first evening of the house party. Who would insist she play parlor games when she was needed to nurse her dear sister back to health?

But Vivian only shook her head, a look of determination claiming her eyes. "Cassie, I need your help."

Cassie squinted at her. "Of course. That is why I want to stay with you."

"No, you do not understand." Vivian's arms were trembling. "We need to switch."

Cassie dropped her arms. "Switch? Why?"

They hadn't switched places in years, not since they'd found it amusing to trick their horrible French governess. And of course they'd done it endless times as young girls, to the exasperation of their mother, but it had only ever been in fun.

Vivian took a deep breath. "You know how I feel about Mr. Hastings, and what my hopes are. But . . ." She swallowed. "But if I cannot be there tonight, I may as well give up now. Miss Tindale is everything that is charming, beautiful, and accomplished."

"So are you," Cassie insisted. "Mr. Hastings knows this." Despite her words, she was far from certain. He hadn't looked particularly thrilled to see Cassie in the hallway, even for the short second he thought she was Vivian.

Vivian ignored her. "You must pretend to be me and ensure that Miss Tindale does not entirely commandeer Mr. Hastings."

"And why can't I do that as myself? I can distract him just as well without going through all this pretense."

"Because I need to maintain my reputation," she insisted. "Who wishes to marry a sickly girl who hides away in her bedchamber?"

"I see. So instead, Cassandra Bell will be the sickly girl who hides away in her bedchamber."

"But you do not care what people think of you."

That was true, for the most part. But somehow it made Cassie uneasy, that the peculiar Mr. Hastings would think of her that way.

"Please?" Vivian begged. "It would just be for tonight.

You know I never stay ill for long. We can both rejoin the party tomorrow."

"This is ridiculous." Cassie rubbed her forehead. "You cannot be serious."

"Why not? No one can tell us apart."

Cassie threw up her hands. "We are not fourteen years old anymore, Viv. There is no possible way I can convince an entire household, not when they already know the *real* you."

"Of course you can," Vivian said, her voice fading. "You know me better than anyone."

"That does not mean I can *be* you."

"But you must. This is too important." Then Vivian's eyebrows lifted. "Think, Cassie. If I am married before the Season, you needn't go to London."

That gave Cassie pause. The both of them knew very well that Mama had only brought Cassie to London because leaving her at home while parading Vivian around would have sparked rumors. But Vivian was the daughter on whom their parents had pinned their hopes for a great match—which, of course, Cassie was perfectly content with. She hardly wanted *more* attention.

And while London had been all good and well in its own way—the food and entertainment, at least—she could certainly do without it. *Especially* if it meant avoiding awkward dances with men she hardly knew or tagging along on never-ending social visits. She much preferred their quiet country home and the company of Grandpapa. He was the only one who laughed rather than cringed when Cassie said something absurd.

If Cassie did what Vivian wanted . . . if she could succeed in helping her sister secure a match with Mr. Hastings . . .

Vivian's shoulders slumped as her energy waned.

"You are going to faint," Cassie said, moving closer. "Lie down."

Vivian jutted her chin. "Not until you promise you'll do it."

Cassie blew out a breath. How could she even be considering this? Vivian was proper and lovely and good. Cassie was . . . not. But could she pretend for long enough to salvage Vivian's hopes for the future?

"One night," she finally said. "I will go to dinner tonight."

Vivian flung her arms around Cassie, who staggered under her sister's weight. "Oh, thank you. I knew you would agree."

"Now into bed with you," Cassie ordered. She helped Vivian to lie back and pulled the blankets up tight around her chin. "And *you* must promise to let me call for a doctor if you are still unwell tomorrow."

"I promise," Vivian said solemnly.

Cassie exhaled. "This will end in disaster, I am certain."

Vivian closed her eyes, as if their conversation had exhausted her completely. Which it likely had. "You'll be perfect, I have no doubt."

No matter. Cassie had enough doubts for the both of them.

Four

THE SECOND ROLAND stepped into the drawing room, he regretted agreeing to his mother's ridiculous plan.

All eyes turned to him. Mr. and Mrs. Marsden and their daughter—who *was* the timid, brown-haired creature he'd vaguely remembered. Miss Tindale and her hawkeyed mother, who stood in the corner, separate from the others. And Mother, of course, who presided over it all with a careful determination.

Roland squared his shoulders and forced a smile. He greeted each guest in turn, making a special effort to converse with both Miss Marsden and Miss Tindale as his mother would want. It wasn't their fault she had arranged this entire debacle, after all. That was also why he'd forced himself to be polite when he'd met Miss Cassandra in the upstairs corridor earlier, even when she'd nearly accused him of sorting through her petticoats.

Though he hadn't been able to resist that last parting shot about her large stash of comfits. He'd rather enjoyed the embarrassment that flashed across her face. He glanced around the drawing room. Where *were* the Bell sisters?

"How was your journey from London, Mr. Hastings?"

Miss Tindale came to his side, smiling brightly as she tipped her head, her brown curls framing her heart-shaped face. Once he might have been immediately taken in by such a pretty face. But after last Season, after months of dancing and flirting and talking, after making every effort to find a woman he could build a life with . . .

Now he was more cautious—and realistic. He'd almost given up the idea of marriage entirely and decided to focus on his work instead, but if these young ladies would be staying at his home for a fortnight, then he might as well follow through on his promise to Mother. He still wanted to marry; he just wasn't certain the Fates agreed with him.

Now he forced a smile to his face. "My journey was excellent. And yours, Miss Tindale?"

"Oh, perfectly lovely. I so enjoy traveling, and the countryside here is beautiful."

He almost laughed. The landscape was drab and bleak in the middle of December. But she was only being gracious. He could hardly fault her for it.

"Are you looking forward to Christmas, Mr. Hastings?" Miss Tindale asked. "I admit I've never been particularly fond of the holiday, but surely your mother has a host of wonderful things planned for us all."

"Yes, I am certain—" he began.

"Good evening!"

The high, breathy voice interrupted him, and he turned to see a halo of golden curls and vivid sky-blue eyes. "Mr. Hastings, Miss Tindale," the young lady said, dropping two bobbing curtsies in quick succession.

"Ah, Miss . . ." He hesitated. "Miss Cassandra, is it?"

She shook her head quickly, as if eager to correct him. "No, sir, I am Vivian."

So this was Miss Vivian Bell. Blast, it was a dreadful task to keep the two of them sorted out. "And where is your sister?" he asked.

"I'm afraid Cassandra is feeling ill today." Miss Bell clasped her gloved hands. "You shall have to make due with just me."

Roland squinted. "Ill? But I saw her only a few hours ago. She looked perfectly well to me."

"Oh?" Miss Bell's eyes widened almost alarmingly. "How odd. I think the journey simply did not agree with her. I daresay she'll be recovered by tomorrow."

At least that would make the sisters easier to keep track of in the meantime. Not that he wished the younger Miss Bell to be sick. In fact, he had almost begun to anticipate meeting her again, to see if she might say anything about their earlier interactions. But it was better this way. After all, Vivian was the one his mother had specifically invited for him.

"How good to see you again, Miss Bell." Miss Tindale slipped seamlessly into the conversation. "I am sorry to hear about your sister, but so long as her condition is not serious, I hope she can join us soon enough."

"Yes, of course," Miss Bell said, and then stood with her mouth slightly parted, as if she knew she ought to say something else, but could not quite manage it. She glanced around. "This room is lovely. I like the—the colors. And the windows." She shifted her weight. "Of course, Miss Tindale, you look lovely as well, with your . . ." She wafted a hand over her own head, indicating that she meant Miss Tindale's elaborate hairstyle enhanced by two tall, white feathers. "And Mr. Hastings, you look—" She broke off, clearly struggling for words. "You also look lovely?"

She had used the word *lovely* thrice in the span of twenty seconds. And he wasn't certain he had ever heard the term applied to a man.

"Thank you, Miss Bell," he said, casting a confused look at Miss Tindale. She, of course, was too practiced in the ways of society to show any reaction save for a slight arch to her eyebrow.

They were all saved from further interaction by Mrs. Hastings's announcement that dinner was ready. Roland excused himself and moved to escort the matronly Mrs. Marsden into dinner, as was proper, yet he could not help a glance back. Miss Tindale had rejoined her mother, but Miss Bell stood with her hands on her waist, shoulders slumped. As he watched, she let out a short puff of air from the side of her mouth, blowing a curl from her face. Then she met his eyes. She straightened suddenly, as if he had caught her doing something rather wicked.

During the Season, Roland had spent—at most—a few hours with Miss Vivian Bell, and he had assessed her to be everything society wished for in a young lady: poised, proper, and polite. But tonight it seemed as though something had set the young lady on edge.

Though, of course, this entire house party could certainly be reason enough. Roland was unsure if Miss Bell, Miss Tindale, and Miss Marsden knew precisely why they'd been invited, but they had to at least suspect. What was he to do, court all three in the hopes that one would somehow be all he was searching for in a wife?

He pushed back those thoughts as he offered his arm to Mrs. Marsden. He could not think that far ahead. He *could* be kind and polite, as his mother wanted.

At least for two weeks.

Dinner was *not* going well.

First, Cassie sat too quickly as the footman pushed her chair in, and she almost dropped to the floor. Thankfully, she caught herself on the edge of the table, and no one noticed.

Then she spilled her glass of wine and stained the white tablecloth nearly the entire length of the table, which *everyone* noticed, though Mrs. Hastings assured her it was nothing.

Why on earth had she agreed to this switch? Her nerves were as frayed as her favorite shawl. She never felt entirely comfortable in company on a normal day, but neither was she ever this incompetent. At this rate, she would out her own charade in an attempt to save her sanity.

She steadied herself with deep breaths. Thankfully, she was seated beside Mrs. Tindale, who was far too focused on her daughter across the table to speak to Cassie. Miss Tindale had somehow managed to secure a seat near Mr. Hastings and had claimed his attention for most of dinner.

Which, Cassie realized belatedly, was exactly the sort of thing she was supposed to prevent while playing Vivian. She'd been so caught up in her fears of being found out that she'd forgotten her purpose. When at last Mrs. Hastings rose to lead the women from the dining room, Cassie followed with new determination. She would do what Vivian would do. She would not let Miss Tindale dominate the drawing room as she had dinner.

And she would *not* use the word *lovely*.

Cassie passed an awkward few minutes making conversation with the shy Miss Marsden, who somehow seemed more uncomfortable than Cassie. Was she always like this? Surely she wasn't also pretending to be her twin sister.

Thankfully the men joined them rather quickly, which was unsurprising, as the male portion of the party included only Mr. Hastings and the elder Mr. Marsden. As soon as Mr. Hastings stepped inside, Cassie excused herself and moved to intercept him. But before she could take two steps, Miss Tindale swooped in like a falcon after a rabbit. How could she move so fast and yet so gracefully? Cassie pushed her chin up a notch. She would not back away. She joined the two of them as Miss Tindale began questioning him about the landscape painting that hung above the fireplace.

"That is our family house in Yorkshire," Mr. Hastings said, clasping his hands behind his back. "Willow Cottage."

"The artist is quite talented," Miss Tindale said. "What pretty colors. I daresay it is something of a masterpiece."

Cassie examined the painting. Were Miss Tindale's eyes going dim? "I would hardly call it a masterpiece," she said. Now was Cassie's chance to set herself apart from the other ladies. "Why, if the house was actually at that scale compared to the coach, even a child would be hard-pressed to make it through the doorways. And the sheep look a bit more like clouds with legs rather than animals."

If Cassie had thought she might impress with her detailed critique, she was quickly proven wrong as she was met by silence and bewilderment.

Mr. Hastings gave a slight cough. "This painting was done by my mother."

Oh, dear.

"That is," Cassie said frantically, "the brushstrokes are skillfully done, as is the general . . . uh . . . landscape." She had *told* Vivian this would be a disaster.

But perhaps Mrs. Hastings had not heard. Cassie glanced behind her—and was met by the woman's fierce scowl from where she sat not ten feet away. Drat. Never mind the spilt wine—she'd gone and insulted the mother of the man her sister hoped to marry.

"*I* think it a beautiful painting," Miss Tindale said smoothly. "If the actual Willow Cottage is half so pretty as its rendering here, I should be very pleased to see it one day."

Miss Tindale sent Cassie a knowing smile. Of course. The minx must have known Mrs. Hastings had painted the picture—hence why she'd complimented it in the first place.

But Cassie held her tongue. She'd already done enough damage to Vivian's reputation tonight as it was.

Miss Tindale turned the conversation to other topics, and Cassie slipped away and retreated to the far corner of the room, where the cold and dark leeched through the windows as she sat primly on a chair. If she could keep herself far enough away . . .

"Are you determined to exile yourself, then?"

Cassie jerked her head up. Mr. Hastings had followed her across the room, leaving everyone else staring in his wake, though they tried to pretend otherwise. He stood beside her, his eyes amused.

She cleared her throat. "Only until I learn a bit of prudence."

"Prudence is all good and well," he said, taking the chair beside hers. "But so is honesty. And I must admit I've often thought the same thing of the cloud sheep."

"I appreciate you voicing your opinion now, rather than two minutes ago," Cassie said dryly.

Mr. Hastings grinned. "Never mind my mother. She'll have forgotten by tomorrow."

Cassie highly doubted that, but then it wasn't *his* head Mrs. Hastings was currently glaring daggers at.

"Be that as it may," she said, "I think it best to keep my head down."

He leaned back in his chair. "Probably wise for the moment. My mother has never been one to enjoy criticism."

"Does anyone?"

"No, I suppose not." Mr. Hastings wore a thoughtful expression. "Tell me, Miss Bell, what qualifies you to appraise artwork? Are you a painter?"

She almost laughed, but she managed to cut the sound off with a cough. No, Cassie was not a painter. But Vivian was.

The only reason Cassie had even thought to mention the flaws of Mrs. Hastings's painting was because of the many hours her sister had dragged her from museum to museum in London.

"Yes, I paint," she said. Was it a lie if it *was* true about Vivian? Cassie hadn't had time to untangle the moral ambiguities of what she was doing. "Though from my unkind words about your mother's painting, you might assume a higher level of expertise than I actually possess."

"As I have no artistic inclinations whatsoever, you still claim an advantage over me." He tipped his head. "And what do you like to paint?"

"Oh." She paused. Why was he pursuing this conversation? She'd just made a fool of herself in front of the entire party. Did he feel sorry for her, or perhaps feel as if he owed her time, having already spent a good portion of the evening with Miss Tindale? "I paint a bit of everything, I suppose." Cassie tried to remember which subjects filled Vivian's canvases most often. "Landscapes, flowers, animals."

"Animals?"

"Yes, we've something of a menagerie at Brightling Place. My father raises hunting dogs, and many of our tenants also raise sheep and goats. And of course there is the parrot."

Mr. Hastings raised an eyebrow. "Why, of course. Because what country estate is complete without a parrot?"

Cassie laughed. "It belongs to my grandfather. He purchased it from a sailor who seemed desperate to be rid of it, for reasons that soon became obvious."

"You are keeping me in suspense, Miss Bell."

Miss Bell. It shouldn't feel so strange to be addressed as such. It *was* Cassie's name too, after all. But as the older sister, Vivian had always been Miss Bell.

Cassie cleared her throat. "We soon learned that the bird knew only a few phrases and repeated them with unbridled enthusiasm—which would not have been so terrible if the phrases had been more . . . appropriate."

Mr. Hastings's lips twitched. "You are saying the parrot dared to use unsuitable language in front of a young lady?"

"*Dares.*" Cassie emphasized the present tense. "My grandfather loves the old bird too much to be rid of it. He used to travel a great deal as a young man, and I believe the parrot helps him relive those times."

Talking of Grandpapa caused an acute ache in Cassie's chest. She'd left Brightling only two days before, but she already missed him dreadfully. There was no one she felt more free with, more herself—save for Vivian, of course. Although lately Cassie felt as though even Vivian was drifting farther away, especially since the Season. Marriage had become of the utmost importance to her, and Cassie could not quite summon the same enthusiasm.

"You are fond of your grandfather." Mr. Hastings watched her with a curious sharpness, one hand rubbing his chin.

"Yes," she said hesitantly. Why did it feel as if their conversation had suddenly turned into an odd sort of test? "Very much so."

He smiled, and Cassie's heartbeat took an unexpected tumble. He *was* handsome, after all, with that dark hair and those brown eyes, long lashes, and sharp cheekbones. Had she never looked at the man closely before? Or had she convinced herself society thought too highly of him and dismissed him without real consideration?

"Or perhaps," he said, "you are simply fond of your grandfather's improper parrot."

Cassie did like the silly parrot—she thought it rather hilarious. But *Vivian* did not. Or at least she did not laugh anymore when Grandpapa brought the bird into the drawing room after dinner. She looked more like Mama, who clenched her jaw with every word that escaped the parrot's mouth.

"I ..." Cassie hesitated. She'd already shown Mr. Hastings perhaps a bit too much of her own personality tonight. She needed to let Vivian take control now. "I admit I did like it when I was younger. But now I find its language disconcerting, especially as I aspire to absolute propriety."

There. That ought to help Vivian's image.

But it seemed to have the opposite effect. Mr. Hastings straightened, and the gleam in his eyes disappeared. "Yes, of course," he said. "I would never insinuate you are less than ladylike."

"No, I did not mean—"

He shook his head. "No matter. I understand." He stood and offered a brief smile. "My mother needs me."

Indeed, his mother was gesturing at him across the room, her scowl from earlier gone, though the hard lines around her eyes remained.

Mr. Hasting offered a short bow, and for a moment his expression softened. "I hope we have more time to talk during the party, Miss Bell. I look forward to knowing you better."

Heat crept across her cheeks. Cassie seldom blushed, but that was due to the rarity of a man's attention more than any other reason. "As do I," she managed with a nod.

He left to rejoin his mother, and Cassie tried not to let her eyes linger on his shoulders, his tall frame, as he walked away.

She did not succeed.

Five

"You must tell me everything." Vivian propped herself up on shaking arms, her face pale, as Cassie slipped into her room that night. "This instant."

"Can it wait until morning?" Cassie pulled pins from her hair, letting her curls loose from their tight constraints. "It is exhausting pretending to be you. How can you be *so* proper all the time?"

Vivian ignored her. "Please. Tell me. Did it work?"

Cassie sat on the bed beside her sister. "For the most part, though you may not thank me for it after hearing the details."

She summarized the evening, from her idiotic *lovelies* to her insult of Mrs. Hastings's artwork.

"And that is why," she concluded, as if presenting a scientific lecture to the Royal Society, "we should never have attempted this in the first place. I only made things worse."

Vivian leaned back, her eyes thoughtful. "Possibly. Well, certainly with Mrs. Hastings. But I can smooth her ruffled feathers with little issue tomorrow."

"If you are well tomorrow," Cassie pointed out. "You do not look the least bit improved. Are you certain this is just from traveling?"

"Quite," Vivian said, though her trembling voice negated her answer. "But what matters is that you were able to distract Mr. Hastings from Miss Tindale."

"Undoubtedly." If looking ridiculous at a dinner party was her ticket to returning home, then she would happily make that sacrifice.

"What did you and Mr. Hastings talk about?" Vivian asked, rubbing her forehead with a wince.

"Nothing of great consequence, I assure you." Cassie frowned, watching her sister. If Vivian was not better by tomorrow, she would insist upon a doctor.

"I must know everything," Vivian said, "so we may transition back seamlessly tomorrow. He cannot know you were pretending to be me."

Cassie sighed. She was right, of course. "We talked of your love of painting."

Vivian nodded.

"And I mentioned Grandpapa's parrot."

Vivian stopped nodding. "The parrot? You cannot be serious."

Cassie shrugged. "It made for interesting conversation."

"But the parrot." Vivian groaned. "That foul creature should have no part in a drawing room, even just in conversation."

"It isn't foul." Cassie straightened. "It is amusing."

Vivian fell back on her pillows. "At least I know you spoke of it, in case Mr. Hastings mentions it."

Cassie shook her head. "Viv, you should not worry about this now. Rest, please."

"All right." Vivian did not resist very hard. "But do not let me sleep all morning. I am determined to go to breakfast."

"Of course." At least this lie was easy for Cassie to make, knowing it was for her sister's good.

If only it could be the last lie she told.

Vivian was worse the next morning.

Upon finding her sister barely able to raise her head, Cassie went to Mrs. Hastings immediately—acting as Vivian, of course—and asked for a doctor. Fortunately, the matron complied without complaint, though she watched Cassie with narrowed eyes.

When Dr. Dutton arrived, he examined Vivian carefully. Cassie took up position at his elbow.

"Can you say what it is, Doctor?" Cassie finally asked. "Nothing serious, I hope?"

The doctor shook his head as he felt Vivian's pulse. "I'm afraid I cannot be certain. She has a fever, but it is not dangerously high. I have seen similar symptoms in other patients recently, and all recovered within a few days."

"A few days?" Vivian paled even more, which Cassie had thought impossible. "I cannot be abed that long. In fact, I need to dress now for breakfast."

She began to rise from the bed, but Dr. Dutton set a gentle hand on her shoulder.

"I'm afraid that will only make things worse," he said. "For your own sake, and for the sake of others, I insist you remain in bed until I pronounce you well enough."

Vivian sank back against her pillows. "This is ridiculous."

Dr. Dutton went to his bag and gathered his instruments. "I'll come again this afternoon to see her," he said to Cassie. "Keep her in bed, and send for me if her condition changes."

Cassie nodded and the doctor left. She turned back to Vivian, who scowled at the ceiling. "I'm sorry," she said, and she meant it. Even if she thought her sister's plan of wooing Mr. Hastings rather silly, she never wanted to see Vivian distressed.

"A few days," Vivian repeated again, defeated. "It is utterly useless. By that time, Miss Tindale will have ensured that no one remembers I exist."

Cassie sat beside her. "Never mind that. We must get you well first. I promise you'll have your chance."

"Yes, you are right," Vivian said slowly, fixing Cassie with a meaningful look. "But until then..."

Cassie straightened. Then she held up her hands. "No. No and no."

"But it is the only way," Vivian pled. "Can't you see? If you simply continue the switch for another few days, no one will be the wiser."

"I was the worst possible Vivian Bell last night," Cassie said stubbornly. "You cannot want that to continue."

"I can, since it is my only option. Besides, you'll grow better at it, I am sure." Vivian took her hand, squeezing it tightly. "Please, Cassie? Just a bit longer. Let me have my chance at happiness."

Cassie knew she should say no. Heavens, she should pretend to be sick right alongside Vivian so she could avoid the rest of the party.

But Vivian looked at her with such desperation. Cassie had never been able to refuse her sister in anything, and this was so important to her. Not to mention, if Cassie *was* successful... She pictured a cozy Christmas back at Brightling, happily tucked away for the winter with no dread for the upcoming Season.

"All right," Cassie said with a long exhale. "I'll do it."

Vivian patted her hand. "Thank you, Cassie. It will be done before you know it." Her eyes widened. "But hurry, you must go down to breakfast before everyone disperses. I am absolutely certain Miss Tindale has already cornered Mr. Hastings."

A few minutes later, dressed in Vivian's white-flowered morning gown, Cassie descended the main staircase, trying to find a new determination. She could do this, she told herself. She knew Vivian better than anyone.

"Good morning, Miss Bell."

Cassie jumped, but it was only Miss Tindale striding across the entry.

"Oh. Good morning." Cassie cleared her throat. "Have I missed breakfast?"

Miss Tindale smiled pleasantly. Well, as pleasantly as a vulture could manage. "They haven't cleared it away yet, but you might hurry." Then her smile turned sympathetic. "How is your dear Cassandra? I understand the doctor was called for this morning."

"She is . . ." Cassie paused. She hardly wanted to add to her sickly reputation. "She should be well enough to join us in a day or two." Perhaps if Cassie wished *very* hard, her words would come true.

"That is good news. Do give her my best wishes." Miss Tindale gave the barest curtsy and brushed past Cassie to reach the stairs.

"And where are you off to in such a hurry?" The words slipped from Cassie's mouth before she could stop them.

Miss Tindale turned back. "Have you not heard? Mrs. Hastings has lost her cat, and she is simply distraught. I am helping in the search efforts, of course. Anything for sweet Mrs. Hastings."

Sweet as codfish, that is. At least Cassie managed to stop *those* words.

"How kind of you," she said instead. But she knew it was more than kindness at play. Whoever found this cat would undoubtedly be in Mrs. Hastings's good graces, and Miss Tindale was planning to take that coveted position.

Unless Cassie found the feline first.

She bid farewell to Miss Tindale and started for the breakfast room, but as soon as the young lady disappeared upstairs, Cassie veered down the ground floor corridor. Eating could wait; winning back her hostess's approval could not.

She searched the library, the dining room, the sitting room, and the billiards room. But after half an hour, Cassie was no closer to finding the creature than she was to flying. She stopped in the middle of the billiards room, hands on her waist. If *she* were a cat desperate to escape an unpleasant and judgmental mistress, where would she go?

A blur of movement caught her eye outside the window. Cassie crossed the room and pulled back the curtains just as a curved, gray tail slipped around the corner of the stables.

She dropped the curtain and nearly ran for the door.

Six

ROLAND KICKED HIS horse, urging his stallion faster as they galloped up the frost-covered hill, the bright winter sun throwing shadows behind the bare trees. If a houseful of guests made him tug on his too-stiff collar, a brisk ride in the chill December air had the opposite effect. His blood pounded through him, filling him with a heat he hadn't felt in months. Riding in Hyde Park was not the same as taking the countryside in hand, mastering the land as he and his mount jumped hedges and waded through streams.

But of course he couldn't do this all day, as much as he wished to. He'd never hear the end of it from Mother if he avoided the party for much longer. He'd already skipped breakfast in favor of a tray in his room. Although, if he was being honest, he wasn't quite sure who he was intent on avoiding. Miss Tindale had proven an apt conversationalist at dinner last night, which was somewhat refreshing after his experience with the majority of vain, single-minded women in London.

And yet, he admitted, it was not her face that came to mind when he thought of last night. No, instead of Miss Tindale's dark hair and porcelain complexion, he saw golden curls and laughing blue eyes.

Roland turned his horse back toward the house, his breath leaving clouds in his wake. Miss Bell had proven a surprise last night, with her dry repartee and entertaining tales of the foul-mouthed parrot. When he tried to remember her in London, he could not recall much at all, save for the fact that he hadn't found himself immediately drawn to her. That had been enough for him then, but now he could not help but think he had dismissed her too quickly.

After entering the stables, Roland dismounted and handed his reins to a waiting groom. But as he turned, he came to a sudden halt. There, in the open stall across the way, was the focus of his thoughts: Miss Bell herself, kneeling as she peered beneath a water trough, the curls around her face nearly even with the floor.

"Come here, you wicked creature," she said in an amused voice. "You think you are quite clever, don't you, hiding under there?"

Roland could not resist. He approached quietly, clasping his hands behind his back. "Good day, Miss Bell."

Miss Bell jolted, banging her head on the trough and letting out a sharp yelp.

"Blast." Roland hurried forward. He'd only meant to surprise her. "Are you all right?"

She squinted up at him, rubbing her head. "I admit, I've been better."

Roland grimaced and crouched beside her. "I am sorry. Truly. May I look?" If she was bleeding . . .

Miss Bell shook her head. "I am fine, I promise."

She did seem fine. There was no sign of the unfocused vision or slurred language that afflicted many of his friends after a bout of boxing. On the contrary, her eyes were bright and purposeful, and her words lacked none of the spirit he'd come to expect from her.

She smelled sweet, like cherries.

He hastily stood and held out his hand to her. "Might I be of assistance, Miss Bell? Are you looking for something?"

"No, I simply enjoy exploring dusty, old stables," she said wryly as she took his hand.

His cheek twitched. "Then you are in luck. Mine is the oldest and dustiest in the county."

Her eyebrows shot upwards, and before she could say anything, he pulled her to her feet. It wasn't difficult, as Miss Bell was as slender as she was unexpected.

As soon as she found her feet, she took back her hand and stepped away. "I am sorry, I should not have said that about your stables. I'm certain they are well cared for."

"I am far from offended, I assure you," he said, crossing his arms. "But I am curious what you were doing just now."

She blew out a breath and gestured at the trough. "I am attempting to fix the rift I created between myself and your mother."

He squinted. "I am afraid I cannot see the connection between my mother and crawling about the stables."

"She has lost her cat," she said. "I am hoping if I am able to return it..."

"She'll forget your mistake of last evening?"

"Precisely."

Roland crouched once again and peered beneath the trough. Two yellow eyes stared back at him. "It is an admirable plan," he said. "My mother loves that cat like a second child." Never mind that it was a wretchedly spoiled creature that hissed at Roland whenever Mother was not present.

Miss Bell knelt beside him. "If only I had a treat to bribe him with."

"Perhaps a few of your sister's comfits," he said with a grin.

Miss Bell looked up at him sharply. "What?"

"Comfits?" he repeated, one brow raised. "Your sister Cassandra had a great deal of them in her trunk."

"Oh. Right. She mentioned that little mix-up." Miss Bell cleared her throat. "Yes, Cassie is very fond of sweets, but I daresay a cat would be more motivated by a bit of milk or meat. Having none on hand..."

She knelt on the stable floor once more, balancing on her elbows.

"Come here, you pretty thing," she said softly, holding out one hand. "Come out and I will take you to the house for some cream."

The yellow eyes tipped to one side, as if the cat was considering the proposition.

"I won't hurt you, I promise." Miss Bell slid her hand closer. "Come on now, be a dear."

Roland sat back on his heels, watching the young lady before him in bewilderment. Everything he had heard about Miss Bell—and had experienced briefly for himself in London when they'd met—told him she was refined and sophisticated. And yet there she was, practically lying in the dirt, talking to a cat.

As he watched, the cat crept forward and licked Miss Bell's extended hand. "That's it, come out," she encouraged it as she slowly drew backwards. The cat followed, stepping into the light—and revealing its gray coat of fur from nose to tail.

Roland coughed. "Miss Bell, I do believe we have a problem."

"A problem?" She stroked the cat's arched back as it purred.

"That is not my mother's cat."

She jerked her head up to stare at him. "Pardon?"

He could not help a short laugh. "My mother's cat, Sir Chester, is black and white, and much more ill-tempered. Actually, you might consider yourself lucky not to have found him."

"Not her cat." Miss Bell turned her eyes back to the cat, now rubbing against her skirts. "Thunder and turf. Though I cannot say I am surprised, considering my unfortunate luck lately." She continued to pet the smooth gray fur.

"Unfortunate luck?" Roland asked. "How is that?" If anything, *he* was the one with bad luck, returning home to his mother's ambush of a house party.

"Well, first Vi—" She stopped, then gulped. "That is, first Cassie grew sick. And then of course the incident with your mother's painting. Now I bungle the one thing that might have redeemed me."

Roland eyed Miss Bell. She focused on the cat, but her back was stiff. Was it worry for her sister? "Might I ask after your sister's health? Will she be joining us today?"

She shook her head. "No, I'm afraid she will need to recover for a few days at the least."

"I am sorry to hear it." He leaned forward conspiratorially. "Though I admit I was intimidated at the prospect of telling the two of you apart."

Miss Bell continued petting the cat, but her eyes took on a new wariness. "I do not think it would be very difficult. C-Cassie and I are quite different in personality, if not in looks."

Roland clasped his hands behind his back. "Really? I spoke with her only briefly when you both first arrived, but it seemed you at least share the inclination to speak your minds."

"Oh." Miss Bell gulped and looked down. "I must assure you I do not normally act like this. I'm afraid I've been a bit out of sorts with Cassie being ill, and then with that . . . misunderstanding last night."

"A misunderstanding with my mother would unhinge nearly anyone," he said by way of reassurance, though he was not sure why he needed to reassure her. Did she think speaking her mind was a negative quality in a woman? He had never thought so, considering he'd had his mother as his example growing up. Mother had a different way of expressing herself—more crafty than outspoken—but she never failed to make clear how she felt about something.

Miss Bell picked up the cat and stood. "I had better go inside and continue the search. Likely Miss Tindale has already found the real Sir Chester."

"Which would be a terrible thing?"

"I suppose not. But I am a bit more desperate for your mother's approval than Miss Tindale."

He nearly asked her why, but he caught himself. A delicate balance existed at this house party. He was certain all the guests knew why they'd been invited—to see if one of the young ladies could tempt him into a proposal. But they couldn't very well talk about it as if it were common knowledge.

Miss Bell sighed and held out the cat to him. He stared at the creature, then at her. "Er, it isn't mine."

"I know," she said with a furrowed brow. "I just thought perhaps you knew who it belonged to."

"The stables, I imagine." He took a step back. He'd been around his mother's cat enough times to be wary of sharp claws. "To keep the vermin out."

"Oh." She brought the cat back into her arms and tipped her head up at him. "You aren't frightened of it, are you?"

"If you knew Sir Chester, you would understand my hesitation," he said.

"Not all cats are horrible." She gave the cat in her arms one last pat before setting him on the ground. "This one is rather sweet, I think."

The cat scampered away, pausing at the stable doors to look back before disappearing out into the cold.

"Might I accompany you up to the house?" Roland asked. They were going the same way, after all. But even if they hadn't, he felt the strangest urge to prolong this conversation with Miss Bell. When they'd met in London, he'd known only the barest details of her, a hurried sketch of her character. Now it was as though each time he spoke to her, that sketch became more detailed, with small spots of watercolor slipping in around her.

He was far too pragmatic to lose his heart on a whim. But if this small bit of intrigue he felt towards Miss Bell meant anything . . . he wanted to see where it led.

"Of course," Miss Bell said. Then she looked down at herself and winced. "If you can bear to be seen with me, that is."

Her white-flowered dress was covered in dirt, and she brushed at her skirts. A few of her golden curls had escaped her coiffure and lay limply against her neck. Though a lovely neck it was, he could not help but observe.

"I think I can manage," he said, offering his arm. Miss Bell hesitated, her gaze flicking up to his. Then she slipped her hand around the crook of his elbow, her touch light.

He led her from the stables and back towards the house, attempting to keep up their easy conversation. He pointed out details of the manor and estate she might find interesting— the addition to the east wing his father had built a decade ago, and the best place to find wild strawberries in the summer. Miss Bell nodded and replied as was appropriate. Too appropriate, really. Was this an attempt to prove him wrong, that she did *not* speak her mind?

Women were odd creatures indeed.

Upon entering the house, Miss Bell drew her hand from his arm. "Thank you for seeing me back, Mr. Hastings."

"Well, it would have been a great deal more awkward if I'd simply followed you here."

A flash in her blue eyes. Amusement. But she turned away before he saw her smile.

"Roland, there you are."

Mother marched across the entry, and in her arms was the long-haired, black-and-white cat. Miss Tindale trailed behind, hands clasped neatly in front of her.

"I see you've found Sir Chester," Roland said. At least he wouldn't be forced to join the search.

"Yes, no thanks to you." Mother frowned at him deeply. Roland knew better than to think she was irritated he hadn't helped look for the cat. No, she was put out because he'd skipped breakfast. "Fortunately, Miss Tindale was untiring in her efforts and located him upstairs."

"I could hardly let the poor creature go missing, not when it distressed you so, Mrs. Hastings." Miss Tindale peered up at Roland through her lashes. "It was the least I could do."

"Your actions are much appreciated." Mother stroked Sir Chester's back. "How glad I am to have such a thoughtful and kind guest in my home."

She did not look at Miss Bell as she spoke, but the slight was obvious all the same. Roland groaned inwardly. Mother and her pride. Miss Bell was their guest just as much as Miss Tindale, no matter the incident last night.

"Yes, thank you, Miss Tindale," Roland said. "And Miss Bell, as well. I found her in the stables, intent on her own search for the cat."

"That is why I am so dirty," Miss Bell added quickly. "I was sorry to hear he was missing and wished to help."

"I see." Mother scrutinized Miss Bell. "In any case, Miss Tindale asked for a tour of the house, and I cannot refuse her in anything since she found my Chester. Roland, would you join us?"

He forced a smile. He did not truly have a choice. "Of course."

Mother turned to Miss Bell. "I am certain you will wish to change, or of course you would be welcome as well." She sounded as welcoming as a bear in its den.

"Yes, indeed," Miss Bell said with a too-bright smile. "Perhaps later."

She curtsied and hurried up the stairs. Miss Tindale immediately claimed his side and began questioning him on the stained-glass window in the library, but his attention stayed on Miss Bell—her bouncing curls and slim shoulders—until her skirts whisked around the upstairs corner.

She did not look back, a disappointment Roland had not thought to expect.

Seven

THE NEXT TWO days passed in an exhausting tumble. Cassie had to take care every second to watch her mouth, her reactions, her very thoughts. She still gave a little jolt whenever someone called her Miss Bell rather than Miss Cassandra—never more so than when Mr. Hastings did it—but her caution began to pay off. She made no more horribly egregious errors.

Though she could not deny the warmth in her stomach each time Mr. Hastings looked at her. But it was hardly her fault that her sister's intended was unfairly handsome.

Which was an entirely new sort of problem. When Mr. Hastings had found her in the stables, she'd been caught off guard and, like in all their interactions before, acted too much herself. He now thought Vivian was *outspoken*, for heaven's sake. That had prompted her careful reevaluation of strategy. She managed the situation instead of attempting to lead it. She stayed with Mr. Hastings and Miss Tindale, offering only the blandest and safest opinions during their conversations. At the very least, she could ensure the other two were not on their own overmuch.

"I am sorry I cannot do more," Cassie told Vivian as she dressed for dinner four days after arriving at Hartfield Court. "But I assure you it's for the best. Once you are entirely well, you can charm everyone."

"If I can ever recover," Vivian muttered from the bed. She

had only just begun to look a bit like her own self, not running to the chamber pot every hour. But her illness left her weak and frail. When she tried to stand, her legs shook and she nearly fainted.

"You will," Cassie reassured her, pulling on her elbow-length gloves. "Dr. Duttle said three more days at the soonest, though, and as much as I wish to relinquish my role as Vivian Bell, I'll not do it at the cost of your health."

"I know," Vivian said with a sigh. "And I am not ungrateful. I know you have done all you can."

"You know I would do anything for you, but I shall be glad when this is over." When Vivian could take her rightful place at Mr. Hastings's side and Cassie could return home to Grandpapa and her quiet life.

She looked at her reflection in the mirror. She wore Vivian's vivid-red dress, which Cassie would never have chosen for herself. But she admitted she looked rather well in it, with her hair swept up to the crown of her head and embellished with a bit of holly she'd found on a walk that morning, which added a bit of Christmas festivity to her look. She wondered if Mr. Hastings liked holly . . .

Cassie tore her eyes from the mirror.

"Enjoy your dinner," Vivian said, a note of sadness in her voice.

Cassie took a deep breath. This house party was all Vivian had dreamed of for weeks, and now she was missing it. The least Cassie could do was keep her thoughts from Mr. Hastings and focus on her sister. "Would you like me to send up a tray? Or just more tea?"

Vivian made a face. "I'm afraid nothing sounds particularly appetizing at the moment."

"Tea it is." Cassie forced a smile. "I will see you after, I promise. I'm certain I'll be able to avoid disaster again."

"Shall we have some music?" Mrs. Hastings called out as the party settled into the drawing room after dinner. "We've hardly had time in the last two days, but I would so enjoy hearing the young ladies sing."

"Of course. That is a splendid idea," Miss Tindale said as Miss Marsden nodded her agreement. "I have just the song in mind."

Unsurprising. She likely had a hundred songs prepared for a moment such as this. But Cassie had no time for petty thoughts. Because Mrs. Hastings's attention then turned to her. In nearly four days of pretending to be Vivian, Cassie had not thought to anticipate *this*.

"Oh, no, I couldn't tonight," she stammered. Her mind scurried to find a plausible reason. "I haven't practiced?" she said, more of a question than she wanted it to be.

"A true artist can create under any circumstances." Mrs. Hastings fixed her with a stare, as if daring Cassie to argue.

"Perhaps I might only play instead of sing." That would be feasible. She could manage a quick, little tune.

"Nonsense. I hear you have an excellent voice, and I should like the opportunity to judge for myself," Mrs. Hastings said briskly.

Cassie forced a little cough. "Truly, I think I might have a sore throat. Perhaps another night—"

"I'll not take no for an answer, Miss Bell." Mrs. Hastings narrowed her eyes. "I insist."

Cassie opened her mouth to refuse, then stopped. *Vivian* would never refuse. So she shut her mouth and managed a weak nod.

The problem lay much deeper than possessing an inadequate singing voice. Really, Cassie could sing well enough—

alone. But whenever Cassie attempted to perform in front of anyone other than her immediate family, her voice ... her voice squeaked. Badly. So badly, in fact, that the last time her mother insisted she sing in front of company—two years ago—her dim-sighted great-aunt Wilmington had insisted there was a mouse beneath her chair.

But when Vivian was known for having a lovely voice, what was Cassie to do?

Miss Tindale began playing her piece, a sweet folk song, her full, steady voice joining the tones of the pianoforte after a few measures. Cassie sat stiffly, hands clutched together in her lap, when Mr. Hastings caught her eye. He furrowed his brow and mouthed a few words at her. But since Cassie was as terrible at reading lips as she was at performing, his message of "Tar ewe all night" was not particularly reassuring.

Cassie shook her head slightly, hoping Mr. Hastings would understand she had no idea what he was saying. She looked again at Miss Tindale—composed, effortless Miss Tindale—and tried to think of a plan. Perhaps she might pretend to faint. But then she would be relegated to her bed like Vivian, which would defeat the entire purpose of this charade. The same was true of persisting with her lie about a sore throat.

Her only choice was to perform—and hope with every bone in her body that her voice was no longer frightened of people.

Miss Tindale finished her song to great applause, and Miss Marsden began her performance, her light and airy voice barely audible above the pianoforte. Cassie's heart thumped faster and faster, nearly leaping into her throat as Miss Marsden curtsied and moved back to her chair.

"Miss Bell," Mrs. Hastings said, nodding to the instrument.

Cassie somehow seated herself before the pianoforte and rested her fingers on the keys. She'd chosen her song, "Whilst Shepherds Watched Their Flocks by Night," very carefully. First of all, it was a song she could recall by memory, as she hadn't brought her music to Hartfield Court. And secondly, she hoped playing a familiar carol would soften Mrs. Hastings's opinion of her. This *was* a Christmas party, after all.

Cassie glanced up for a brief moment, spotting Mr. Hastings at the back of the chairs. He had stood sometime during the other performances and now crossed his arms, eyeing her in an unnerving way.

She pressed her fingers down into a chord, played a few measures. At least her fingers remembered the notes well enough. Then there was nothing for it but to start singing.

"*Whilst Shepherds wa-atched their flocks by night.*" The first line went fairly smoothly, though her voice cracked slightly on a high note. She went on. "*All seated on the ground.*"

That wasn't bad, really. Her voice was not nearly as confident as Miss Tindale's, but neither was anyone covering their ears.

"*The Angel of the Lord came down and glory shone all round.*" Perhaps she could do this. Survive, that was. Another few stanzas and she could retreat to her chair.

"*Fear not, said he—*" Her voice jumped, leaping into a squeak that would have made dogs howl. She swallowed hard. "*Fear not, said he for mighty dread—*" Another squeak, higher and louder. Cassie's eyes flew up and she locked gazes with Mr. Hastings for a brief moment. He straightened, alarmed, no doubt, by the blazing panic on her face.

But all she could do was finish the song.

"*For mighty dread had seized their troubled mi—*" The

sound that next escaped her mouth would have put a dying animal to shame. Cassie slammed shut her mouth, her hands frozen over the keys. What was worse, fleeing in embarrassment or continuing to sing in embarrassment?

A crash sounded across the room. Someone gasped as the entire party turned in their chairs, and Cassie stood abruptly, the stool skittering away from her knees.

"Blast." Mr. Hastings put his hands to his waist, looking down at the floor near his feet, where shattered pieces of ceramic lay.

"Roland." Mrs. Hastings stood, her face aghast. "My vase."

"I am sorry, Mother. It was an accident." He sounded truly apologetic. "I know you liked it."

Mrs. Hastings pursed her lips, as if holding back a scolding. "No matter," she finally managed, then called for servants to clean up the mess.

Mr. Hastings turned to Cassie and—he winked. *Winked.*

Had he done it on purpose?

The party settled back in their chairs, and Cassie cleared her throat. "Perhaps I might finish another time. I find my nerves are a bit rattled."

"Of course, dear," the matronly Mrs. Marsden assured her, and Cassie hurried back to her seat. Safe. For now, at least.

Mrs. Hastings still did not look particularly happy, especially as the guests broke into groups for cards and conversation. It would be best for Cassie to avoid her the rest of the night. In fact, it would likely be best to avoid everyone for the remainder of the night.

When all eyes were occupied, she slipped from the drawing room, grateful the door's hinges were far better oiled than her voice. She couldn't go upstairs yet; Vivian would be full of questions as to why she was so early. Cassie retreated down the hallway until she found a rounded alcove lined with windows. She sat on the ledge and leaned against the cool glass, closing her eyes.

But laughter echoed down the corridor, invading her quiet. Cassie peered around the corner. A figure stood outside the drawing room, shutting the door behind him. Broad shoulders and a mess of dark hair. Mr. Hastings.

She shrank back into her alcove. Perhaps he would go upstairs and bypass her altogether. But his footsteps came closer until he rounded the corner and spotted her.

"There you are." His eyes flickered in the candlelight. "I wanted to see you were all right."

His kindness tugged at her heart. He was concerned—for her.

She forced a smile. "Yes, perfectly all right. Better now that I do not have to sing."

He stepped forward. "Are you certain? I am sorry my mother pressed you so. If you *do* have a sore throat—"

Cassie shook her head fervently. "Oh, I'm not ill, I assure you. It's just this cold weather."

He nodded, looking out the window. "I daresay it will snow soon, which would delight Mother."

"I did not take your mother for an enthusiast of snow." Cassie wasn't particularly fond of the stuff herself. It was lovely, she supposed, but she did not relish the feel of it melting in her boots.

Mr. Hastings gave a short laugh. "I would not word it that way. She thinks snow is unfailingly romantic, and that it will surely make me fall in love at last."

Cassie blinked. What was she to say to that? Perhaps a change in subject was best. "Thank you." The words nearly burst from her.

He raised an eyebrow. "Thank you?"

"For earlier," she said quickly. "For distracting everyone so I did not need to finish my song."

"Oh, that." He sat on the window ledge across the alcove from her. He was not particularly close, but Cassie's pulse ticked faster. "I'm afraid I cannot claim credit for rescuing you. I was born clumsy, you see."

A smile tugged at Cassie's lips. "And you somehow happened to shatter a vase halfway across the room?"

"It's a dreadful curse," he said with a grin.

"Well, I shall thank you all the same, especially since your mother seemed upset at the loss."

He waved that off. "She'll be glad for it when we go to London again and she has a reason to shop for another."

"You'll attend the Season, then?" Why did that thought make London suddenly more appealing?

Mr. Hastings shrugged. "If I must."

She wanted to press him further, ask why he seemed reluctant to go. Because it looked as if they had that very much in common. But Vivian *adored* London, so it would not make sense for Cassie to suddenly have developed a dislike for it. She sighed. This pretense was getting more and more difficult by the day.

"Why the sigh?"

"Nothing," she said hastily. What would he say if he knew she was ruminating over the unexpected difficulties of convincing him she was her sister?

He narrowed his eyes, and she scrambled for something else to say. "That is, I admit I am missing home, and my family. I've never spent Christmas away before."

"But you have your sister, at least."

"Yes, of course. But I shall miss my grandfather especially."

He nodded. "You said you are close to him."

He remembered that? She'd mentioned it days ago.

"Yes," she said, tugging up her gloves. "He always makes Christmas special. The song I played is a favorite of his, and he insists I play it every year."

Mr. Hastings smiled. "My father loved Christmas as well. We often hosted a dinner on Christmas Day, and Father enjoyed having his friends and family around him." His smile faded. "You said the other day that your grandfather's parrot made him feel young again, helped him relive his favorite memories. I think Christmas did that for my father."

Cassie wrapped her arms around herself, trying to remember what she knew of the Hastings family. When had the elder Mr. Hastings died?

"Your father . . ." she began, uncertain how to phrase her question.

"He died a year ago, before Christmas." Mr. Hastings leaned forward to place his elbows on his knees. "It makes this time of year difficult, especially for my mother." He swallowed. "Though I also miss him, of course."

She hardly knew what to say to that. She bit her lip, ready to make an attempt, but thankfully he spoke before she could say something horribly inadequate.

"This house party has been good for my mother, though," he said. "She takes a strange amount of joy in planning menus and activities."

"What does your mother have planned for tomorrow?" she asked. "I feel I ought to be prepared, for obvious reasons."

Mr. Hastings grinned, and the unexpected seriousness of their conversation lifted. "I'm sorry to say I haven't the faintest. I find it better to leave the planning to her, because she does everything how she wishes no matter what I say. Saves me a great deal of time and effort."

"If you had your say, what would we be doing?"

"We wouldn't be having this house party, to start."

She blinked. "Oh."

He grimaced. "I am sorry, I did not mean it like that. I've enjoyed the past few days, for the most part. But I will admit I had no hand in organizing this party, as I had no idea of its existence until the day I arrived from London."

Was that why he had been in a bad humor when their trunks had been switched? But she could hardly blame him. She hadn't wanted to come either, after all. She almost said that aloud but again stopped herself. Because *Vivian* had wanted to come.

"Then besides the preferable option of there being no house party at all," she said lightly, "what activity would you choose for tomorrow? Because if the host does not enjoy himself, I cannot think why a house party would be worth the effort."

He laughed. "You and my mother have very different views on house parties." He seemed to consider the question more seriously. "Anything outdoors, I suppose. I cannot stand to be cooped up, even when it is cold." He paused. "Perhaps archery."

"Are you good at it?"

"If you had asked me as a youth, I would have boasted endlessly about my prowess with a bow. But now I cannot say I've touched one in years."

"That sounds like a problem to be rectified," she said. "We have the time now, after all."

He leaned back against the window. "You underestimate my mother's abilities. You've seen how good she is at filling all seconds of the day."

"True enough." But she could not help but think that if he was forced to attend every event, he might as well enjoy one of them.

Voices echoed down the corridor as the drawing room opened once again. "Roland?" Mrs. Hastings called.

Roland—Mr. Hastings, that was—raised a finger to his lips and grinned. Cassie held her breath. She wanted to be caught in a compromising situation even less than he did. Although perhaps that was *one* way for Vivian to achieve her marriage goals.

Footsteps moved towards them, and the two of them dared not move. Cassie's eyes went to his, as if pulled by a current. He stared back at her, the amusement in his expression shifting to something... different.

"Roland?" Mrs. Hastings called again, a sharp edge to her voice.

But Roland did not move. That is, his body did not. His eyes, however, wandered her face, slowly, curiously. And she found she could not look away.

Mrs. Hastings's footsteps moved, back inside the drawing room. When the door shut behind her, it snapped the pull between them, and Cassie drew herself backward, bracing her hands on either side of the window ledge. What had *that* been?

Roland cleared his throat. "I am sorry for making you hide. But I thought we both needed a respite from my mother."

"You are not wrong," she murmured, still attempting to collect her thoughts. She'd never felt... felt... *whatever* that had been between them. She looked back up at him, as if to test herself, to see if it would happen again. He offered a slight smile, and although her stomach warmed slightly, she did not wish to fling herself into his arms like she had only moments before.

It was his fault, she decided, for being so kind and good-looking. Why, he likely had ladies flinging themselves at him with every flash of his smile. She only needed to be on her guard, that was all. At least with the two of them together out here, she was assured Miss Tindale was most certainly *not* with him.

"So tell me," Roland said, as if his mother had not just nearly caught them together, "what activity would you choose for tomorrow, if you could?"

"I hardly know," she said. "I'm afraid I'm not quite as fond of the outdoors as you."

"Still," he said. "If you had all of tomorrow to yourself, what would you do?"

Cassie knew what Vivian would want to do—pay visits, shop, attend parties and dinners. But for once she wanted to give an honest answer. "First, I would sleep far too late into the morning. Then I would eat my fill of pastries and chocolate, perhaps read a book or spend time with my sister. And then I would go in search of that little gray cat in the stables."

"The cat?"

"Yes," she said. "After the stress I caused it the other day, I daresay it deserves a treat."

Roland stayed quiet a moment. "I think that sounds like a wonderful day," he finally said.

And Cassie couldn't help thinking the only thing that might improve it was if he was there too.

Eight

WHEN CASSIE WOKE the next morning, it was with a smile. She padded to the window and parted the curtains, looking out at the gray skies and light mist of rain.

And yet still Cassie smiled.

She should be exhausted. She couldn't say how late she and Roland had stayed in that alcove the evening before—had the clock struck one o'clock, or perhaps two? The other guests had eventually made their way upstairs and gone to bed. But not the two of them, not tucked away in their peaceful seclusion. They'd talked and laughed—quietly—long into the night.

They'd talked of everything. Cassie had shared amusing stories from growing up a twin, and Roland told her more of his Christmas memories with his father. Their topics ranged from literature to opera, with time allotted for the latest scandal about the prince regent and the tendency of Roland's butler to cough precisely three times upon entering a room.

They'd talked so much that Cassie had forgotten to be on her guard.

Her smile faded, and she let the curtain fall back into place. She thought over all she'd said last night—or at least she tried to. They'd spent hours together, but it had felt more like minutes. Had she said anything to give away her true identity?

Likely small things here and there. But he wouldn't really remember all that anyway. Would he?

A knock came at the door, and Cassie went to answer it, throwing her dressing gown around her shoulders.

"Vivian," she scolded upon seeing her sister leaning heavily on the doorframe. "What are you doing out of bed?"

"You didn't come to see me last night," she said in a weak voice. "I was worried."

"I was tired, is all." Cassie ushered her inside. "Come sit down before Dr. Dutton sentences you to longer in bed."

Vivian lowered herself to an armchair. "How was dinner last night?"

"Well, I was forced to sing, so I'll let you imagine the rest."

Vivian's eyes widened. "You sang?"

"No, I croaked, but luckily my song came to a sudden end."

She shook her head. "Heavens, Cassie, sometimes I cannot decide if this deception is worth all this trouble."

"You and me both," Cassie said. "Though I've thought so from the beginning."

"It's no use changing course now," Vivian said with a frown. "I shall have a mountain of things to fix when we switch back, but that should be soon enough. I feel much better today."

"You can barely stand," Cassie pointed out. "The doctor said at least two more days."

"Soon enough," Vivian repeated, rubbing her forehead. "And what of Mr. Hastings? Did you talk with him last night?"

Cassie coughed. "Yes, of course. That is my job, after all. Distracting him."

"And what did you talk of?"

Everything and nothing. The grandest ideas and the silliest details.

But she could not tell Vivian all that. And she especially could not tell her about the way Roland had looked at her last night.

"Operas came up, I believe," she managed instead.

"That seems safe enough." Vivian frowned. "Though I hope you did not give him the impression I liked them overmuch."

"I would never," Cassie said with a laugh. "I've entirely ruined your singing reputation, but your opinions of opera are intact, I assure you."

"Good," Vivian said. "Less work for me." She stood carefully. "I am going to lie down, but please come see me later. I am dreadfully bored."

Poor Vivian, shut away at a house party with nothing to do but rest and read the books Jennings had brought her from the scarce library. "Of course," Cassie said. "You know I will."

Vivian left, and Cassie dressed quickly, pinning her hair up carefully. Far more carefully than she had in the past.

Another knock at her door. Vivian again? "Come in," she called, tugging at a curl in the mirror.

A maid appeared, carrying a tray. "Pardon me, Miss Bell, but I was sent with a tray for you."

"For me?" Cassie turned on her chair. "You do not mean my sister, Miss Cassandra, who is ill?" Surely this tray was meant for Vivian.

"No, miss, for you." The maid set the tray on the little table before the fireplace. "Mr. Hastings himself asked it to be sent."

Cassie went to the table. The tray was near to bursting with a variety of pastries and a steaming cup of chocolate. Her mouth dropped.

"Thank you," she said to the maid, who curtsied and departed. Cassie sat at the table and took a sip of the chocolate, the sharp bitterness and warmth mixing delightfully together.

He'd remembered.

Such a small thing shouldn't bring her so much pleasure, but it did. Cassie often felt forgotten behind her sister, which she truly did not mind. She loved Vivian and hardly blamed her for it.

But to be seen like Roland saw her...

She straightened. No. He did not see her as Cassie. He saw her as Miss Vivian Bell, save with a few quirks Cassie had unwittingly added. She could not allow herself to begin to think he cared for her. That would only lead to pain.

But she still had to continue on this path until Vivian recovered. She simply needed to sort her feelings better. Roland could be nothing more than a friend, her future brother-in-law.

She picked up a pastry covered in red jam and took a small bite. It was delicious, of course. And quite suddenly, despite her confusion and trepidation over the entire affair, she wanted to repay Roland's kindness. He gave so much of himself, to his mother and his guests and now to her, that he deserved some happiness all his own.

But what? He'd mentioned archery the night before, but as she looked out the window, large drops of water began hitting the glass. They could hardly shoot outside in this weather. How else might she surprise him, as he had surprised her with breakfast?

An idea took root in Cassie's mind, then began to grow and blossom. She grinned. Perfect.

Roland looked again at the note in his hand as he slipped down the back stairwell. *Ballroom at one o'clock,* it said, with no name or any clue as to its writer. He'd studied it a hundred times since finding it slipped under his door after his morning ride, and he'd also studied each of the young women when the party had gathered to play cards after breakfast. Miss Tindale had acted her usual proper and insightful self, Miss Marsden had hardly peeped out a word in his presence, and Miss Bell...

Well, he knew who he hoped had sent the note. Because he hadn't been able to keep his eyes from Miss Bell all morning—the graceful curve of her neck, her fair curls bouncing as she laughed.

And from the many times he'd met her eyes, it seemed she wanted to look at him as well. The hours they'd spent together the night before in the secluded alcove had danced through his mind since they'd parted. He'd hardly slept for thinking of it, for thinking of *her*. He tried to force his hopefulness away; a few conversations did not a love match make. Even if they had been wonderful conversations. Even if he'd never spoken so freely with another person besides his father.

Roland drew in a deep breath as he approached the ballroom, stuffing the note inside his jacket pocket. Thankfully, the ballroom was quite out of the way, or he would not risk meeting whoever had sent the note. But still, he looked up and down the corridor to ensure he was alone before stepping inside. Dim light seeped through the windows, the sun hidden behind the clouds and falling rain. He closed the door behind him. Was he here first?

"You are late," said a teasing voice.

He turned to see Miss Bell crossing the room, dressed in a simple blue day dress. Even with the muted light around them, her eyes shone with a brightness that made his heart lighter.

Roland grinned. "I think being late is well within my rights, when I hadn't the faintest idea who extended such a mysterious invitation."

"Ah, but the mystery made it more exciting, did it not?" She stopped a few paces from him, her lips curving upwards.

"True enough." He crossed his arms. "Though perhaps your reason for inviting me was intrigue enough."

Her expression turned earnest. "Not so very intriguing, no. I only wanted to thank you for your thoughtfulness in sending me breakfast. It was thoughtful of you, and I was surprised you remembered, considering."

"Considering we spoke for nearly five hours last night?" He spoke quietly, as if they stood amidst a packed ballroom and not the empty one now surrounding them. "I find it hard to forget anything you say, Miss Bell."

She looked down, looping one arm behind her back to grasp her other elbow. "I . . . I enjoyed our conversation," she said.

"As did I." Roland could have said a great deal more, but there was no need to rush anything. If there was something between the two of them, they had time enough to discover the truth of it. The house party was only half over.

Miss Bell cleared her throat. "Anyway, I did not entice you here simply to thank you. I also wished to offer a surprise of my own."

"And what is that?"

"I wanted to give you the activity you wished for last night, but since it is raining . . ." She waved a hand to the far end of the ballroom.

Roland turned. Across the room, below one of the chandeliers, stood an archery target—one he recognized immediately, even if he hadn't seen it in over a year. He stared.

"I managed to bribe a footman to set it all up," Miss Bell said quickly. "The room isn't very long, so I doubt the distance will be much of a challenge for you. And the footman wasn't entirely certain which equipment was yours, so he brought the lot of it."

Roland let out a soft laugh. "You've set up an archery range? Here in the ballroom."

Miss Bell swallowed. "I'm sorry, that was terribly forward of me, wasn't it? I should have asked permission instead of—"

He stepped forward and took her hand, lifting it between them. She stopped, her eyes focused on their hands.

"No, you should not have asked permission," he said. "That would have defeated the purpose of a surprise, would it not?"

She raised her gaze to meet his. "I . . . yes, quite right."

With her small, warm hand in his and her vivid-blue eyes staring up at him, Roland's pulse leaped within him. He wanted to tell her this was the kindest thing anyone had ever done for him. But something in her wide eyes held him back.

"Good," he managed instead, reluctantly releasing her hand and stepping back. "Now, you ought to prepare yourself to be dazzled. I cannot be held responsible for any swooning once you witness my skill in archery firsthand."

Miss Bell laughed, a bit breathlessly. "I shall try to restrain myself."

They moved to the opposite wall from the target, where a long table had been laid with bows and arrows. Roland shot Miss Bell a sidelong glance as they walked. She absently rubbed the palm of her hand—the hand Roland had been holding not moments before. He allowed himself a small grin.

"I hope you have everything you need," she said as they reached the table. "I cannot say I am a great expert in the essentials of archery."

"So your skills are limited to critiquing art and taming cats." He moved to the bows, finding his favorite and gripping the handle. "I shall need to remember that."

"Why is that?"

He raised his eyebrow mischievously. "To remind myself you are not perfect."

She let out a sound crossed between a snort and a guffaw. "I think I provide you with reminders enough."

She had no idea how much her "reminders" charmed him. What she saw as embarrassing mistakes, he viewed as endearing eccentricities.

He set his bow down and picked up his stout leather brace before slipping it over his left arm and buckling it.

"I am sorry I do not have a brace or glove for you," he said as he next slipped on his shooting glove, a three-fingered contraption that buttoned at the wrist.

Miss Bell watched his motions with interest. "Oh, no matter. I had not intended to join you, only observe."

"We will see about that." Roland flexed his gloved hand. It had been so long. Would he even be able to properly string his bow?

"You do not want me to handle any sort of weapon, I assure you," she responded. "Someone would likely lose a finger."

He laughed. "I would be much more likely to lose a finger persuading a stubborn cat from beneath a trough."

"We each have our strengths, then." She nodded at his bow. "Come, Robin Hood, let me see this ability you've so boasted."

Roland took up his bow again, feeling the weight of the smooth, cool wood, nearly as tall as Miss Bell. He grasped the free end of the string and placed the bow in position, his right hand on the center of the handle, the bottom of the bow placed on the ground against his foot. In one swift movement born from years of practice, he pulled at the handle—the bow bending as it braced against his foot—and quickly slipped the eye of the string over the nock.

"That looked difficult," Miss Bell observed, stepping closer to examine his handiwork.

He laughed. "As I was trying to make it look effortless, I must count it a failure."

She grinned. "I was only attempting to save my true amazement for the actual shooting."

"Then ready yourself, madam," he said, taking an arrow from the table and stepping away. "For you shall not be disappointed."

Roland tested the strength of the string, and, finding it sound, nocked the arrow to the string and raised the bow. Drawing the arrow back to his ear, he squinted one eye. He held his position another few seconds, making small adjustments in his form and aim, then released the arrow.

It flew across the ballroom and hit the target with a dull thunk on the outer white circle. He'd barely managed to hit the target.

"Well," came Miss Bell's amused voice from behind him as he lowered his bow. "If I cannot trust your word that you are an accomplished marksman, what can I trust?"

"The first shot hardly counts. You must allow me some practice."

She leaned back against the edge of the table. "And how much practice do you require? One year? Two?"

"Your teasing will get you in trouble sooner or later." He walked back toward the table.

"So long as it is later, I do not mind overmuch," she said with a playful tilt to her head.

He'd planned to take another arrow from the closer end of the table, but at her words, he could not resist a change in direction. He moved straight at her, slowly. Her eyes widened as he stopped before her. She did not move from her position, though she straightened.

"And if trouble finds you sooner?" he said in a low voice, placing one hand on the table beside her.

She barely breathed, her eyes fixed on his. "I daresay I can manage a little trouble."

Roland dipped his head closer to hers, their faces inches apart. Her mouth parted, and he forgot that he was teasing her back, that he did not actually mean to kiss her. He forgot all the cautions he had given himself and the reminders that he needn't rush anything. Because in that moment he wanted nothing more than to close the distance between them and claim those soft pink lips as his.

Nine

CASSIE STARED UP at Roland. She dared not move—giving any freedom to her limbs would surely result in her leaning forward and discovering what all the fuss with kissing was about.

His coffee-colored eyes flicked over her, and for a moment the teasing in his expression was replaced by a look she'd never seen on a man. At least, not on a man looking at *her*.

Then he flashed a grin and leaned closer. She inhaled a sharp breath, but he simply reached behind her, took an arrow from the table, and stepped away.

"Allow me ten shots, Miss Bell," he said, nocking the arrow on his bow. "You can resume your teasing if I haven't improved."

"You may count on it," Cassie somehow convinced her voice to say. She did not move from where she leaned on the table, not trusting her legs to support her weight.

It took him less than ten shots before he hit the gold center circle. He did not crow in victory but sent her a sly smile and offered a bow as she applauded. They spent the next hour—or two or three, she couldn't tell by the light—talking as Roland reacquainted himself with his long-neglected archery skills. Just as last night, their conversation ran the gamut in terms of topics, and never was there an awkward moment between them. It was difficult to remember to be Vivian, to respond as she would. Talking with Roland was like stepping into a swift winter wind. It swept her away, twirled her about, and made her head feel light and dizzy.

And like a winter wind, she had no idea where she was headed.

Cassie pushed that thought away, concentrating again on Roland's laugh, his quick wit and dancing eyes. She simply wanted to enjoy the here and now.

When at last the light outside the windows began to fade slightly, Roland let out a sigh and lowered his bow. "I think that is the most escape we can hope for today. Mother is no doubt wondering where I am, full of lectures about neglecting my guests."

"*I* am a guest," Cassie pointed out. "So you needn't feel guilty."

He came back to the table and laid his bow down. "Believe me, guilt is the last emotion I am feeling at the moment." He said it lightly, but somehow his voice still carried a note of meaning. Cassie's heart quickened, and she ordered it to calm. He could have meant a million different things.

Roland crossed his arms. "But before we abandon our pleasant sojourn here, I must insist you take a turn."

"Those words will be etched on your gravestone," Cassie warned.

He fought a grin. "They will be well worth it if you are as bad as you say. Then at least you can provide the both of us with some entertainment."

"How can I refuse such an offer when it includes guaranteed mocking?"

"Oh, I do not guarantee it. That depends entirely on your lack of skill." He picked up a smaller bow. "Here, use this. It was mine when I was a boy, so it will be easier to draw."

"I suppose I could try," she said reluctantly as he strung the bow. She didn't particularly want to make a fool of herself, but archery seemed to make him happy. And for reasons she was not very clear on, she wanted to make Roland happy.

"I have every faith in you." He held out the bow with a gleam of mischief in his eyes.

"All right." Cassie took the bow and a few arrows. She moved closer to the target and set the arrows on the ground. He remained at the table, no doubt in fear for his life.

She had used a bow and arrow before, but not often. Neither she nor Vivian had a special fondness for archery, so revealing her lack of skill was thankfully not adding to the deception. Cassie nocked an arrow on the string as she'd watched Roland do, then raised the bow. Drawing the arrow back to her ear, she stared down the length of the smooth wood and aimed at the center of the target.

She released the arrow, and off it flew. That is, until it skittered to the floor not twenty feet away.

"So it wasn't false modesty." A laugh hid in Roland's voice.

Cassie gave an exaggerated huff. "I allowed you ten shots, so I expect the same courtesy."

"Of course. Unless you wish for my help?"

She'd been bending to fetch another arrow, but she nearly fell over as she spotted him approaching from the corner of her eye.

"No, no," she said hastily, finding her balance. "No, I will be perfectly fine on my own, thank you."

He gave her a strange look. "As you wish," he said, thankfully returning to the table.

Cassie let out a breath of relief as she turned back to the target. Her heart was already a mess, her stomach made of twisting currents. It was best if he stood far, *far* away.

She raised the bow again, this time pulling back the string farther. She didn't mind his teasing, not when he took hers so well, but she wanted to impress him all the same. *This* arrow would make it to the target. Aiming the tip of her arrow, she tried to keep her arms as steady as possible. She relaxed her right hand, preparing to release.

"Roland?"

Cassie's arm jerked at the voice. She yelped at the same moment that her arrow tore from her fingers—

—and buried itself in the polished wood of the open ballroom door, not inches from Mrs. Hastings's wide, white eyes.

"Heavens," the woman gasped, clutching a hand to her heart as she staggered back.

"Mrs. Hastings," Cassie squeaked, nearly dropping her bow.

Mrs. Hastings stared at her, then her eyes flew to the target on one end of the ballroom.

"Mother, are you all right?" Roland crossed the room, his brow dipped in concern.

Mrs. Hastings waved off her son, her eyes flashing dangerously. "What," she said, her tone sharp as a cat's claws, "is happening here?"

Roland cleared his throat. "I thought this might be a diverting way to spend the rainy day," he said before Cassie could speak. "I set it up, and Miss Bell happened upon me. I invited her to join me."

Cassie felt as if an evergreen tree had fallen across her chest. She clutched her bow in both hands and focused on breathing. He was taking the blame for her. She tried not to think of the risk to her reputation—to *Vivian's* reputation. The two of them alone for hours. *Again.* What had Cassie been thinking?

"Miss Bell would do well to think twice before accepting such an offer in the future." Mrs. Hastings's eyes narrowed. She did not believe them, that much was obvious. But what could she do? She did not like Cassie. She would hardly demand Roland march her down the aisle when there were no other witnesses to their breach in conduct.

"It was only an accident, Mother," Roland said.

"I am very sorry for the fright I gave you, Mrs. Hastings," Cassie quickly added.

Mrs. Hastings drew herself up to her full height. "Dinner is soon. I suggest, Miss Bell, you go upstairs to dress, or you'll be late."

"O-of course," Cassie stammered. She nearly scurried out into the corridor before remembering she still held the bow. She turned back. Roland was already stepping forward, arm outstretched to take it from her.

"I am sorry," he murmured, so his mother could not hear. "I will try to clear this up."

"Thank you," she whispered. "I did not mean to cause any trouble."

One side of his lips curved up into a wicked grin. "And here I thought you liked a bit of trouble."

Cassie could not help the tiniest smile in return. He did not seem overly concerned. Perhaps he could set this all to rights. She bobbed a curtsy to both him and Mrs. Hastings and tried not to run as she left the ballroom.

Ten

Roland watched Miss Bell leave the ballroom, her footsteps echoing in the quiet she left behind. There had been such panic in her eyes when he'd taken the bow from her. He wished he could have said more to reassure her, but with his mother present, he could not manage more than a few whispered words.

"Roland."

He faced his mother, who scrutinized him with very real worry.

"What were you thinking, being alone with that girl?" she asked. "Anyone might have happened upon you, and then what?"

He ignored her insinuation, though his stomach flipped at the thought. Couples had been forced to marry for far less. Yet he could not quite convince himself that would be so terrible a thing. With Miss Bell, at least.

"You mustn't blame Miss Bell," he said instead. "I take full responsibility. And besides, I thought you would be glad to find me spending time with our guests."

Mother huffed. "Yes, perhaps I would have been a week ago."

"And what has changed? Did you not invite her for this very reason?"

She paced to the nearby window and looked out over the

dreary, rain-soaked landscape. "I did, but now I am doubting my own judgment in regards to Miss Bell's suitability."

"Because of the incident with the painting?"

Mother turned sharply. "No. Well, not entirely. That, of course, did not endear her to me, but since then everything I have seen has only given me more qualms. She has acted more like her unruly sister than the proper miss I knew her to be in London, and I cannot account for it."

"Have you not thought to consider that is why I like her now?" he said. "I met her in London as well, if you'll remember."

Mother eyed him, as if fully understanding how careful she must be. They were at odds; they both knew that.

"I believe you think you like her," she said. "And I admit she is not the worst sort of girl you could marry. She is pretty enough, and from a good family. But she is not accomplished or poised or any of the things you need in a wife." She paused. "She is not the woman your father imagined for you."

Roland stepped back, jaw tight. Of course she would bring Father into this. "Not the woman Father imagined, or not who *you* imagined? Because if I remember correctly, he did not make me promise to marry a woman you approved of. He only wanted me to marry."

"Yes, but he hadn't any idea who you would set your sights on."

Roland shook his head. "You do not know the first thing about Miss Bell."

"And you know her so well?"

"Yes," he said simply. "I do. And since we've a week left to this party, I plan to use it as you intended: to see if Miss Bell is the woman I could spend the rest of my days with."

He strode past her and escaped to his study, where he could be assured of a few moments of peace before dinner. He paced before the window, the raindrops leaving wistful trails as they tumbled down the glass.

Why was Mother so against Miss Bell? Yes, the young lady had slighted her painting, but she had done everything in her power to win back his mother's approval. She had searched for the blasted cat, performed a song when she clearly had not wanted to, and been all that was kind and helpful. But Mother had seen none of that—only Miss Bell's apparent mistakes.

Roland wouldn't stand for it anymore. Not when he knew Miss Bell's—Vivian's—true nature. That she was thoughtful and interesting and intelligent, and that she only wanted to please.

And she was beautiful. He could not deny it. He leaned his shoulder on the windowsill, lost for a moment in the memory of those alluring blue eyes, her golden curls tumbling about her neck as she turned to look at him over her shoulder. He'd always thought Miss Bell pretty. But having come to know her better in the last week . . . Her character had become her beauty, more so than any dress, jewels, or rouge ever could.

He'd begun this house party so reluctantly that he could not believe he had reached this point.

That he could almost admit to having fallen in love.

Once Cassie made it to her room, she dropped onto her bed, her body overcome. The entire afternoon with Roland flashed through her mind—their conversation and teasing, his tempting nearness, and how little control she had over herself whenever she was around him. She hugged a pillow to her chest, trying to keep the heat there at bay, certain it would start a fire if she let it escape. What Roland made her feel, and the person she became when she was with him—she wasn't Cassie or Vivian. She was someone else, someone new. And she liked that someone.

Almost as much as she liked Roland.

Cassie groaned and buried her face in the pillow. The truth she'd been attempting to hide for days now stared down at her, like the hot sun in mid-July. What she felt toward Roland was not brotherly affection or friendly camaraderie. If she knew any better, if she'd had any experience whatsoever, she would even come close to calling it ... well, love.

But she couldn't love Roland. It was impossible. *Vivian* was in love with Roland Hastings, and Cassie was just a poor substitute. She was not at all what such a man needed in a wife. He needed someone to help him further his connections, move upwards in society. Vivian would do that a thousand times better than Cassie ever could.

But that was beside the point. No matter what Cassie had imagined between her and Roland, it could never come to pass. She would never betray her sister, not when Vivian deserved every happiness, especially this one she'd long set her heart after.

And Roland ... If the intensity in his eyes when he looked at Cassie was any indicator, then he felt something for her in return.

But the person he thought her to be did not exist.

Cassie managed her breathing, her head formulating a plan even as her heart struggled in vain to stop it. Vivian would be well in a day or two. Until then, Cassie would play a new part. The path she had been walking had proven too perilous. Now she would be careful. She could not avoid him completely, but neither would she seek him out or send him notes or exchange secret smiles with him.

That was for Vivian to do.

Cassie set her jaw. This was the right decision, for her, for Vivian, for Roland. She knew that. But the ache in her chest refused to dissipate, and she closed her eyes against the hot tears that fought to be free.

Eleven

MISS BELL WAS avoiding him.

Roland could easily tell, though she still smiled and conversed with the others that night after dinner as she always had. But when she looked at him, it was as though her eyes did not quite see him. Like he'd become an uninteresting painting on the wall or a statue gathering dust in the corner.

Had Miss Bell seen the risk they'd taken in the ballroom, and was she afraid to repeat it? Had her feelings changed? Or perhaps had the looming figure of his mother daunted her more than he'd realized?

The last was the likeliest. Mother was an intimidating figure even when one was not already in her black books. Roland wanted nothing more than to take Miss Bell aside and make her listen to him. She had to know that he did not care what his mother thought of her and that he only wished for her to be herself, forever and always.

But he did not want to push her. If she needed time, he would be patient.

When he awoke in the morning, the drizzle of rain had turned to spiraling white flakes that fell lazily to the earth, covering the grounds in a layer of snow. Mother was all enthusiasm, and she planned an entire day of snow-related activities: sleigh rides to the pond, ice skating, and hot tea when they returned.

Roland felt a lift in his heart. Snow was hopeful. Snow was renewing. And surely sometime in all the busyness, he would find a chance to pull Miss Bell aside and speak to her.

He waited at the base of the stairs as the party gathered in the entryway, all abuzz over the snow and the festivities. Miss Tindale found his side and chattered away, though he could hardly say what she spoke about. His responses were meager at best, and though he was sure he was being rude, he could not take his eyes from the top of the stairs.

But Miss Bell did not appear.

"Are we ready?" Mother adjusted the cloak around her shoulders. "Come then, the sleighs are waiting."

Miss Tindale looked up at Roland, no doubt expecting him to offer his arm. But he only stepped quickly to his mother's side, taking her arm before she could follow Mr. and Mrs. Marsden outside.

"What of Miss Bell?" he asked. "Are we not to wait for her?"

"She said she wishes to spend the day with her sister, who has been dreadfully lonely." Mother looked far too smug about her news.

"And I am sure you did nothing to discourage her," Roland muttered.

"What, dear?"

Roland sighed. "I only asked after Miss Cassandra. Is she nearly recovered?"

Mother nodded. "Yes, the doctor was by again today. He says she'll be able to join us tomorrow."

How strange that would be, to have Miss Bell's identical sister at her side. Not to mention, it would be even harder to catch her alone.

Miss Tindale huffed as she moved past him and out the open door.

"You have *other* guests besides Miss Bell," Mother said shortly. "You would do well to act as if you remember."

She swept after Miss Tindale, and Roland rubbed his neck. What a mess this was. How could he give Miss Tindale or Miss Marsden the attention they expected when he knew his heart was taking another path entirely?

He could be kind, at the least. Polite, but nothing more.

Roland glanced up the stairs one more time, as if Miss Bell might suddenly appear, her lips quirked in that inviting half smile. But no one came. He took his hat from the footman and set it firmly on his head, determination growing inside him.

Miss Bell could try and avoid him, but he wouldn't let her. One way or another, he would find a way to see her.

Cassie crossed her arms as she stared out the window, the twirling snow barely visible in the growing darkness. She'd watched the party return from their winter escapades not an hour ago, laughing and invigorated. In the twilight, she hadn't managed to pick Roland apart from the rest. Was he also laughing? Had he missed her today?

"Are you planning to dress for dinner soon?"

Vivian's voice stirred Cassie from her contemplation. She turned to her sister, wrapped in a blanket and seated beside the fire.

"No, I thought we could eat together, if you'd like." Cassie took the chair beside Vivian. She had not the energy for dinner, not when she knew their charade was at an end. Dr. Duttle had come that morning, and he'd delivered the good news that Vivian had made a full recovery. Starting tomorrow, she was free to rejoin the party.

Cassie's end of the agreement was fulfilled. She had

played Vivian as best she could, and now her sister could return to her place come morning. There was no point in going to dinner tonight.

It would only hurt Cassie more.

Vivian eyed her curiously. "Are you so weary of pretending to be me that you prefer even more solitude after an entire day together?"

"*Yes*," Cassie insisted. "Not only am I quite finished with this deception, but it has been too long since we spent any significant time together. And when you join the party tomorrow, I'll lose you once again."

Vivian reached over and took her hand. "You won't lose me, Cassie."

Cassie shook her head. "But I will. Or, at least, I'll lose what we have now. When you marry Mr. Hastings"—she nearly choked on the words—"things will never be the same. And I understand that is the way of life, but does that mean I cannot mourn the change?"

Vivian squeezed her hand, a soft smile claiming her face. "I do not think I deserve to have you as a sister. I have been so focused on my future, on my own plans, that I think I have neglected you. But I shall try harder to show you I love you, no matter what may come. You have done so much for me."

What had she done for Vivian, really? Made a mess of her reputation, abandoned her to spend time alone with Roland, and spun a web of lies.

"In any case," Cassie said, clearing her throat. "Let us spend the evening together without thoughts or worries for tomorrow. Just like we used to."

"Another round of backgammon, then?" Vivian suggested with a grin. "We are caught in a tie, and I should like to beat you soundly."

Cassie forced a laugh and moved to set the pieces again

on the table. But her smile did not reach the depths of her heart, which felt more like the storm outside.

After another two hours of games and talking, Vivian declared she needed to rest in order to make the most of the next day. Cassie bid Vivian good night and stepped out into the corridor, cold and lonely without the warmth of a fire. Hard as it was to pretend nothing was wrong, Cassie far preferred the distraction of her sister to an empty room and wandering thoughts.

"Miss Bell."

She froze, her hand still on the doorknob. Not now. She turned slowly to see Roland stepping from the shadows, his dark, unruly locks falling over concerned eyes.

Cassie managed a quick breath, trying to reclaim her equilibrium. "Should you not be at dinner?"

"I pled exhaustion after the long day," he said, crossing his arms. "And I did not want to miss my chance."

"Your chance?"

"To intercept you before you hid away from me again."

"I wasn't hiding—"

He held up one hand. "I do not blame you in any way. I only . . ." He paused. "I missed you."

Cassie's heart thumped wildly, as if it might grow wings and burst from her chest. Roland had missed *her*.

He moved closer, the candlelight flickering over the lines of his face, his wide jaw and straight nose. "Come with me."

It was not a question but not quite a command. "Come with you where?"

He smiled and held out his hand to her. "I believe it is my turn to surprise you."

Cassie stared at him, then his hand. She couldn't. She shouldn't. After what had happened yesterday in the ballroom, there was too much risk—both to her reputation and her heart. And what about Vivian? How could she think to—

"Please?" he said, his voice soft as the gently falling snow outside. She met his eyes once more, and the hope there destroyed all her defenses.

She slipped her hand into his.

His smile broadened. "I want to show you something."

He tugged her with him as he started down the corridor, and she needed no further encouragement. His firm, warm hand in hers sent continuous tingles up her arm and straight to her chest. One more night, she reasoned with herself. After all she'd endured in the last week, she deserved one more night of happiness. Then tomorrow . . .

But she would not think of tomorrow. Not with Roland guiding her through the quiet, dark corridors, and her pulse racing like a colt at Newmarket.

"Here we are," he finally said. She sent him a questioning look, but he only opened an unremarkable door and ushered her inside.

A fire sparked in the grate across the room, leaving most of the room in shadow. Cassie moved to the center, turning to gain her bearing. A little bed near the window, neatly made. A row of tin soldiers arranged on a low table, and a shelf full of books and blocks. "The nursery?"

Roland nodded. "My nursery, when I was a boy."

"If you wanted to play soldiers, you only needed to ask."

He grinned. "I did not bring you here to play soldiers, though the idea is tempting." He moved across the room to the large window above a padded bench. He opened the window, and cold slipped into the room, surrounding her like the cool waters of the lake near Brightling.

She shivered as Roland turned back to face her. He grimaced. "I should have had you bring a cloak."

"Then I might not have come," she said dryly.

He chuckled, taking the blanket from the bed and

coming to her. She inhaled a sharp breath as he wrapped the blanket snugly around her shoulders.

"Better?" he asked.

She cleared her throat. "Yes. Good."

He nodded and moved back to the window. "Come on."

"Where are we—"

But he did not wait for her to finish her question. He climbed through, ducking under the windowsill, then turned and offered his hand once again.

She could leave. Return to her room with her heart still intact. At least, mostly intact.

But she needed to know why he'd brought her here. She needed to know what here *was*.

She took his hand and stepped up onto the bench, holding the blanket closed with her free hand. He helped her over the windowsill and onto the small ledge below the window, which extended at a slight angle a few feet before dropping off. The snow drifted around them, though they were sheltered by the angle of the walls.

Roland helped her sit and then took his place beside her, one elbow propped on his upright knee.

"I used to sneak out here as a boy," he said, "to hide from my nursemaid, or whenever I felt particularly daring. I thought it might provide us an excellent view of the snow, since you did not go out with us earlier."

He spoke with no hint of judgment, but Cassie straightened. "I could see it very well from my window."

"That is hardly the same thing as experiencing it."

"No, this is much colder."

He laughed with a shake of his head. "You cannot hate snow so much," he said, gesturing to the snowflakes, which swirled about in a complicated dance only nature knew.

"I do not *hate* it." She brought her knees to her chest and wrapped her blanket around them. "But it is wet and inconvenient, and generally I prefer to be inside near a fire."

"And now?" he asked. "Would you rather be inside now?"

He was looking at her—she could see it from the corner of her eye. But she did not dare look back at him, knowing the strength of his gaze. "No," she said, focusing on the snow gathering on the roof just beyond her slippers. "No, I am quite content where I am."

They sat in silence for a long minute, the snow falling around them in a silent chorus. She could hardly feel the cold anymore, what with Roland's arm brushing hers.

"Will you tell me why you've been avoiding me?" he finally asked. "I've dared to guess that it involves my mother."

Cassie bit her lip. She hadn't thought she would see him again before tomorrow, and then only as Cassandra, not Vivian. She hadn't begun to formulate a response to such a question.

"I admit your mother is part of it," she said. "But it is far more complicated than that."

"Complicated how?"

She shook her head. How could she tell him the truth, that she was not the girl he thought her to be? That she had been lying to him almost their entire acquaintance?

"I am sorry, I should not press you," he said. "I only wanted the chance to . . ."

He paused, and then she did look at him. He stared steadfastly out into the snow, as if searching for the right words to appear.

"To what?" she whispered.

His eyes met hers, and Cassie had to gulp a breath. How could his eyes hold both such intensity and warmth?

"To tell you what I think," he said simply. "And what I

think is that you should not care one whit what my mother says or believes. Because the reasons she has decided to dislike you are the very reasons I do like you."

Cassie did not move. Indeed, she *couldn't* move, not with his words still lingering in the air around her.

Roland turned so he faced her directly, stray snowflakes clinging to his dark locks. He slipped her hand from where she clutched her knees and held it in his, his thumb brushing over her knuckles.

"You are all a woman ought to be," he said. "Compassionate. Sincere. Determined." He offered a smile. "You surprise me at every turn, and not just with archery ranges in the ballroom."

She gave a choked laugh, and he tightened both his hands around hers, warming them as if she held a fresh cup of tea.

"You mustn't allow my mother's voice into your head," he said in a near whisper. "She has no place there, nor between us."

"But you cannot pretend she has no influence in your life," Cassie said with a catch in her voice. "I would not want to come between you in any way."

Roland fixed her with a stern look. "I have yet to allow my mother to dictate my life, and I do not plan to start now. My choices are my own."

"I did not mean to say they were not," she said. "Only that ... well, problems follow me wherever I go. I have not made your life any easier since I arrived." It was the closest she could come to the truth. She *had* complicated his life, toyed with his emotions and desires. And he had no idea.

"No," he admitted, "my life has not been easier. But that has everything to do with an unwanted house party and nothing to do with you. Because you ... you have made it all worthwhile." He raised her hand and pressed a soft kiss to her knuckles. A shiver swept across her. "You have made me remember what is possible, in life and love."

Love. Oh, he should not have said that word.

"Roland," she whispered. "I cannot . . . you mustn't . . ."

He silenced her protests with another kiss, this time on the soft skin inside her wrist. Her blood pulsed hot in her veins.

"Roland," she tried again, weakly.

Then she could speak no more, because he was kissing her. He pulled her close, wrapped one arm around her waist, the other behind her neck. But his lips—oh, his lips. Why had no one ever told her how absurdly wonderful kissing was? Cassie's arms wound about his neck, the blanket falling from her shoulders. She kissed him back, not stopping to think, to doubt. She only knew she wanted this, more than she'd ever wanted anything—she wanted his kiss, his gentle words, his *love.*

His hands moved to caress her cheeks, leaving a trail of fire behind. She leaned into him, needing to be closer, and he responded with a new intensity in his kiss, an urgency that stole the breath from her lungs. But she did not pull away, not until he drew his mouth from hers, breathing deeply as he kissed her nose, her cheeks, her closed eyes.

"Vivian," he murmured.

Cassie's eyes shot open, and she jerked back, staring at him. *Vivian.*

He stared back, his brow furrowed. "What . . . what is wrong?"

Everything was wrong. Everything.

"I have to go." She scrambled to her feet, holding tight to the windowsill so she did not slip on the slanting roof.

"Let me help you," Roland protested.

But she clambered back through the open window

without his help, barely finding her feet before stumbling toward the door.

"Vivian, what did I do?" He caught her, taking her arm before she could disappear into the dark corridor. "I'm sorry, I should not have kissed you like that. I thought you felt the same."

"I *do*," she said, the words tearing painfully from her throat. "I do. But you must let me go. Please. If you care for me at all."

He hesitated, still holding her arm. But she pulled away, and he let her go. She did not look back as she darted out of the nursery.

Twelve

WHY ON *EARTH* had she gone with Roland tonight? She had known it would only lead to more heartbreak, and yet she had followed after him without question. She had hurt him, and herself, in the process.

What was she to tell Vivian? How could Cassie face her, knowing she'd kissed the man her sister hoped to marry? Surely she had broken every rule of sisterhood. She was only meant to distract Roland, not *fall in love with him.*

Her eyes burned with tears, but she swiped at them angrily, refusing to let them fall.

"Miss Bell."

Cassie came to a sudden halt. Mrs. Hastings stood in the corridor ahead, still dressed in her evening finery.

"Mrs.—Mrs. Hastings," Cassie stammered. "Is dinner over already?"

"Quite," she said. "Hardly reason to prolong such an event when my son did not even bother to show for it."

Cassie said nothing, only tried to control her breathing. But Mrs. Hastings moved closer, her narrowed eyes roving over Cassie's face.

"You were with him again, weren't you?" she asked quietly.

Cassie clenched her jaw. She did *not* owe this woman any answers.

"I see." Mrs. Hastings stopped an arm's length away. "At least you are smart enough not to admit it."

Hostess or not, Cassie was finished with this conversation already. She was finished with this entire evening.

"I beg your pardon, Mrs. Hastings," she said stiffly. "I am tired, and I am going to bed. Good night."

She moved around the older woman, and she had nearly made her escape when Mrs. Hastings called after her. "Oh, Miss Cassandra?"

"Yes?" Cassie said shortly, spinning back.

A look of victory spread across Mrs. Hastings's face, and Cassie realized her mistake.

"I knew it," Mrs. Hastings breathed. "I knew you were the wrong sister."

"No," Cassie said weakly. Her mind would not work; her breath caught in her lungs. "No, you do not understand. My sister truly is ill, and she—"

"I do not care that she is ill," Mrs. Hastings said. "I only care that she is not *you*. I haven't the faintest idea what drove you to take her name in the first place, but Roland never need know."

Cassie shook her head. The woman was making no sense.

"My son thinks he is in love with you." Mrs. Hastings approached slowly, her eyes fixed on Cassie. "But of course, that is only an illusion. We both know you are not right for him, for this life. You could never be what he needs. Could you mingle with the highest of society? Stand beside him at balls and dinner parties, ready to help him make his way in the world?"

Cassie clutched a hand to her stomach, the roiling there so intense she thought she might be sick.

"No," Mrs. Hastings said. "No, you could not. You would embarrass him, and yourself."

"What do you want from me?" Cassie finally said.

"Switch places again." Her voice grew cold. "I would prefer he marry into another family altogether, but Roland has shown no liking for the other young ladies I invited. He is already in love with who he thinks is Vivian Bell, so that is who we will give him."

Switching back had always been Cassie's plan, the goal from the start. But now that she knew her intentions lined up so neatly with Mrs. Hastings's, she felt a forceful resistance to it.

"And me?" Cassie asked, gritting her teeth. "Shall I simply fade to the background, pretend as though nothing happened?"

The matron hesitated, then she set her jaw. "No. I would have you leave altogether. Your being here would only complicate things. We will say Cassandra's condition was not improving and she wished to recover fully at home."

Cassie turned away, hugging her arms tight around her chest.

"You know this is the right thing to do." Mrs. Hastings almost sounded sympathetic. "I always intended your sister for Roland, not you. You were never more than a placeholder."

Why did she have to be right? Cassie knew it to be true. But a voice inside begged her to reconsider, to imagine the possibilities. She could tell Roland everything, admit to Vivian what had happened. She'd never intended to fall in love, after all. It had been an accident. Could Roland love someone who had deceived him so completely? Could Vivian ever forgive her?

She took a shuddering breath. No. It was useless. She could never hurt her sister like that. And *if* Roland had begun to see her true self, and perhaps even care for her, Mrs.

Hastings was right. Cassie could never be a proper wife to him. Not like Vivian could.

She had to give Vivian and Roland the best chance at happiness she could. She loved them both, so how could they not love each other?

Cassie turned back to Mrs. Hastings. "I will go," she said softly. "In the morning. Roland will never know." And Vivian would never know Cassie's true feelings.

Mrs. Hastings nodded. "I'll have a carriage readied for you at first light."

Cassie nearly thanked her, an instinct from years of etiquette lessons. But she bit her tongue.

Mrs. Hastings took a step and then paused. "I did not want to hurt you," she said. "But it is for the best."

Cassie could not be there a moment longer. She spun on her heel and ran until she found the safety of her room, the quiet crackling of her fire.

She did not bother to call for Jennings to help her pack. After lugging her trunk to the base of her bed, she began tossing in dresses and shawls haphazardly. Everything would be dreadfully wrinkled, but that hardly topped her list of concerns at the moment.

After emptying her wardrobe, she moved to her desk. Upon seeing her package of cherry comfits, Cassie's will nearly broke, remembering Roland's gentle teasing. But she squared her shoulders and tossed the package into her trunk. She would throw them out when she arrived home.

When there was nothing left in her room save for a traveling dress for tomorrow, Cassie stood with her hands on her waist, breathing hard, fighting the tightness in her lungs. But she couldn't fall apart now, not when one task still remained—the most difficult of all. She sat at the writing desk and pulled out a piece of paper.

So much had happened since she'd come to Hartfield,

and soon this house party would be nothing more than a memory, bittersweet and inescapable.

"Leaving?" Vivian had been inspecting herself in the vanity mirror, but now she spun to face Cassie. "What do you mean, you are leaving?"

Cassie sat on the bed, one hand steadying herself on the bedpost. She had to be convincing. "I am tired, Viv. Of the pretense. And you know I have never enjoyed parties. Now that you are better, there is no reason for me to stay. I can go home for Christmas."

Vivian shook her head. "But I need your help. What if Mr. Hastings mentions something you haven't told me? What if—"

"Everything you need to know is in here." Cassie pulled the letter from her reticule. "Read it, please."

Vivian took the letter, but her eyes did not leave Cassie's. "What happened?" she asked quietly. "Something has changed since last night."

Cassie sighed. "I have simply had enough of this house party and want nothing more than the quiet seclusion to which we both know I am better suited."

"You know I do not believe you in the slightest."

Cassie gave a sad smile. "Of course. But I also know what I am doing, I promise."

Vivian looked far from convinced, but Cassie stood and embraced her. "I wish you every happiness with Mr. Hastings," she whispered. "He is a good man, and I know you will be happy together."

Vivian pulled away, her eyes glossy with tears. "I hope so, but I do not think I shall ever be truly happy until you are settled as well."

Cassie shook her head. She was quite cried out, having shed more than her fair share of tears during the long night. "You may be wishing for that a long while yet." Vivian frowned, but Cassie did not want to prolong this conversation any more than necessary. "Goodbye, Viv. I hope to hear good news from you soon."

Vivian kissed her on the cheek, and then Cassie hurried from the room, down the stairs, and out the front door, where a coach awaited her. The footman helped her inside and closed the door behind her, the thud echoing in her ears with resounding finality.

She looked back at the manor as the coach started away, as if she might catch a glimpse of Roland at a window, or riding from the stables. But she saw no one.

Cassie curled into the corner of the coach, her eyes unseeing as they drove through the snowy landscape. Surely Vivian was reading the letter now. Cassie had tried her best to explain all that had happened between her and Roland. She'd written of their late-night conversation in the alcove, the archery range in the ballroom—and their kiss on the roof in the snow. She could hardly keep all that a secret now, not when Vivian needed to know everything.

She'd written that she'd been too embarrassed to tell Vivian all this in person, and that of course Roland had only kissed her because he believed her to be Vivian. There was no doubt in Cassie's mind, she'd said, that Roland Hastings loved Vivian Bell.

The only thing she did not tell her sister was how much Cassandra Bell loved Roland Hastings.

Cassie closed her eyes, remembering briefly those few moments of bliss from last night, when Roland had kissed her.

When she'd felt absolutely and completely loved.

Thirteen

ROLAND DID NOT sleep.

To be fair, he did not really try. He sat before his fire for hours, poking at the ashes as his memories wound about in circles. Vivian, her cheeks rosy and eyes bright, looking up at him. The sweetness of her lips on his, her soft hair and skin. And then the look of utter panic that had overtaken her features as she scrambled back through the window.

Away from him.

And yet.

And yet he clung to what she'd said, that she *did* feel the same way toward him. Had he simply pushed too far, too fast? He hadn't meant to kiss her. He'd only wanted to talk. But how was he supposed to resist her sitting there beside him in the snow, impossibly beautiful, unreasonably adorable?

He could not begin to explain his actions to himself, let alone to her. This house party was to have been a thing to endure, but he could never have anticipated Vivian. He'd fallen for her so quickly—though *falling* was not the right word. He'd plummeted into love. Plunged. Really, it was his own fault she'd run off. First his mother's actions and now his impulsive kiss.

He needed to fix this. He needed to reassure her he did not expect such ardor in return, even if his heart was already hers. He would give her the time she needed to decide.

The ashes of his fire were nearly cold when sunlight began drifting through his curtains. Roland dressed and escaped for a ride, hoping to cool the fever that had taken control of his body since last night. When he returned, he paused in the entryway when he heard female voices coming from the parlor. Was Vivian inside? How might she react to seeing him?

He took a deep breath. They would see each other sooner or later, and perhaps it was better to do so in a group setting. He only wanted to show her that his affections remained unchanged despite her reaction last night.

Roland stepped inside the parlor and stopped short. Vivian sat across the room, dressed in a pretty pink gown, her fair hair glowing in the sunlight. But that was not why he stared. Vivian sat beside his mother, and both women were *smiling*.

Mother looked up. "Ah, there you are, Roland. We thought you'd deserted us again."

Her pointed slight at his missing dinner last night barely registered in his mind. He focused instead on Vivian, who stood upon his entering. She clasped her hands tightly, her blue eyes fixed on his.

"Good morning, Miss Bell," Roland said quietly. "I trust you slept well."

She nodded. "Yes, very well, thank you."

There was something strange in her posture—her shoulders were too stiff, her back as straight as the arrows they'd shot in the ballroom. But of course she would be ill at ease, considering their meeting last night.

"Won't you join us?" Mother asked, smoothing her skirts nonchalantly. "The others are still eating breakfast, but I am sure they will come in soon."

Roland glanced at Vivian, but she nodded without

hesitation. "Yes, please join us. Your mother has been telling me amusing stories from your childhood, and I should so like to hear your side of them."

Feeling somewhat reassured—she hadn't run away, at least—he pulled a chair closer to them and sat beside Vivian.

"And what mistruths has my mother been telling you?" he asked. "Surely not the story about the grasshopper again."

Mother gave a titter. "How can I not share that one? You decided my sewing basket would make the perfect home for the creature, and forgot to tell me before I discovered it inside!"

Vivian laughed, but it was not the unbridled, joyful sound he'd come to expect from her. No, this laugh sounded forced, practiced almost. But then, they *were* seated beside his mother. He could hardly expect her to act as she did when it was just the two of them.

"I would have been so affrighted to find a grasshopper among my thread," Vivian said, leaning forward. "I admit I have no fondness for wildlife."

"Save for cats," he said with a grin, hoping to put her at ease.

"Cats?" she repeated.

"And parrots, of course." A hint of his confusion found its way into his voice. Did she not want him to discuss such a thing before his mother?

"Oh. Of course, parrots." Vivian gave a sudden nod, as if recalling a long-forgotten fact. "My grandfather has one, though I would not advocate it as a proper pet."

"Decidedly not," Mother said. "But I am glad to know you have a fondness for cats, considering my own."

"Y-yes," Vivian stammered. "I adore cats. They are quite . . . pretty."

Something was not right. Roland squinted at Vivian.

Nothing she had said was wrong, but it was more *how* she said it.

"Is your sister joining us today?" Roland asked, watching her closely. "I hope she has made a full recovery."

Vivian blinked rapidly, as if she'd gotten something in her eye. "No. No, I'm afraid Cassandra has decided to return home. She is feeling better, but not yet up to enjoying the house party."

Roland nodded. "Ah, a pity I did not get to spend much time with her. But perhaps I shall send her a package of cherry comfits to assuage her disappointment."

"Comfits?" Vivian furrowed her brow. "An interesting gift. Very... thoughtful. I am certain she would be glad to receive it."

He stared at the young lady before him, at her carefully folded hands, her pursed lips, and her guarded eyes. The golden curls and blue eyes were the same, but nearly everything else was different.

And then it all connected in his head, his thoughts flying faster than a sparrow on the wind.

"You are not Vivian," he said slowly.

Her mouth parted, but she did not speak.

Mother gave a nervous laugh. "Of course this is Miss Bell. Who else would it be?"

But Roland shook his head. "This is not the woman I spent the last week with."

Mother stood, face reddening. "Roland, you are being ridiculous, and quite rude to Miss Bell. I insist you apologize—"

"No." The young lady stood as well, and Mother gaped at her. "No, please do not apologize. You have nothing to feel sorry for, while I have everything to regret." She took a deep breath and looked Roland straight in the eye. "I *am* Vivian

Bell, but not the one you came to know. That was my sister, Cassandra."

Cassandra. Her name repeated in his mind, again and again.

"She pretended to be you?" he asked, perplexed. "Why?"

Mother sat again, holding a hand to her forehead, and Vivian's cheeks grew pink.

"I . . . I am embarrassed to admit I formed an attachment to you during our time in London. When I grew ill during our journey here, I begged her to take my name and—" She closed her eyes tightly. "I asked her to ensure that the other young ladies did not monopolize your time."

Roland leaned back in his chair, head spinning. His memories skimmed over the last week; he remembered all the little oddities and inconsistencies he'd noticed in Miss Bell—Cassandra. Her competitiveness with Miss Tindale, her struggling to appear more proper than she was. And her *singing*.

Then, to everyone's surprise, including his own, a short laugh escaped him.

"This explains so much," he said, shaking his head. "In truth, I cannot believe I did not guess it sooner. I simply assumed she acted strangely because she was nervous." Another realization struck him, and he turned to his mother. "Nervous of *you*, Mother. Tell me you did not know about this."

Her face paled. "No! Of course not." She paused. "That is, until last night."

Roland narrowed his eyes. "What happened last night?"

"I . . ." She swallowed. "I may have encouraged Cassandra to return home. I thought it best, considering her entire character was a deception from the start. But Miss Bell here—"

"That was *not* for you to decide, Mother." Now Roland was on his feet. He turned to Vivian. "Miss Bell, I am certain you are all that is sweetness and gentility, but—"

"But you are in love with my sister," she said softly, understanding growing in her eyes.

Roland hesitated. He did not want to hurt this lovely young lady, when she was guilty of nothing but setting her sights on the wrong man.

"It is all right." Vivian looked down at her clasped hands. "After spending just a few minutes with you, it is quite obvious how you feel about her. I had my suspicions after reading Cassie's letter this morning, but I wanted to see the truth for myself."

"She wrote you a letter?"

"Yes, explaining all that happened." She cleared her throat. "And now I must be clear about a few things. Cassie is my dearest friend, and I have no doubt it was her sincerity, her cleverness and compassion, that endeared her to you." She took a steadying breath. "If there is any chance Cassie returns your feelings, then you must go to her."

Roland forced himself to breathe, memories from last night on the roof slipping through his confusion. Miss Bell—Cassie—returning his kiss before running away. He understood now why she'd done it. She hadn't wanted to hurt her sister.

He stepped forward. "Where is she now? You said she decided to go home."

"Yes." Vivian's smile faded. "She left early this morning. It is a two-day journey."

He strode to the window, inspecting the ground. It would not be easy traveling in the snow, especially once it began to melt and mud took its place. But surely he could make better time on horseback than by coach. If he hurried, perhaps—

"Roland."

His mother's voice snapped him back to attention. She stared at her hands, held tightly in her lap.

"Roland, I . . ." She shook her head. "I thought you were making a monumental mistake, and I saw it as my duty to correct you." Mother finally raised her eyes. "Cassandra Bell is not who I would have chosen for you, but if she is who you want, I will resign myself to it. She is determined and intelligent, and that will have to be enough."

That was as close to an apology as he had ever heard from his mother. He nodded, though far from ready to forgive her completely. "If she will have me."

"You will never know," Vivian said, "if you do not give her the chance."

Roland inhaled an unsteady breath. Was he ready to propose? Not even a fortnight ago had he considered such a thing possible.

But Cassandra had changed all that. Her ringing laugh danced through his mind, her gentleness and her spirit, the ease with which they conversed for hours on end. And he knew this was what he had been searching for. What his father had wanted for him.

He looked at Mother. "Father would have liked her," he said softly.

Her eyes misted, and she turned away. "Then what on earth are you waiting for, my boy? Go and claim your lady."

He turned to Vivian, his mind racing. She raised her chin, though a flash of pain still echoed behind those familiar blue eyes. "You must go," she said, her voice firm. "That is my wish for you, and for Cassie."

He stood still, trying to grasp all that had happened in the last few minutes. If he knew anything about Cassandra, it was that she cared for her sister above all else. It would be no easy task to convince her to accept him when it might injure Vivian.

Roland looked at Vivian. "I do not wish to take advantage of your kindness, Miss Bell, but if you are willing, I would be grateful for your help."

She pulled back her head in surprise, but then she nodded. "Of course, Mr. Hastings. Anything."

Fourteen

CASSIE HAD EXPECTED some relief upon arriving home, but the sight of the familiar columned portico and brick exterior brought her nothing but emptiness. That and exhaustion, of course, after two days of bumping around in a carriage with nothing but her thoughts for company.

The footman helped Cassie down from the coach. There was no snow here at Brightling, nothing to hide the depressing drabness that was December. She climbed the front steps, pulling at the ribbons of her bonnet as she stepped inside. "Mama?" she called. "Papa?"

"Cassandra? Is that you?"

She did not think there was anything that could make her smile at the moment besides her grandfather's voice. Cassie hurried to the study, which Grandpapa claimed as his refuge. He sat in his great leather armchair, the same as always: a glass of whiskey in one hand and a book in the other, his disorderly gray hair at odds with the tidiness of his clothing and those sparkling blue eyes.

He set down both the glass and the book at her appearance, his eyebrows raised. "Cassie?"

"I am sorry to intrude upon you, Grandpapa," she said, her voice breaking. "I know you did not expect me for another few days."

"Never mind that." He stood and moved toward her, his face crinkled in concern. "What is wrong?"

She shook her head fervently. She could tell no one what had happened, not even her grandfather. There could be no chance the truth would make its way to Vivian.

"Nothing," she said brightly. "Just a long journey, that is all. I grew bored of the house party, and Vivian was getting on well enough, so I decided to return for Christmas." She forced a smile. "I know how you love Christmas."

"That I do." Grandpapa scrutinized her, then pulled her into an embrace. "I missed you, child. Your parents are dreadfully dull company without you and Vivian around."

Cassie managed a laugh. "And where are they? They haven't abandoned you?"

"I could only dream," he said, pulling away. "No, they've gone to town for some errands. I expect them back soon."

Cassie nodded. She could tell her mother she had done everything in her power to give Vivian the match she'd dreamed of—even if it had broken her own heart in the process.

"I'll have the maid bring us tea." Grandpapa moved to the door.

"I can do that," Cassie insisted.

"No, no," he said hastily. "You stay here. Keep Arnold company."

She hadn't noticed the parrot in the corner of the room, quiet as he was. Usually the creature squawked constantly and made a great deal of noise, but not today.

"Stay here," Grandpapa said again, a strange look in his eye.

Cassie furrowed her brow. "All right."

He disappeared without another word. Odd. He must really have missed her.

Cassie wandered to the fireplace, warming her hands as

she took in the comforting adornments of her grandfather's study. The rows of books, the paintings featuring sights from all over the world, the broad windows that let in the waning afternoon light. She let out a long breath. At least she was home.

"Mary."

Cassie spun before she realized it was not a real voice. It was only Arnold in his cage, stretching his bright-red wings. She went to him, head tilted.

"Mary?" she repeated. "Have you finally learned a new word, then?" Or a name? Perhaps they had acquired a new maid in her absence. Mother had been searching for one when they'd left for Hartfield Court.

"Mary," the parrot squawked again. "Mary."

Cassie smiled faintly. If nothing else, she could spend her Christmas entertained by this silly parrot and her loving grandfather. She would need such distractions, dreading as she was the news that would surely come from Hartfield soon. Cassie bit her lip, fighting her own mind from turning where she knew it should not turn—back to Roland.

Footsteps sounded behind her, and she cleared her throat against the persistent lump there. She did not want Grandpapa to suspect anything.

"It seems Arnold has made some progress in my absence," she said, reaching a finger inside the cage to stroke the bird's tail feathers. "But who is Mary?"

A sigh and a short laugh. "I should have believed your grandfather when he said it was useless."

Cassie stiffened. That was *not* her grandfather.

She swallowed, then turned slowly to peek over her shoulder. Roland stood just inside the door, hands clasped behind his back, a half smile toying with his lips. She stared at him, all of him, from his polished boots to his dark hair. It *was* him, wasn't it? Surely she wasn't so desperately in love as to imagine him.

"What—" Her voice cracked, as if she were again performing at the pianoforte. "What are you doing here?"

"I admit you posed an interesting challenge, leaving hours before I did." He moved further into the room, his eyes never leaving hers. "It meant a late night and an early morning, but I managed to arrive about two hours ago."

Cassie gripped the back of her grandfather's armchair to steady herself. What was happening? He should be in Hartfield, with Vivian.

"I know everything," Roland said softly.

A new panic gripped her. Did he know who she really was? Had he discovered her deception and come to punish her for it?

"I know," he said, his voice full of meaning. "I know you are Cassandra Bell. I know you pretended to be your sister for the entire house party."

Cassie took a sharp breath. "Roland—"

"I know you kept the truth from me, even after it became clear there was something between us."

"I am so sorry—"

"And," he interrupted, "I know you only did so with the best of intentions. To help your sister."

She blinked. He smiled and stepped closer.

"I know that, despite your name," he said, his voice quiet and sincere, "you are the same woman I talked with for hours. You are the same woman who reassured an anxious cat and who performed the worst rendition of a carol I've ever heard."

Roland took two more steps to her side, holding both her hands in his, pressing them against his chest.

She finally found her voice. "But I deceived you. I made you believe I was Vivian."

He shook his head. "I would not care if your name was Hephzibah. A name does not a person make."

She wanted to smile at his jesting, but her unbelieving heart did not allow it. Cassie closed her eyes. "You did not have to come all this way."

"Actually, I did. But you were right, the blasted parrot is completely useless. We—meaning your grandfather and I—finally convinced the creature to say one of the necessary words, but now it seems to be the only word it knows. And truthfully, I first thought to come on Christmas, like my mother suggested. But I simply could not wait."

Cassie opened her eyes again. "You must know I haven't the faintest idea what you are talking about."

"Marry," Arnold squawked again.

And then she understood.

"Marry me," Roland whispered, his eyes searching hers. He pulled her closer, still holding tight to her hands. "I have been searching for you for a year, and now that I have found you, there is no hesitation in me. I want you by my side, just as I want to be at *your* side, always."

Cassie gaped at him, surely the most unbecoming prospective bride in all the world, with her mouth wide as a saucer. Marry him? Her mouth fought to form the word she wanted so desperately to say. But she could not say yes. Not now.

"I cannot," she whispered. "If you know why we switched, then you must know I could never hurt my sister."

Roland's expression shifted, and a gentleness claimed his eyes. "I thought you might say something like that." He reached inside his jacket and withdrew a folded note.

She took the note with a trembling hand and opened it.

Cassie,

There is no doubt in my mind that you would do anything to ensure my happiness. Now you must let me do the same. Please, be happy.

All my love,
Vivian

Cassie exhaled a shaky breath. Oh, Vivian. She must have written this note even as her own heart broke.

Roland's warm hands came around hers, still holding the note. "Vivian," he said quietly, "understands completely. She told me the truth herself, and she told me to come here."

Cassie lowered the note and set it on the nearby table. She could only imagine the selflessness of her sister to make such a choice.

"She wants this for you," he said. "But you must decide if this is what *you* want."

"But . . . but your mother," she protested. *Why* was she speaking of his mother? "How will this ever work?"

He grinned, a slow spread of his lips that brought flutters to every inch of her body. "There is a reason dower houses are built, Cassie."

Cassie. *Cassie.*

She could not have stopped herself if she tried—and she certainly did *not* try.

Cassie propelled herself upward and kissed him with such force that he staggered back a step. But then he caught her in his arms and kissed her back, his lips firm and demanding against hers. Every emotion she'd felt since leaving Hartfield came roaring through her, channeling into this moment, this kiss. Her heart pounded furiously in her chest, as if shouting aloud that it had been claimed, and her hands wandered from his chest to find the scruff of his neck, rough after two days of travel. She quite liked that, and she pulled herself even closer. His arms tightened around her, his hands exploring her waist and back.

It wasn't as though she hadn't enjoyed their first kiss on the roof. But *this* kiss was so much more—it was confirmation of all she'd convinced herself she could not have. From the moment she'd met Roland, she'd fought every rush of attraction and every meaningful connection. Now she felt it all, deep in her soul. She was meant to be here, with Roland.

Still wrapped in each other's arms, they shared one more slow, tantalizing kiss. A blissful sigh escaped from Cassie, and she felt Roland's lips curve upward beneath hers.

"That was my way of saying yes, in case you were uncertain," she whispered.

"Really?" he teased. "I thought perhaps we'd stepped beneath some mistletoe."

She smiled and pulled back slightly as her fingers toyed with the hair at the nape of his neck. "I must clarify one thing, however."

"And that is?"

"We will *not* be naming any children Hephzibah."

He laughed, drawing her hand to his lips and kissing it twice. "You shall have no argument from me, I assure you." Then he gave a dramatic exhale. "Now, I am certain your grandfather is waiting to hear the good news."

Cassie grinned. "He can wait a few minutes more. I think you are quite right about the mistletoe, and we should not risk any bad luck."

Roland grinned back. "If you insist."

His expression softened, and he turned her chin up with gentle fingers. Cassie slid her hand up his forearm, not looking away. She hadn't even realized she'd wanted this—love and marriage—until she had it. Until it was solid and absolute. And knowing she had Roland, that he loved her in return, was more happiness than she'd thought to imagine for herself.

"I love you, Roland Hastings," Cassie whispered. "I thought you should know."

He swallowed, then bent again slowly and met her lips with impossible tenderness. Cassie leaned into him, into the comfort of his arms and the promise of their future.

The End

Joanna Barker was born and raised in northern California. She discovered her love for historical fiction after visiting England as an eleven-year-old, and subsequently read every Jane Austen book she could get her hands on. After graduating Brigham Young University with a degree in English, she worked as an acquisitions editor before devoting herself full-time to writing. She enjoys music, chocolate, and reading everything from romance to science fiction. She lives in Utah and is just a little crazy about her husband and two wild-but-loveable boys.

Visit her website here: AuthorJoannaBarker.com

PROMISE ME AGAIN

-Annette Lyon-

One

December 3, 1823
Audbury, the Cotswolds

"How much farther to the lower pasture?" Jacob asked, running off after another sheep who refused to stay with the flock.

Miriam heard the sound of his boots slipping, followed by a thud as Jacob landed in a very muddy spot of grass. He let out a mild expletive, which made her laugh out loud. Her reaction apparently made him blush, as he was now nearly as red as her father's spring tulips. "Lily giving you trouble?"

"I do exactly what you've shown me, but they don't obey." He sat up and reached for his hat, which had fallen to the side.

"Maybe you should try singing," Miriam said, trying to sound lighthearted.

"Should I, now?" Jacob said, his voice playful.

She shrugged but knew it didn't look as offhand as she'd hoped. "Well, I know *I* could never run away from you after hearing you sing." Now it was her face that was turning red, if the flush burning its way up her neck and cheeks was any indication. So much for *not* sounding forward or flirtatious. She turned away, looking skyward at any invisible guardian angels who'd abandoned their duties of making sure she didn't make a fool of herself. Would that she hadn't said anything about his singing—which truly was heart-meltingly amazing—and called to the ewe.

She called to Lily, who stopped in her tracks and spun around as if Miriam had promised the sheep an apple. The old ewe nearly bowled her over, but Miriam, fortunately, managed to stay upright. For a moment, anyway. No sooner had Miriam regained her footing than Lily nudged her again, as if looking for the unpromised apple. This time, gravity had its way, and Miriam found her boots slipping. The next thing she knew, she was lying on the hard, wet ground, her hip aching with the shock of the fall.

Jacob, still on the ground, crawled over to her in a rush. "Miriam! Are you hurt?" All humor had left his face and voice, and while the color from before remained, the cause was no longer embarrassment but deep concern.

She tried to respond, to assure him that she was quite well, if slightly bruised, but Lily intervened one more time. She charged at Jacob like a guard dog protecting her mistress, running so fast that she practically went through him. Indeed, he was suddenly airborne, and though the whole matter couldn't have taken more than a blink or two, Miriam noted his expression of stunned fear before he crashed to the ground beside her. After the thud, he let out a groan, then rolled to his side, away from her, so she couldn't see his face. His shoulders began shaking silently.

Now it was her turn to worry. Caring nothing for muddying her work dress further, she crawled to him. "Jacob? Jacob, are you hurt?"

At his side, she touched his arm and shook him by it. "Talk to me. Please."

The shaking only increased, which compounded her worry. Right as her eyes threatened tears, Jacob rolled onto his back, and the cause for the shaking was perfectly clear: he was laughing so hard, he could scarcely breathe. Jovial tears ran down his face.

The ridiculousness of the situation came over Miriam—it could, now that her worry over Jacob was eased. "I suppose this is rather silly," she said. "Lily is so old that I don't know why Father bothers sending her from one grazing spot to the next. She doesn't ... exactly ... produce the best ... wool." She found her own shoulders shaking. She covered her mouth with a hand to hold back the laughter, but giggling—followed by full belly laughs—emerged anyway.

Soon they were lying on the hard ground, side by side, laughing uproariously. After a time, their amusement died down, and Jacob's hand found hers. As if he'd read her mind, he began to sing—it was a simple folk tune, but as usual, her insides turned to melted butter as she listened.

His voice, combined with their entwined fingers, made everything else feel trivial, as if the only people who mattered in the world were her and Jacob, right in that moment, forever. But saying such a thing might be a bit *too* much, so when he finished the song, she settled on speaking something equally true, if not as colorful or passionate. "I could stay here comfortably all day, even with the cold mud." Her face turned to the side so that she could look at him. He did the same, and when his eyes met hers, her insides melted.

"For my part, I'm quite comfortable at the moment," Jacob said in a voice that warmed every nook and cranny of her soul.

"As am I."

He pushed himself up slightly on one arm, and with his free hand, he reached over and smoothed back some wisps of her hair that must have escaped her braid in the ruckus. While in some respects his touch felt like a dream, it was solid and real. He wasn't some ethereal, dreamlike visage. No, Jacob Davies was every inch a real man, with her right now, here on one of the rolling green hills in sheep country.

"However," Jacob went on, tracing a line with his fingers from her hair down to her chin, "your lips are a bit pale." This he said while gently brushing her lower lip with his thumb. "You'll catch your death of cold if I keep you out here much longer, and that wouldn't do." He gazed into her eyes for several seconds, neither of them moving despite his suggestion. He leaned down. Miriam closed her eyes and waited for his kiss.

But instead of enjoying a kiss stolen in privacy, they were pulled apart when the unmistakable sound of whistling tore through the air. More specifically, the whistling of Norman, the elder Davies brother. Miriam's eyes flew open, and they withdrew from each other, sitting up so as not to be discovered in anything that could be interpreted as an unseemly position. After all, Norman did not approve of Jacob having so much as a friendship with Miriam, much less a "romantic entanglement," as he put it.

They scrambled to their feet, each action accompanied by more of the same annoying trill that marked Norman's call for Jacob. If he were to find them not only together but alone, far from any possible chaperoning eyes, and lying beside each other? And all of that *while kissing?* Well, perhaps the resulting apoplexy would result in Norman fainting to the ground. That was wishful thinking, of course. Miriam was frantically smoothing her muddied skirts and hoping Norman hadn't seen them.

Jacob threw her a look of apology, then turned to his brother, jaw clenched with frustration before quickly schooling his expression into a polite one. He raised an arm and cheerfully cried, "Ahoy, brother!"

Norman rode up on his horse, slowing to a walk as he drew near but saying nothing for several moments, even waiting for several breaths to speak after he'd stopped completely. The silence was painfully awkward—which, Miriam realized, was likely his intent. Norman nodded at Jacob and offered Miriam something that might have resembled a nod.

"Mr. Davies," Miriam piped up, stepping closer to the horse. "Your kind brother has been most gentlemanly today. You see, he's been helping me move my father's sheep to the lower meadow."

From his perch in the saddle, Norman looked about and almost seemed disappointed that there was indeed plenty of evidence for her statement. The clearest evidence, of course, was the flock of sheep heading down the hill, and stubborn Lily still standing nearby, not having followed her flock mates.

"Has my dear younger brother been of such noble service, then?" Norman's brows rose, and his lip curled arrogantly. "Tsk-tsk. If Father could see you now."

"He'd be quite happy with how I've turned out, thank you very much," Jacob retorted. "Father was always kind and willing to help others."

Miriam wanted to say more, to defend her dear Jacob, but knew in her gut that nothing a sheep farmer's daughter could say would sway Norman Davies, and any attempt might only make matters worse. But she was sure of one thing; the late Mr. Davies *had* approved of her as a match for Jacob. She'd heard him say so with her own ears only a week before his death.

He'd even hinted not so subtly to her, without either son in the room, that he wished Jacob were the elder son, because he didn't quite trust Norman. He'd exhausted his strength before saying more, so Miriam didn't precisely know the whys or wherefores for their father's mistrust, but she suspected it surrounded the family's finances.

Norman slipped off his horse and, letting the reins go slack, stepped close to Jacob, stopping when they were nearly nose to nose. The brothers were of almost equal height, with Jacob having perhaps an inch on Norman. Each brother folded his arms and stared the other down. Miriam gulped. She glanced at the sheep, all of which seemed to be happily grazing patches of old grass. Even Lily had decided to lie down and now appeared to be sleeping. Why couldn't the animal be a nuisance at a convenient time?

"May I help you with something?" Jacob demanded. "Why are you here?"

"I came to fetch you to the house to discuss a matter of business that's of utmost importance."

Jacob's eyes narrowed, as if he was studying Norman's face for what he was really thinking. *Had* he seen anything that could be interpreted as untoward? Miriam wanted to say he hadn't; keeping such a detail to himself didn't seem to fit with Norman's personality. But he did appear awfully pleased with himself...

"I'll come as soon as the sheep are securely in the pasture."

"You'll come now." Norman took half a step forward, which was all he could take, because now their toes really were touching. A thick vein on his neck throbbed.

The absolute last thing Miriam wanted was for the brothers to come to blows right there on the hillside. She stepped forward and, in the same cheerful tone Jacob had used before, said, "I was just telling your brother that we were almost there. Wasn't I, Jacob? That is, Mr. Davies?" She looked to him, but the brothers' eyes remained fixed on each other. Miriam continued as if all were well. "I'll be fine here navigating the last few hundred yards. You two head back to Stonecroft Cottage to discuss whatever it is you men need to discuss." She twirled her hand at the wrist to punctuate her words.

Norman's only response was to correct her with the name he preferred. "Stonecroft *Hall.*"

"Yes," Miriam said, trying not to stammer. "Stonecroft Hall." When she got no other response from Norman, she took a step backward and raised a hand in farewell. "Well, I'll be off, then." Then, unsure whether Norman Davies would think a wave too low or impolite, she dipped a curtsy. "Good—good day!" she finished, then turned about and walked to the sheep. At her call, they bleated in protest but gradually got to their feet in a group and followed her down the hill.

Head high and standing tall, she yearned to look back, to catch Jacob's eyes and whisper a farewell to him, but she daren't with Norman there. Instead, with each step, she prayed for two things: first, that she wouldn't slip again—at least, not while the Davies brothers were still watching—and second, that Norman would not try to interfere in her and Jacob's relationship.

With each step, she grew less and less sure of avoiding either.

Two

JACOB RELUCTANTLY WATCHED Miriam's figure recede down the grassy hill.

"Come on, then!" Norman said, annoyed. He bumped Jacob's shoulder as a way to get him moving.

He took half a step forward, in the direction of Miriam, which only made sense, as gravity pulled him that direction, but Norman's intent had been to fetch him home to Stonecroft Hall, formerly known as Stonecroft Cottage.

Only when Miriam had disappeared from view, which did not take long, did Jacob fetch his fallen hat from the ground, put it on his head, and turn on his brother. "Happy now?"

Norman's gaze looked down the hill, then back at Jacob, and his lips thinned and curled. "We shall see." Without waiting for Jacob to respond, he turned about and headed back in the direction he'd come from. Ten paces away, he paused and looked back. "Come on, then," he said again, as if calling a dog.

Jacob ground his teeth but *came along*, keeping a gap between himself and his brother ahead. He had absolutely no interest in exchanging niceties about the weather, or worse, carrying on a conversation, until absolutely necessary. Unfortunately, their father's death last month had made a lot of things absolutely necessary. It had also given Jacob a singular regret: that he hadn't proposed to and married Miriam before his father's passing. Joseph William Davies would never know his grandchildren, nor they him.

Not that Jacob could have given his father grandchildren quickly; he and Miriam had first exchanged words of love only a few months before. While he knew in his heart that he wanted to spend his life with her, he wasn't confident about her having reached a similar conclusion—at least, not yet. And now the brothers were in mourning. Holding a big wedding wouldn't be proper anytime soon.

They reached Stonecroft Hall all too quickly, a ten-minute walk that felt both never-ending because it took him farther from his beloved Miriam and much too fast because he dreaded any "urgent" conversation his brother would insist upon having.

Their house was one of the larger ones near Audbury, though that didn't exactly mean they lived as kings. Father had done well for himself as a merchant, having abandoned the sheep and wool trade years before many sheep farmers lost everything. Father had guessed correctly that future success lay in selling imported goods like tea and silk, which he arranged to be transported from the shipyards of London and sold at towns along the way. He and his men had stopped at towns with residents who eagerly awaited his shipments.

Their father had been away much of their adolescence. Their mother had succumbed to pneumonia shortly after giving birth to a stillborn child that would have been their little sister. So in their youth, the boys spent weeks at a time alone while their father was away on business.

Norman had always assumed the role of the one in charge, with authority to order Jacob about whenever Father was away. Jacob had reluctantly gone along with Norman's orders for years. Then they had left boyhood behind, and

Jacob grew both taller than his elder brother and fully capable of caring for himself with or without his brother's supervision. That was when he had stopped obeying his brother altogether.

For his part, Norman had been trying to regain control over Jacob ever since, to no avail. Though Jacob wouldn't have thought it possible, Norman's efforts to regain his role as patriarch had redoubled in the last month. The result was less that Norman had any control over Jacob and more that Jacob sought every opportunity to flee Norman's presence and to flout any expectations his brother might have for his own life and actions.

In the house, Jacob followed his brother up past the parlor and into their father's study. *Norman's study now,* he remembered with an ache, and he found a set of shiny new leather chairs. "Where are Father's chairs?" he demanded.

"Oh, those old things?" Norman sat on one of his new chairs, making the fresh, shiny leather squeak. "They were dry and cracked, and the style was so old-fashioned. I sent them away when these ones arrived this morning!" He leaned back in his chair, rested one leg on the other knee, and steepled his hands. "The leather is exactly the color of my favorite port."

"Lovely," Jacob said, and hoped sarcasm didn't come through his voice. He'd loved his father's old chairs, and he would have happily taken them into his room. Those chairs held a lifetime of memories for the family. The only clear memory Jacob had of his mother was of sitting in her lap on one of those old chairs, listening to her read a fairy tale. He had countless memories of Father in them. From those chairs Father had given, and they'd received, advice and guidance—never with coercion, the likes of which Norman tried to burden Jacob with nearly every day. When Jacob was but four years old and horribly ill, Father had held him in one of those chairs and sung to him beside the fire all night long.

How could Norman have tossed them away like so much rubbish?

"Now, let's discuss what I've brought you here for." Norman uncrossed his legs, leaned forward, and clasped his hands, resting them on the desk blotter. Jacob struggled to pay attention; every object, every sound, even every smell in the room flooded his mind with memories and emotions, making it hard to focus on his brother's words. The red wallpaper Father had chosen for this room five years ago refused to be ignored; Jacob could not block it out. The new chairs clashed abominably with the wallpaper. Father wouldn't have selected a bright red if the chairs in the room were to be dark red.

Jacob cleared his throat, trying to draw his attention back to his brother. "Yes, do tell me, what is so important, then?"

"Naturally, as the elder son, I am taking over Father's business operations. It's my duty."

"Naturally," Jacob repeated, again hoping his voice sounded neutral. They both knew that Father had long worried over Norman's ability to spend and gamble away money. Father had wished the property were not entailed, and Jacob suspected that he would have preferred to bequeath the house and his possessions to him, the more responsible son by leagues.

"I have spent the time since the funeral reviewing Father's records," Norman went on. "I have come to the determination that several significant changes are needed. First and foremost, I will be moving operations closer to London."

Jacob's brows drew together. "Whatever for? We have so many customers between here and the city; selling along the way as Father did makes perfect sense."

"Perhaps," Norman said, his voice taking on an oily feel. "But only if one has low ambitions."

One of Jacob's eyebrows shot up at that, and he resisted

the urge to call his brother out for defaming their father's name. "What do you mean?" he asked instead, through his teeth.

"The greatest profits are not to be found in lowly country villages," Norman said with a patronizing tone. "I suppose Father knew as much, but he never acted upon that knowledge." He waved both hands about the room. "Just think, we could have lived in a house five times the size of Stonecroft Hall, with dozens of servants."

Again, Jacob's loyalty for his father reared its head. He swallowed against the angry knot in his throat. "I suppose our father wanted to ensure that his sons had a consistent life, seeing as they'd already suffered the loss of their mother and sister."

"Perhaps," Norman said with a dismissive nod. "God rest their souls." Blasphemy if Jacob had ever heard it. Norman meant no such thing.

Jacob's first instinct was to argue, to insist that Norman not move the business to London, but then he caught himself. If Norman lived in London and coordinated the family business from there, he would no longer be pulling the puppet strings of Stonecroft in Audbury. Perhaps...

An idea sparked in Jacob's mind. "Could I continue to live here after you've settled in London? You'll be letting a flat, a far grander place than this, and I can continue to maintain the property so that the house and land don't fall into disrepair. You'll be able to return whenever you wish."

Norman tilted his head and smirked. "My dear brother, *why* would I ever want to return to this old place? I'll take my new chairs, but as far as the rest of the place, I'll be quite happy to leave it all behind."

Back on the hilltop when Norman had called Jacob home, if he'd given a hint of this wonderful news, Jacob would have run. But Norman wouldn't view the situation as having the potential to give Jacob everything he'd ever wanted. In fact, Jacob knew he'd better not let on just how much he wanted to live in the house with Miriam, or Norman might deliberately find a way to sabotage their happiness.

"So I could have the house—and a family—here?" Jacob asked. Had he sounded too excited about the prospect?

"Not exactly." Norman pushed his lower lip out slightly as he thought, then added, "Not at all, in fact."

Jacob braced himself, gripping the armrests of the infernal chair, whose dyed leather was so new it still reeked. "Go on."

"You'll be coming with me. I'll have servants maintain the house here. We'll need to keep it so that we are still considered residents of the county."

What, in the name of all that was holy, was Norman talking about?

"Now, I know you're not the ambitious type, but I do know you have a soft little heart in that chest of yours for the less fortunate, though most of their situations are due to their own deficiencies. You see, when the business increases its profile and reputation, I'll be able to position you so that you'll be able to become a member of Parliament, representing our own little county." He sat back and crossed his legs again, clearly pleased with his cleverness. "Think of the good we could do together, with my brains for business and your heart for politics."

His brother intended to put Jacob into Parliament and control him from there? Jacob shook his head, "Norman, no. I—"

"No, no," Norman said, stopping Jacob from saying a word. "You and I will rise above our sad family legacy and create a new one. To be a Davies will *mean* something."

The whole thing sounded wrong to Jacob. Could his brother intend genuine good to come from this scheme? If he succeeded in getting Jacob elected as an MP, could he find a way to control Jacob's votes and actions there? Or could Jacob realistically influence the law according to his conscience? He didn't have the slightest idea how Parliament functioned, so for all he knew, Norman might be able to vote in Jacob's place as a surrogate—and vote exactly opposite of how Jacob would wish.

None of that mattered, because Jacob didn't want any of it. He wanted to live here in Audbury, with Miriam as his wife and, in time, with their children. Barring that, as the town's population kept growing ever scarcer as the wool industry floundered, they could move elsewhere. He could find work in carpentry, or as a farmer, or perhaps in a factory somewhere. He hadn't anything inside him pushing him to become rich or famous or influential. He wanted a simple life with the woman he loved.

"May I think on all of this for a spell?" Jacob knew better than to tell Norman no outright.

"Very well, but there is an additional matter to discuss."

Jacob had moved to stand, but he settled back in the new leather chair. As before, it squeaked under his movement. "Yes?"

"The matter of your future wife."

"Well, that's settled, or it will be soon." Jacob hoped it would be, anyway. He nearly blabbered on about Miriam, proposals, and plans, but he stopped himself just in time. Norman tended to worm his way into one's mind and settle in, making one feel a bit mad—and sound it.

"To become a politician of any sort, and to have any influence at all as one, you must possess certain characteristics."

"Yes," Jacob said, drawing out the word.

"You must be able to read and write, to speak well."

"Father paid for our schooling at Harrow. I'm well acquainted with reading, writing, and elocution."

"You must dress well and have impeccable manners," Norman continued, as if he hadn't been interrupted. "And ..." His pause seemed oddly meaningful. Jacob's stomach tightened as he waited, refusing to show his nerves to his brother. At last, Norman went on. "You must have a wife at your side who exhibits all of those things and more. She should be of at least a respectable lineage and most certainly *not* of low birth."

Jacob stood in one quick motion, a flame of rage erupting in his middle. "How *dare* you insult my future wife in such a manner?"

His outburst served only to make Norman smile; Jacob immediately cursed himself for losing control.

"The truth is, dear brother," Norman said, "Miriam Brown is not a suitable choice for the wife of a future MP." Norman was fortunate to have the desk between them, for without it, Jacob might have done something he would have later regretted.

"I will marry Miriam Brown," Jacob said evenly. "You cannot stop me. I will not be your puppet, having you pull my strings for the rest of my earthly life. I will never be an MP."

"As the head of this family, I do not and will not approve of a marriage between you and anyone of such low stock." Norman held out his hands helplessly, as if the matter were entirely out of his control. "Even if she wore the finest Paris fashions to a ball in London, imagine the moment she opened her mouth and said two words. Everyone would know she was lowborn. They'd be able to say with remarkable accuracy how much her father earns a year, entirely based on the way she speaks, not to mention how she eats and otherwise comports herself."

"You and I grew up here, poor. There is no shame in that."

"We were not precisely what I would call *poor*, but that's beside the point. Father saw to it that we were properly educated, and that meant sending us away from this"—his lip lifted in what might have been an expression of disgust—"sad little village."

Being sent to a boarding school for four years hadn't felt like a gift to Jacob at the time; it had felt like a way for Father to unload the very real burden of two rambunctious adolescent boys. Norman had returned with a much more polished manner of speaking than Jacob had. They'd both learned the "proper" way of speaking, and Jacob could not deny that when traveling or otherwise around people he didn't know, he spoke as his professors had insisted upon. Speaking like a boy from the countryside did not open doors or win favors; Norman was right about that much.

He was also right about Miriam in that she hadn't had the benefit of that kind of education. Half a dozen words from her mouth were enough to reveal where she was from and give a very good sense of how much money her family had. Yet Jacob bristled at the unfair, harsh realities of the world he lived in: England was a place where one's background did matter, and a person had just one opportunity to make a proper impression after opening one's mouth. If that impression placed you firmly in the lower classes, that was where you forever would belong.

Jacob could picture what Norman had painted: if Miriam were to attend a ball in London, she would be laughed at, ridiculed. Likely behind fans and in whispers and hushed laughter—but that fact wouldn't lessen the humiliation one whit. Norman was right on that count, a fact Jacob loathed.

I'll never put my sweet Miriam into such a situation.

"You move to London and do whatever you feel you

must with Father's money and business," Jacob told his brother. He snatched his hat from the floor, where it had fallen moments before. "But I want nothing to do with any of it. I am a grown man. You are not my father, and I don't need your permission or approval to marry the woman I love." He turned and strode toward the door, but before he crossed the threshold, Norman called after him.

"I'm warning you—"

Jacob's step halted at the door, but he didn't turn around.

"Abandon your foolish designs on Miss Brown," Norman said. "She is *not* part of your future."

The words felt like arrows hitting their mark on Jacob's back. He didn't turn to confront his brother again. Ample experience had taught him that no amount of debate would do any good. Instead, he straightened his posture, cleared his throat, and left the room entirely. He continued down the hallway, then headed for the front door, needing to breathe free air and escape the suffocation that Norman left in his wake. Jacob walked and kept walking, expecting his anger to subside quickly, but it did not.

By the time he returned home, the sun had set and night lingered in the corners, waiting to descend upon the land. Jacob was no less angry at his brother, but the time outdoors was not wasted exercise; he returned home with a firm decision made. It was time to contact his solicitor about drawing up a marriage contract so that he could properly propose to Miriam.

He paused before entering the house, his glove on the handle. An urgency flooded through him. Norman *would* interfere, somehow prevent the marriage if he could. Jacob spun on his heel and went right back to the road, turning toward the humble house where the Brown family lived.

He'd propose to Miriam right away. Norman be damned.

Three

MIRIAM STIRRED THE stew again, checking for the tenderness of the meat and vegetables. "Dinner is almost ready," she called to her father in the next room.

She wiped her hands and crossed to a different, much larger pot, where her and her father's clothing was being laundered. She stirred that pot too, eying the clothing inside—aprons, petticoats, men's shirts, and other white fabrics—and wondered whether to add more bluing. No matter how much she worked, there always seemed to be more to do about the house or the garden, or there were sheep to be cared for—more so now that her father's health wasn't what it once was. The wintry cold of December had sunk deep into his bones and joints as it did every year, and he'd taken to his bed, scarcely able to walk from the swelling in his knees and pain in his hips.

Truly, it was a wonder the two of them managed as well as they did without any outside help. Granted, they *had* to manage; they could not afford to hire even one servant; the closest they got to that was occasionally giving an extra coin to the Smith boy down the road to run a quick errand for them.

A burst of wind kicked up outside, sending a haunting sound like an ethereal voice wrapping itself around the cottage, whispering things only those from another realm could understand. Miriam left the laundry pot to empty the bug trap, but the sound made her pause. Winter was coming, and with it, rain and snow. She glanced at the corner of the roof above the fireplace; it had begun to leak with autumn rain showers, and they lacked the money they would need to cover the considerable cost of re-thatching the roof.

Before she could chase away the worry, a knock sounded on the door. Darkness had already blanketed the village, as it always did early in the evening so close to Christmas. She went to the door and opened it, curious and not knowing what to expect. Opening the door let in a chilly breeze, but the sight of Jacob standing on the other side made her smile and care nothing at all for the cold.

"Jacob!" she said, feeling her smile pulling wide. "Come in, or you'll catch your death of cold." She stepped aside as he entered, closing the door behind him. "I didn't expect to see you again today."

Goodness, might he interpret that to mean she didn't *wish* to see him? Because the opposite was true.

He seemed to be avoiding her eye—very unlike Jacob. Was he uncomfortable around her? Perhaps she shouldn't have invited him inside; gossiping old ladies who heard of it might flap their tongues, though Jacob was always a perfect gentleman.

"May I speak with Mr. Brown?" Jacob said. He'd removed his cap, and now his fingers seemed to be worrying it so much, they were liable to rub a hole into the wool. He glanced up, and their gazes caught. He smiled, and his cheeks bloomed with color.

Dear Jacob. That smile would forever lighten her heart—and make it patter.

"You wish to speak with my father?" She'd heard him

well enough, but the reality of what that meant, what his blushing cheeks meant, suddenly came over her. Her hands flew to her mouth, and her eyes pricked with happy tears. "Do you mean..."

"Yes." Jacob stepped forward and reached out. She happily placed her hands in his and closed the gap between them even more. "I'm here to ask him for your hand. If you'll have me, that is."

"Of course!" Miriam said, her heart beating so crazily that it might as well have been a group of boys banging on drums. "I want nothing so much as to be with you."

"We must marry quickly because—" Jacob's voice cut off, and his lips pressed into a tight line.

Miriam felt quite certain she knew what he was going to say. Perhaps not the specifics, but the general concern. "Norman?"

"He wants me to become an MP, and our marriage does not factor into his plans." Jacob took a deep breath and sighed worriedly. Brow furrowed, he went on. "My brother has always been difficult."

"That's putting it mildly."

"Indeed." Jacob swallowed hard. "He's clever, and he's done plenty of things in the past to destroy my hopes or to make me a laughingstock or to control my decisions. All our lives, he's been little more than a conniving fox for me to constantly outwit. If I lost the game of wits when we were young, I took the blame for some mischief he'd done, or he got the last sweet Papa brought back from London. But now..." The shake of his head worried Miriam, and she braced herself as he went on. "So much more is at stake than the last piece of candy or foregoing supper as a punishment. If he has his way, I'll lose *you*. And I will not risk that."

Concern combined with her love for Jacob, the two

emotions twining together like a plait. "What are we to do? The banns must be read for several weeks, but surely he can't declare that we are of close relation or name any other legitimate reason we should not wed. He cannot stop us from marrying."

"I don't know what he'll do, but he will try to stop it from happening, which is why we must act quickly."

A sound turned their heads to the doorway leading to her father's bedchamber. He stood there, leaning on the doorframe and a cane, looking weak of body and troubled of spirit.

"What are you doing out of bed?" Miriam said, hurrying to his side. "I'll bring you supper soon."

He waved her away. "I'm not going back to bed quite yet." He eyed Jacob and nodded toward him. "Did I hear you correctly, that you came this night to ask for my daughter's hand in marriage?"

Once more, Jacob swallowed and nodded. "Yes sir, I did."

"And your brother objects?"

"He does."

"Well, I do not object." He smiled at that.

"Thank you, Father." Miriam walked to him and kissed his cheek.

"I want your happiness more than anything." Her father lifted a hand from the doorframe and stroked her cheek with his trembling thumb. "I won't be around much longer, and I want to go to my eternal rest knowing that you are cared for and loved."

Jacob stepped closer. "Thank you, Mr. Brown. I will do everything in my power to ensure that your daughter is both happy and cared for. It will be my life's work."

"Good." Her father shifted, and Miriam went to his side to help him walk back to bed. He paused in his step and tossed one more comment over his shoulder at Jacob. "If I can aid you in thwarting your brother's intentions, please let me know, and I'll do it."

"I will," Jacob said. His face already looked lighter than it had when he'd entered, when a weight had pulled at the corners of his eyes.

A few minutes later, her father back in bed, Miriam and Jacob sat on the settee and discussed the possibilities.

"A new law went into effect last month," Jacob said. "It provides a way for a couple to marry more quickly, without the banns needing to be read for three weeks."

"That's possible?" Miriam asked, not doubting him but amazed. "Truly? How?"

"A bishop must provide a license, and representatives of the bride and groom must swear that there are no impediments to the marriage, which must occur within three months of the license."

That seemed far too simple, yet Miriam wanted to hope. "That's all? A license can replace the banns? A bishop can grant a license without any other requirement?"

"Well, there is a payment that must be made to ensure that the sworn statement is correct, but I have the money. Though the estate was entailed to my brother, my father was able to leave some money for me. I'll use that."

"But that money should be saved," Miriam began. She knew all too well how quickly fortunes could change, and if one had money, one should save it for the inevitable difficulties of life.

"This is the only way I can see to thwart Norman's plans, whatever they may be."

"But if we marry here, couldn't he cause, I don't know, some problem in town to prevent it from happening?"

"Yes, which is why I intend to go on a trip to Harton first thing in the morning." At her confused expression, he explained. "The ceremony must occur in a parish where one party has lived for a fortnight. The law used to require a much longer period. But I'll get a license and stay in Harton for two weeks, and then you and your father can join me there for the ceremony."

"Would your brother become suspicious of your up and leaving, right before Christmas?"

"Not at all. We have an aunt and uncle in Harton who have invited us for the holiday, not wanting us to spend Christmas alone after our father's passing. I can certainly slip away some morning and meet you at the church."

"Goodness, Jacob, this is all almost too wonderful to be true!" So much had happened in just a few moments—she'd become engaged to the man she loved more than life itself, he'd found a way for it to happen despite his brother's protestations, *and* it would occur in only two weeks.

"I will leave for Harton in the morning and arrange for the license after that. We'll need someone to represent your father—I can hire a solicitor for that. And we can draw up the contract to make sure all is as it should be. What do you say to marrying on the morning of Christmas Eve?"

"So soon?" Miriam's mind was spinning with the news and happiness and the idea of so much change. "That sounds divine."

Jacob's voice lowered slightly, and his eyes took on a hint of concern again. "It would have to remain a secret, as much as possible, with only our witnesses present. It won't be anything grand, with flowers, music, a luncheon after, or any of the other things a regular wedding should have and, no doubt, all brides hope for—"

Miriam stopped his words with a kiss, then pulled back. "I've long hoped for *you*. All that matters for our wedding is that you and I will be there, together, and that we'll be bound as husband and wife for the rest of our lives. Nothing else is of any consequence, even if it means I end up wearing an old dress covered in mud stains because of an ornery sheep." She tilted her head to one side and then the other. "Though I believe I'll be able to manage something a bit nicer than that."

Jacob leaned in and rested his forehead against hers. She breathed him in, feeling the tension and nerves in her body ebb away like the outgoing tide. "I love you, Miriam Brown."

"And I you, Jacob Davies."

Four

THE VERY NEXT day, after serving her father breakfast, Miriam was scrubbing dishes when a knock sounded at the door. She wiped her hands on a linen dishcloth and went to see who their visitor was. Upon opening the door, she found Jacob, a carriage behind him and a small package in one hand.

"I had to see you before I left for Harton," he said.

From the carriage, Norman called, "Hurry now. We haven't all day."

Miriam and Jacob ignored him, embracing one last time for the next fortnight. "I'll miss you so," she said, arms about his neck.

"And I you," he said. "But just think: when we meet again, it will be at the Harton chapel to be *married*."

She pressed her forehead against his. "How can I wait so long?"

"We must, and we shall," Jacob said. He gave her hairline a tender kiss and then held up the package. "This is for you."

"What is it?" she asked, taking it in her hands. Whatever the paper held, it was soft, likely made of fabric.

"It's an engagement gift. I hope you like it."

"Ahem!" Norman said from the carriage.

"You'd better go," Miriam said, holding the package to her chest protectively.

"I'll see you soon. Promise."

"Promise." She went onto her toes and kissed him lightly one last time before Norman knocked the side of the carriage with his walking stick and cleared his throat in annoyance.

Jacob winked before heading to the carriage and waved before stepping inside, to which Norman grunted and rolled his eyes. After the carriage had gone, Miriam went inside and opened her gift: a beautiful wrap of silk, likely something the late Mr. Davies had procured in his trade with India. The fabric was smooth and seemed to move almost on its own. She put it around her shoulders and took in her appearance in the looking glass over the washbasin in her bedchamber. The bright-blue accents made her pale-blue eyes seem deeper and prettier.

"Miriam?" her father called. She hurried to his bedside to see what he might need. Instead of making a request of her, however, he held out a hand.

"Here. These are for you."

Unsure what he meant, she put her hand below his, and into her palm he dropped a handful of coins. "Buy yourself a new gown."

"Where in the world did you get this?"

"I've been saving a penny here and a penny there for just such a day as this. You deserve a proper wedding dress, and while this isn't enough for a gown fit for a queen, I hope it's enough for something a bit nicer than you would've been able to wear otherwise."

To think that he'd gone without medication and comforts, all to provide more for *her*.

She curled her fingers around the coins, her love and gratitude for her father washing over her. Just when she thought it impossible to love him more, something like this proved otherwise.

That afternoon, she walked to the next town over, Whitefold, where the nearest dressmaker was located. She had her new wrap about her shoulders and a reticule with her father's coins in her hand. Hopefully the dressmaker would have the time and materials to create a dress for her; she imagined that Christmas was a common season for new requests.

As she stepped into the shop, a bell at the top of the door jingled, announcing her entrance. She took in shelves that held bolts of beautiful fabrics of different types and colors, and a counter where a woman was looking over samples of lace. At the back of the room was a raised area where a young woman stood, getting a dress fitted to her by the dressmaker— Mrs. Fulsome, she assumed. At least, that was what the sign outside read.

The dressmaker took a handful of pins from between her teeth and called, "I'll be right with you."

Miriam nodded in acknowledgment and whiled away her time waiting by meandering through the shop, admiring various fabrics, and looking for what she might choose for her wedding dress. It would have to be something she could wear to church and on special occasions; she could not spend so much money on a gown to be worn only once. If she'd had the time, she would have made her wedding dress, as she had made her others. But thanks to her father's generosity and forethought, she would get something new.

Soon Mrs. Fulsome—for so she indeed introduced herself a few minutes later—came to Miriam's side, and they began looking over fabrics and making plans. Miriam chose velvet and chiffon in complementary greens for the top and the skirt, hardly able to believe she would own such a luxurious gown.

"And it *will* be ready by the twenty-third?" Miriam asked.

Mrs. Fulsome nodded as she wrote down notes about the order. "It certainly will be. I've had much shorter periods in which I've had to do more. This dress will be a joy to create for you." She looked up at Miriam and must have sensed the latter's concern, for she added, "I'll plan for it to be ready two days early, just in case we stumble upon any delays." The door jingled as she finished with, "Don't you worry your pretty head. You'll have the dress in hand no later than the twenty-third, and likely sooner."

"Thank you," Miriam said, but then, suddenly aware of a new customer having entered, leaned in and whispered, "if you could keep details confidential—"

"Understood," Mrs. Fulsome said with a wink. "Have a lovely day."

"You as well," Miriam said, and turned toward the door, only to lay eyes on Norman Davies. She'd assumed that he and Jacob had both left for Harton that morning, but Jacob must have gone on ahead of his brother. Her throat tightened, and her heart sped up. "Mr. Davies," she said with a nod, and she moved to walk past him.

He stepped to the side, blocking her way. "Miss Brown," he said, "may I have a word?" He gestured toward the door.

Dread pooled in her middle. She wasn't about to go outside and speak with Norman without witnesses. "Very well," she said, clasping her hands at the front of her skirts. "We may speak here. Isn't that so, Mrs. Fulsome?"

The dressmaker's eyes slid from one to the other and back again. "I suppose you may . . ."

Norman's face darkened, and his eyes narrowed. He stepped further into the room, then turned so that his back faced the dressmaker. When he spoke, it was in a whisper, but his tone was as threatening as if he'd yelled. "I know what game you're playing, Miss Brown, and I will have none of it."

Miriam's knees quaked, but she kept her face resolute, refusing to let him see her nerves. For once, she was grateful for skirts that concealed things like trembling limbs. "I am playing no games, Mr. Davies, but I can assure you of one thing: my life is mine to live, and you will not have a say in anything I choose to do or not do."

She noted a flicker of something in his eyes, as if he'd expected her to be made of mettle as weak as clay and was impressed to learn otherwise. His expression hardened so quickly that she half thought she'd imagined the increase of his opinion about her.

"My brother is to have a life and a career far beyond this miserable countryside, and I intend to ensure that lowborn chattel such as yourself will not stand in his way."

"Once again, Mr. Davies—"

"You will *not* stand in his way," Norman repeated, speaking right over her. This time, the venom in his voice silenced her. He nodded toward the counter where she and Mrs. Fulsome had decided on the details of her dress. "I know why you're here—a sheep farmer's daughter suddenly ordering a fancy new gown for herself? You must think me a dolt to not know what you're planning. Make no mistake; there will be no wedding."

Had he observed and merely guessed? Or had someone else told him of their plan? Did he believe they were planning a regular wedding here, in Audbury, after Christmas—and after the reading of the banns?

He mightn't know about the new law, she thought suddenly. *He doesn't know we plan to marry in a matter of days, not months.*

The realization strengthened her resolve and helped her stand with a straighter posture as she addressed him. "Your brother's life and future are his own, as are mine. He will make his own choices, just as I shall. And you, Mr. Davies, will quite simply have no say in the matter." She wrapped her shawl more tightly around herself and walked to the door. "Now I must return home to care for my father. Good day, Mr. Davies."

With that, she opened the door, stepped outside, and walked down the street, making sure to keep her chin high and her steps brisk. Norman was no doubt watching her. For both her sake and for Jacob's, she refused to allow Norman to find any weakness in her. Let him think what he would about their impending nuptials. He would be wrong, and before he could attempt anything to prevent the marriage, the ceremony would be over and they would be the victors.

She and Jacob loved each other more than she'd believed possible. Their love could conquer anything, including a misanthropic, jealous elder brother.

Even so, as she marched away, head held high, hot tears streamed down her cheeks.

Five

NEVER HAD A fortnight felt so infernally long as the one leading up to Miriam's wedding day in Harton. Despite Norman's attempts at cowing her, she was near to bursting with happiness. Aside from the interminably long wait, the only negative about her sudden and brief engagement was that Jacob was not with her, which meant that she could tell no one about the reason for her happiness. She could not reveal her true breadth of joy at all, for fear of sparking curiosity and rumors. And in a village as small and tight-knit as Audbury, curiosity fed rumors like dry straw feeding a fire—and it spread as quickly. Her greatest comfort was at home with her father, where she could talk about their future; naturally her father would live with them at Stonecroft Cottage. He would also travel with her to Harton and stand in as her witness to the ceremony, though truth be told, he might well be *sitting* as her witness.

However, as departure day approached, worries began to mount, though one by one, Jacob eased them from miles away. First he sent word that he would hire a stage for them—a blessed relief, as she'd feared they would have to ride in one of the mail coaches. Not only would that have meant tight and uncomfortable traveling conditions, but it would have posed a particular challenge for her father for a different reason entirely. Mail coaches often demanded that passengers disembark and walk up hills to save the strength of the horses and keep the stage on the proper schedule. But while her father was not prone to complaining, he was, quite simply, unable to walk.

When Jacob's letter arrived with details about their private stage, for no one but her and her father, she held the letter to her heart and found happy tears leaking from the corners of her eyes. Jacob truly did know her and her heart—so perfectly that he spent money he surely could not spare to ensure that she and her father would be comfortable and safe on their travels.

Oh, how she loved him in return. She was not yet his wife, but she vowed in that moment to always keep his wellbeing, safety, and comfort as her highest priority, as he clearly did hers.

On the twenty-second day of December, the stagecoach arrived, rumbling to a stop before the humble Brown family cottage. The driver and footman helped Miriam and her father into the carriage and then carried their two small trunks to the back, where they were strapped in tightly.

Miriam had never seen so elegant a carriage—had never seen *anything* made at such obvious expense and of such beauty. The padded interior, though not new, felt nothing short of luxurious and extravagant; Miriam found herself running a hand along the leather surface of her bench. Her finger traced the curves of the woodworking, then stopped on the glass of the window, wondering at how much such panes must have cost. Her breath made the glass fog, so she used the side of her hand to wipe it clear again, then chuckled at her own behavior.

"I must look like a child in my wonderment. It's only a

stagecoach, but . . ." She shrugged and laughed again. "It's a stagecoach. For me and for you, hired by my dear Jacob, to bring us to him, and—" Her voice cut off; she did not quite dare to speak about her pending nuptials, for fear of tempting fate.

"'Twill be a wonderful . . . *Christmas*, I daresay," her father said, smiling back with an understanding twinkle in his eye, as if he knew her thoughts.

They said no more about the purpose of their journey, a silent agreement to rejoice silently until they reached Harton and appeared at the parish chapel at nine o'clock on the morning of Christmas Eve.

Miriam looked about and noted two lap rugs. She unfolded one, which she arranged on her father's lap to keep him warm. "I understand that travel by stage is much faster than even a few years ago, thanks to better roads," she said, tucking the rug about his legs to keep as much cold air as possible from reaching him and making his rheumatism act up more than it already would.

"Indeed," her father said, "though I pray we won't encounter any slippery patches of snow or ice."

"As do I." She smiled and sat back on her bench opposite him, where she began arranging her own lap rug.

The driver walked from the back of the stagecoach, heading toward his seat up front, stopping at their door. He opened it, noted that they'd already used the lap rugs, and said, "The weather has been mild so far this winter, so no need to fret; we shouldn't come upon any bad roads."

Miriam and her father exchanged startled looks. The driver had clearly heard their conversation. She was particularly glad that she'd stayed silent about the impending nuptials, and if her father's wide eyes under his raised bushy eyebrows were any indication, he was surprised to discover that anything they said could be easily heard without the carriage.

"Thank you," Miriam said, sure to smile at the driver. "That is most assuredly a comfort."

He tilted his head and touched his hat. "Happy to help, m'lady. Barring a storm, we should arrive in Harton shortly after nightfall."

"Thank you," she said again, still feeling too wary to enjoy being called *m'lady* for the first time in her life.

He climbed to his seat, the footman took his at the back—to act as a lookout, Miriam supposed—and then the coach lurched forward, and they were off. The crunch of the wheels on the stones of the road, combined with the clip-clop of the four horses' hooves, created such a volume of sound that Miriam felt quite certain that neither the driver nor the footman could eavesdrop any longer. Goodness, she and her father had to practically yell to understand each other.

The constant rocking and swaying, which were novelties at first, began to wear at Miriam. Within a few hours, she felt positively green and certain that she knew what seasickness must be like. Across the way, her father slept, head backward, jaw hanging open as he snored. He felt well enough to sleep; that was something to be grateful for. It was also enough to allow her to rest, and she found herself yawning, having difficulty keeping her eyes open. Who knew that merely *sitting* in a stagecoach for hours could be so exhausting? She leaned her head against a pane of glass and closed her eyes, trying to rest as the cool glass eased her nausea, eager for sleep to claim her if but for a few minutes.

She would get through this journey; yes, she felt so nauseated from the motion of the stagecoach that when they stopped to change horses and got some tea, she couldn't eat. Just as well; she mightn't have been able to keep a meal inside her. But the resulting hunger certainly didn't help her feelings of sickness or the headache that had formed behind her eyes and now throbbed.

At least this is but one day's trip, she reminded herself, still keeping her eyes closed. *We'll be there soon, and I'll sleep in a warm bed tonight. And Jacob will be there waiting for me.*

Anything was tolerable if she knew that it would end, and that when it did, Jacob would be there waiting for her.

She must have slipped into a much deeper sleep than she'd anticipated, for the next thing she knew, Miriam was jolted awake as the coach slammed forward and to a stop with such force that it might have run straight into a wall of stone. Her father inhaled sharply and drooped in his seat. She reached forward and helped him up to the bench beside her, where he clung to her, breathing shakily.

What had happened? The carriage tilted dangerously side to side as she tried to gain her bearings but began to lose sense of which direction was up. She heard shouts from the driver, and horses neighing with what sounded like fear, and the carriage jerked and then tilted to one side. Miriam embraced her father; her heart raced with fear.

Outside, the world was nearly dark, with only a few deep-purple shadows visible, and those unclear shapes—trees, buildings, people—were all a blur. What little she could make out through the window changed by the second as the coach continued to jerk and sway but make no forward progress.

Miriam looked around, searching for her father's cane with which to signal the driver for help. There it was on the floor of the coach, at her feet. She couldn't reach it without releasing the hold on her father, which she would not consider. She held on even more tightly with one arm and then raised her other fist, using it to knock as hard as she could on the roof.

"Help! What's happening?" she called.

It did no good; the horses neighed out of control, the driver unable to control them. The only thing he said was a string of orders directed toward the horses, interspersed with words that under other circumstances would have made Miriam blush. As she sat fearing for her life, she listened carefully for any information that would give insight to what she should do and what was happening, caring nothing for such curses.

The wheels creaked as they turned for the first time since their abrupt stop, pulling the coach forward with a lurch. A good sign, she hoped; perhaps they were past a patch of mud or something else that had caused them to stop and struggle.

Another jolt. The sound of the coach's wheels on wood instead of gravel or earth—were they crossing a bridge? The stagecoach slammed to a stop once again and tilted once more, this time more and more, until Miriam and her father were thrown against the side. She whispered a grateful prayer that it wasn't on the side with the door, which might have come loose and opened under such a force.

The noises grew louder, and the sound of splintering wood joined the others, along with screeching metal. Something snapped—a spoke of a wheel, part of the bridge? Something else broke. The driver bellowed.

Suddenly, the sensation of falling came over them. Miriam held her father in her arms and prayed. The last thing she knew was an enormous splash into black, icy water, before she succumbed to the darkness.

Six

As Christmas Eve arrived, Jacob could not sleep. He lay wide awake in his uncle and aunt's house, staring at the ceiling well before dawn. How could he sleep when in but a couple of hours, he would pledge his love and life to Miriam, and he would become her husband?

At last the sun crested the horizon, so he allowed himself to get out of bed and begin his morning ablutions. He took extra care shaving his whiskers to be sure he didn't draw blood. Miriam deserved a handsome groom, and while he wasn't boastful enough to believe he was anywhere near what would be considered *handsome*, he wanted to look as good as he possibly could for their wedding.

His boots were freshly polished—something seen to by cousin Martin's valet overnight. Jacob dressed in a new suit bought especially for the occasion. His hair, by some miracle of the fates, lay flat for once, and soon he was ready to leave. He quietly walked to Martin's bedchamber and knocked, apparently waking him, as evidenced by the groggy voice saying, "Come in."

Martin, someone more like a brother to Jacob than Norman ever had been, was indeed still abed. He chuckled at seeing Jacob. "A bit eager, are we? I'll call Collins and hurry, though I don't think the vicar will be ready before nine o'clock."

True to his word, Martin got ready quickly with the help of his valet, Collins, and soon the trio were walking from the family estate of Branbourne Manor toward the chapel. Martin was the only person Jacob had entrusted with the secret of the wedding. Collins knew now as well, but that mattered little now that he was with them along the way. Martin would be one of the witnesses to the ceremony. The other, of course, would be Mr. Brown.

As they walked, Jacob took care as to where he stepped, avoiding muddy spots as best he could so as to preserve the polish and cleanliness of his boots. He dearly hoped his hat wouldn't muss his hair too much.

"Do you suppose they'll arrive early too?" he said, voicing his hopes.

"If they do, you won't be able to see her," Martin shot back, and when Jacob looked pained at the thought, Martin grinned. "That would be bad luck."

"But if we're all there before nine o'clock, perhaps the vicar will be willing to perform the ceremony early."

"Perhaps," Martin said, in what seemed far too calm a tone.

"Perhaps?" Jacob said. "*Perhaps?* The events of this day will transform my life, yet you speak as if we're doing nothing but taking a stroll to a regular Sabbath service."

"And *you*," Martin said with a laugh and a teasing shove, "speak as if the entire world should sense and acknowledge the import of this day."

Jacob shrugged, acknowledging his cousin's point, but he couldn't quite escape the feeling that the world around him was vibrating with anticipation, as if the trees and frosted grasses *did* know. Intellectually, he knew that such thinking was foolishness, but it was truly how he felt.

"You do have the license?" Martin asked suddenly.

"I do." Jacob had made sure of that fact no fewer than a dozen times already, yet he reached up and felt for the folded paper in his breast pocket again anyway. "Thank you for checking."

As much as Martin might enjoy teasing, Jacob knew that the question showed how much his cousin really did care about this day.

The walk to the chapel couldn't have been more than a quarter of a mile, but it certainly felt like several miles. They found the vicar, who was surprised to see them more than an hour earlier than anticipated. Even so, he happily agreed to perform the ceremony early in the event that the bride and her father arrived early.

"May I see the license?" the vicar asked.

"Yes, of course," Jacob said, and suddenly had fumbling fingers too nervous to slip the paper out of his pocket with anything less than several seconds' effort. "There you are."

The elderly vicar settled a pair of spectacles on the end of his nose and peered through them, reading over the license and nodding as he read it. "Everything looks to be in order," he said, then eyed Jacob. "You are the groom? And you are the witnesses?" He gestured to Jacob and then Martin and Collins.

"I'm one of the witnesses," Martin said. "The bride's father will be the other."

"Very good." The vicar sat at his desk and took up a pen and paper, on which he recorded the witnesses' names, though for his part, Jacob wasn't sure of Mr. Brown's full given name.

"We can write that information in later, when they arrive," the vicar said. "You are welcome to stay here in my office or to wait in the chapel through that door. If you'll excuse me, I think I'll go finish my morning cup of tea while we wait."

"I think we'll wait in the chapel," Jacob said. "Thank you." He gave a half bow, holding his hat, and as soon as the vicar left, he ran his fingers through his hair. He looked to Martin with worry. "Did I save my hair from looking like a hat has been on it, or did I muss it up?"

"It looks fine," Martin said. "But Collins here can fix it right up if a problem arises. Can't you?" He turned to the valet, who bowed with a nod.

"I can and will, Mr. Davies."

Martin stepped forward and took Jacob by the shoulders. "Breathe, man. Everything will turn out right. You'll see. But only if you breathe. She won't want to marry a man who faints before he meets her at the altar."

At that, Jacob laughed and realized that he had indeed been holding his breath. "Let's go wait in the chapel, then."

They selected a pew and sat on the bench there, the echoing interior of the chapel, with its fine stained glass and impressive ceiling, making them speak in reverent whispers.

Jacob's knee kept bouncing up and down; he simply *had* to expel some of his nervous energy. He checked his pocket watch again and again. At last the vicar entered, wearing his robes and a few minutes early. Still no sound of a carriage or steps outside that would indicate Miriam's arrival.

The church bells rang, chiming nine times. Still no Miriam, no Mr. Brown.

They waited longer. And longer. At half past nine, Jacob felt nearly driven mad as a hundred possible reasons for Miriam's tardiness crept through his mind. Perhaps she didn't wish to marry him after all. Maybe a highwayman had attacked the stagecoach. What if her father had fallen ill and couldn't travel? All of these possibilities and more muddied his thoughts and increased his worry.

The bells rang out ten times. She was more than an hour

late. By law, the wedding had to take place before noon. Was their coach damaged? If she arrived after twelve, they would simply marry tomorrow, on Christmas. Was that legal? He'd have to ask the vicar.

At long last, steps sounded at the back of the chapel. Jacob stood and whirled about in a single motion, his heart nearly leaping from his chest. But instead of seeing Miriam and her father, he found Norman.

Jacob's stomach dropped to his toes. How had Norman found out, and where was Miriam?

"There has been an accident," Norman said.

"What are you doing here?" Jacob demanded.

"The butler said that you had come this way earlier, so I set out in search of you because of the news. I felt sure you would want to know."

A heaviness seemed to wrap around Jacob's chest, making it hard to breathe. "What . . . news?"

"As I said, there has been an accident. A stagecoach fell into a river while crossing a bridge. Two passengers perished: an elderly man and a young woman."

Jacob felt his head shaking and a moan threatening to escape from his throat. "No. You must be wrong. It's not—"

"The victims are Mr. Brown and Miss Brown." Norman sighed. "I am sorry, brother."

With that, Norman turned about, replaced his hat, and left. Jacob dropped to his knees onto the cold stone floor. Miriam could *not* be dead. Her father was well. They would be here any moment.

They had to be.

Jacob was vaguely aware of Martin's voice and the weight of his hand on his back. "I'll go learn what I can, see what this is all about. I'll report back as quickly as I can."

Unable to speak his thanks—barely able to breathe or think—Jacob nodded.

"Collins," he heard Martin say, "see to it that Mr. Davies returns to Branbourne Manor. Stay with him until I come back."

"Yes, sir."

The sound of Martin's boots moved quickly across the stone floor as he hurried out of the chapel. The cavernous space was silent once more, empty save for himself and his cousin's valet.

Empty, as Jacob's life would be without Miriam in it. He felt as if his heart had been carved from his chest, leaving a hole that would never be filled.

Seven

MIRIAM'S EYES FELT like lead, heavy and immovable, but warm, as if the sun were shining on her face. So different from the searing cold of the water. The water that had brought darkness and excruciating pain with it.

What had happened? She couldn't remember anything but a fleeting sense of terror in the stagecoach. She'd been embracing her father, but that made no sense; hadn't he been sitting on the opposite bench?

She tried to open her eyes and succeeded in part, but she immediately turned her head and closed her eyes against the blinding sun that was indeed streaming in from a window. The movement sent a cascade of pain shooting through her body, from her head to her toes. It didn't leave, however, only settling in her legs with intense throbs impossible to ignore. How had she not noticed that pain? What had happened to her legs? Were they caught under something?

"Where..." She tried to speak, but the single syllable was all that she could manage.

"There now," a female voice said, and a figure drew near. "Lie still," the woman said, arranging a blanket about Miriam's figure.

She was lying on a bed, she realized, but not her own. The sunny room was unfamiliar, as was everything here, including the woman.

"You're at the home of Dr. Wilson, dear," the woman said, finally answering Miriam's question, but the answer only elicited more questions from her confused and tired mind. Her expression must have said as much, because the woman went on. "You were in a stagecoach accident, and your legs are broken. The swelling will need to go down before the doctor can set the bones properly. They're much better than even a day ago, which is excellent news."

A stagecoach accident. So she did remember something of what had happened, but even those images in her mind were blurry and getting fainter. She swallowed, which felt like a herculean task. "My father?" she said, forcing her eyes open again.

The woman hesitated a moment, and Miriam thought she saw a flicker of worry pass through her eyes before she said, "You need to rest up and regain your strength. I'll fetch you some broth, and if you can tolerate it well, I'll find you something more substantive to eat for supper."

"Miss—"

"Wilson. Mrs. Wilson."

"My father. Where—"

The doctor's wife interrupted again. "Oh, I believe it's also time for another dose of laudanum, so I'll be sure you get that as well." She patted Miriam's hand, which rested beside her on the bed—what might well have been the only part of her that didn't ache—and scurried off.

Was Mrs. Wilson deliberately not telling Miriam about her father's condition? Was he in this house? Could she see him? He had to be in far more pain than she was. They should be together. Her presence would ease his suffering, even if she couldn't minister to him herself. She'd ask Mrs. Wilson as soon as possible.

A heavy footfall sounded outside the door of her room,

followed by the figure of a man in dark clothing, wearing a coat and holding a hat. The brightness of the room put his face in shadow until he stepped across the threshold, at which the man's appearance resolved into fine detail. Norman Davies.

Her heart leapt with hope. If Norman knew of the accident, surely Jacob did too, and he'd be along shortly. Perhaps he'd visited her already, before she awakened. How long had she been unconscious?

"Looking better, I see," Norman said, stepping closer to the bed. She wished she could step backward to increase the distance between them. He looked too pleased, too satisfied with himself, for his visit to be something she should celebrate. The hope that had flared in her chest now felt extinguished.

"Where is Jacob?" she asked. Goodness, her throat was dry. Would that Mrs. Wilson would return quickly.

Norman sat at the base of her bed, shifting the whole only an inch, but plenty to send a new dagger of pain through her legs—and her foot. Was it broken as well?

"I am here to broker a deal with you, Miss Brown," he said, not answering her question.

Frustration mounted inside her, but she felt so weak that she could not do much about it, or about him. She managed a single word as a reply. "Never."

Norman chuckled and stroked the side of his hat, acting as if she were foolish and he'd expected that very response from her. "You don't know what I have to offer. You may well be eager to agree when you hear the terms . . ." He lifted his face to hers and then tilted it to one side as if in thought. "And when you hear about what your future would hold otherwise."

Miriam wanted to scrub the arrogant smirk off his face, but she also needed to know what he was talking about. "Tell me."

"I knew you were intelligent." Norman stood, placing his

hat where he'd been sitting. Miriam wanted to kick it onto the floor, but she didn't dare, both because she simply had to hear what Norman was going to tell her and because she feared causing herself more pain or damage by such an action.

"I understand that your rather unfortunate stagecoach accident occurred on the way to a clandestine wedding ceremony you and my younger brother planned."

"Entirely legal." She lacked the strength to form full sentences, but she had to say something in their defense.

"Legality is a different thing entirely from morality or ethics." Norman raised his brows and gave her a pointed look, then carried on, hands clasped behind his back as he walked to the window. "You see, my brother is foolish and does not act in his own best interest. His future is to be an MP."

"He doesn't want that."

"He, my dear, will have no choice in the matter. I will be letting out Stonecroft Hall, and with no source of income, he will live with me in London. As I'm sure you're aware, he spent all of his meager inheritance on this foolish plot to marry you without my knowledge." He huffed and shook his head.

Miriam wanted to contradict him, to argue, but her mind was still foggy, like an early morning over the hills. She knew important things were on the horizon, but she could not make them out, let alone find the words to express them. Was this a result of the accident or the laudanum?

Norman turned from the window and faced her. Once more, he looked dark, the sun putting his features in shadow, but now she could see every inch of his expression, every wrinkle and sneering part of his face. "Here is the reality of the situation, Miss Brown. You are now a cripple. You've broken both legs and seriously damaged your right foot. You will likely never walk again without the aid of a cane at best, but if the kind doctor is to be believed, and I paid for the best—yes,

I am paying for your care—he believes you will be lame for the remainder of your life, likely whiling away your years in a wheeled chair and requiring constant attention."

Her eyes widened at his words—he'd tossed so much information at her, facts and details that upended her entire future, and did so as if he'd merely emptied a bag of marbles and watched them roll about as she tried to gather them up.

"Surely you can see that Jacob deserves to have something more from a wife than a cripple who cannot go to dances, cannot so much as go for a stroll, and who, perhaps, might be unable to bear him children. You would be an embarrassment and a disgrace. How would Jacob be able to find a place in society, even if that path is not as an MP, if he has a sickly wife who cannot be seen in public? Would you condemn him to such a life as that?"

More marbles dumped onto the table of her mind. She couldn't keep track of them all. She shook her head, feeling tears trickle down her cheeks. "Please, stop."

"I am nowhere near finished," Norman said. His voice grew more intent, losing any sense of polite softness that he'd feigned before. "Miss Brown, unfortunately, I must tell you that your father did not survive the accident."

"No. That can't be. Please—" But she knew it was true. Her father already had poor health. If the cold didn't take him, the water might have, or other injuries, like the ones she'd sustained. She couldn't bear to imagine the possibilities. "What happened?"

"He was buried three days ago in Audbury. I thought that bringing his body to the home he loved would be best."

"Th-thank you. That was very kind of you to do." So unlike Norman, yet there it was, a kind act, something that had cost his time as well as pounds, no doubt. Yet to think that he was buried without her present to witness it . . .

"I am not the monster you likely believe me to be, Miss Brown," he said. "I know my brother and I have not always been in agreement on much, but I believe you and I can be in agreement on the future. You might have been able to make him happy, but that was then. Do you truly believe in your heart that you could make him happy now? If I set aside any objections to your union, and if I were to pay for a lavish wedding for you, could you marry Jacob now, knowing that you will cause him pain? That you would be a burden to him, both physically and monetarily, for the rest of your life? That if you could bear him children, you would be unable to care for them?"

Miriam hated every word Norman said—yet he spoke truth. And she was loath to admit it. She felt sobs threatening to rack her body.

"Tell me this, Miss Brown: do you love Jacob?"

"Of course I do. I love him with all my heart."

"Then you would never do anything to hurt him, to hold him back from happiness and success?"

She hated Norman more than she ever had, but again, he was speaking truth. "I can't marry him," she said with a whimper. "I'll die here, and he will be able to carry on." The words were wrenched from her heart, but she knew they needed to be said.

"I am glad to hear you say so," Norman said, a softness back in his voice, one that Miriam knew better than to think was actual kindness or concern. This benefited him as much as anyone. "To show my gratitude, I will ensure that you are cared for, not just in some hospital, but for the rest of your life, so long as you never contact my brother again. He has been told that you perished with your father. I think we'd both prefer for him to believe that than to think that you refuse to marry him. After all, if he knew the truth, he would feel obligated to marry you, and I'm sure you do not want to be a wife out of charity and pity."

Tears fell freely from her eyes. She wiped at them, but more took their place. She shook her head. "You're right. It's best if he believes I'm dead."

"I will arrange for a flat for you in Bath, with a live-in caretaker. You will be able to go to the Roman baths, soak in them to gain some relief and strength in body. I hear the water is medicinal as well, though you'll never regain full use of your legs, of course."

She pictured herself being pushed in a wheeled chair along the streets of a city she'd never visited, by a woman she didn't know. Would the baths be at all healing? Would her caretaker be someone she could call a friend? How lonely a life could she expect for herself? It wouldn't be the life she'd hoped for and expected. In some ways, she'd likely have more money and better clothing and living spaces than she would have as Jacob's wife. All the same, she would have chosen a poor life with Jacob as the one richer in spirit, one that provided a wealth of joy and happiness that no amount of money could provide.

"Here is the agreement, then: You never return to Audbury—the people there will believe that you and your father both perished. You never contact my brother again. And in exchange, I will ensure that you have the best care, a beautiful place to live, and money in your pocket. Agreed?" He held out a hand. She stared at it.

Only minutes before, she'd been so sure she'd never come to any understanding with Norman, let alone agree to something as unthinkable as cutting Jacob from her life.

Slowly, as reluctantly as she had done anything or ever would do anything else in her life, she reached out and shook his hand. "Agreed," she whispered.

Eight

January 10, 1824

A KNOCK SOUNDED on Jacob's bedchamber door. He groggily opened his eyes to a bright morning sun as a servant entered. Not Collins, but a man who could have passed for the man's brother. He carried a breakfast tray to the bedside table, gave a quick bow, and said, "Good morning, Mr. Davies."

"Morning," Jacob managed.

"How are you feeling this morning?"

Jacob tried to sit up, but a wave of dizziness and a pounding in his head made him rethink the decision, and he lay back onto his pillow. "Where am I?"

"Branbourne Manor, of course."

"Oh, yes," Jacob said, though his mind felt fuzzy, as if he were waking from a night of flowing alcohol. He covered his eyes to block more of the light and tried to remember. The last thing he could recall was falling to his knees onto the stone floor of the chapel . . .

Miriam was gone. So was her father. He was not married after all.

"Norman must be pleased," he murmured.

"What was that, sir?"

"Nothing," Jacob said. He lifted his hand slightly to look at the man. "What was your name again?"

"Archibald Lipton at your service, sir."

In the distance, church bells rang out. "Mr. Lipton, what time is it? Have I missed Christmas morning mass?"

The man put on a slightly pained smile. "M'lord, you've been sick for over a week. You missed Christmas entirely."

"Sick," Jacob repeated. "Sick with what?"

Lipton shrugged. "I don't know the details, sir. I've been caring for you and administering medicine as the doctor instructed. You'll have to ask him or your brother about details. But I'm glad to see that you've regained some of your strength."

Jacob was determined to sit up. He raised himself onto his elbow, getting up slowly. "Please order a carriage for me. I need to return to Audbury as soon as possible."

"Regretfully, that isn't possible at the moment."

"Why not?" Jacob asked, brow furrowed.

"You're far too weak to travel, but even if you'd fully recovered, Branbourne Manor is under quarantine. Your cousin Fanny came down with measles right after Christmas. No one is allowed to leave for another week."

That news had Jacob sitting all the way up. He swung his legs off the side of the bed—an action so quick that he had to catch himself until he could get a bit more strength. "I must leave," he insisted. "I've been in this room since Christmas Eve, haven't I? I attended no parties. Surely I didn't contract the illness." But he had to go to Audbury, find out what had happened to Miriam and her father, give them a proper burial.

"Alas, everyone within the walls of Branbourne Manor is under quarantine until further notice." Lipton didn't sound particularly sad over the fact. He left and closed the door behind him, leaving Jacob sitting on the bed, mad with worry and desperation.

Where were Miriam and Mr. Brown's remains? Had they

been laid to rest? And how could he have not been present for such an occasion? Might they have been placed in paupers' graves, without so much as a personal headstone to mark their final resting places? He could not allow that to happen. At the very least, he needed to find out where they were now and arrange for their return to Audbury, where they could be laid to rest in the church graveyard. Then, one day when he had enough money, he would pay for a proper headstone. Then, no matter how long that took, he would know where they lay and be able to visit.

How had life come to this? His eyes burned with unshed tears, feeling dry and hot. His head pounded, likely from worry and illness. Whatever he felt, surely it was better than whatever Miriam and Mr. Brown had experienced in their final moments.

They were gone. She was gone. He could not imagine any kind of future without Miriam in it. Without her, he *had* no life. He had nothing tying him to Audbury. No reason to do or be anything.

Needing to learn more, to *do* something, he dressed and shaved—far more slowly than ever before, as he still felt shaky—then left his bedchamber to find his brother and nearly knocked Norman over in the hall.

"Where do you think you're going?" Norman asked, brushing himself off as if he'd been tossed onto the dusty ground.

"Looking for you, actually," Jacob said.

Norman tugged at the cuffs of his shirt and then looked at Jacob. "Well, you found me."

"I need to find Miriam and Mr. Brown. I need a carriage—no, a horse will do—and some money so I can give them a proper burial. Only a loan. I swear I'll repay every penny. With interest, of course." The words came out of Jacob in a rush, and when he finished, he found himself breathing heavier, as if he'd run a mile down the road rather than plead for a favor from his brother.

"I am not giving you a loan," Norman began.

"But—"

"Stop," Norman interrupted, raising a hand. "Listen to me. Haven't you been informed of the quarantine? You cannot leave."

"But—"

"I have taken care of the Browns. Of all of it. You needn't worry yourself about anything in that regard."

Norman's kind words took Jacob aback. He didn't quite dare believe his brother's sudden altruistic spirit. "I don't understand."

"I knew you would be fit to be tied over it all, and when you fell ill upon hearing the news—"

"What exactly did I fall ill with?"

"A broken heart?" Norman shrugged. "The doctor couldn't say for sure, but you were mad with delirium."

"Whatever it was, I'm well now, as you can see," Jacob said. What "medication" had he been given for days at a time? "I must go find them, bring them back to Audbury."

Norman stopped Jacob's effusion by placing a firm hand on his shoulder. "Listen to me."

"What?" he said, his tone less demanding.

"Martin was kind enough to lend me the use of Bertram, one of the stable hands. I have instructed him to find the, eh, *remains* and personally see to their transport back to Audbury. There, Bertram will give a letter I wrote myself to Pastor Wright so they can be properly buried."

"You—you'd do that?"

"I've *done* that." Norman looked pleased at Jacob's reaction. He lifted a shoulder and let it fall again. "You were unwell, and I knew you would worry."

"Th-thank you." Jacob stammered, not entirely able to comprehend his brother's generosity. "I couldn't bear the idea of them being buried in a mass grave. If I can't be present for the burial, at least I can know that it's taking place in Audbury. Or *has* taken place?"

"Likely has by now," Norman said. He released Jacob's shoulder. "I haven't yet ordered a headstone. I wanted your input on the text before I sent the order to the mason."

Whatever had birthed this version of his brother, Jacob did not know, but he was grateful for it. "Thank you, truly. I can never repay you the kindness."

"Ah, well, we'll see about that." Norman patted his back and led him toward the guest bedchamber Jacob had been staying in. "Doesn't look like you've eaten yet. Go. Eat and rest. I'll let you know more when I hear word from Bertram."

"Very well." Jacob stood there in bewilderment for a moment, hardly recognizing this smiling man as his elder brother.

Perhaps he had ulterior motives, believing that Jacob would agree to the plans of him becoming an MP in exchange for the generosity. The prospect didn't disgust him as it once had, but as he went back into the room and closed the door behind him, he knew that he'd make a sorry MP now. He wouldn't care enough for any cause to debate or fight for it, not while he grieved Miriam. The people deserved a leader. A man with a broken heart, stuck in the past, was not that leader.

Jacob crossed to a small bookshelf in the corner and selected a volume of poetry by Lord Byron. He sat in a padded chair beside the window and began to read. Perhaps he'd find some catharsis in the words of passion and love contained within the pages.

He tried to read, but the words swam in his vision and their meaning wouldn't resolve into anything. After several attempts, he closed the book and set it aside. Perhaps he did not deserve any kind of catharsis, any relief.

After all, if he hadn't been so selfish as to plan a clandestine wedding, Miriam would yet be living. He had orchestrated the journey on which she had died. He would never see her face. She would never draw another breath. She'd died, and it was entirely his fault, a fact he would have to live with for the rest of his life.

Nine

THE TIME SINCE the accident could be counted in days, thought the time felt much longer. Jacob had been confined to his guest bedchambers, unable to leave the room for any reason. Early each morning, a young servant boy came to start a fire in the hearth. Later, Lipton brought him food and drink throughout the day and cleaned the chamber pot, took soiled clothing to launder, brought books to read.

His sounded like a life of gentlemanly leisure, but Jacob had nearly lost his mind. His sanity's only salvation was the window that overlooked rolling green hills that reminded him of Audbury. And, yes, of Miriam. Thinking of her brought the greatest mixture of happiness and bitter sorrow he could have imagined. When the days and nights grew particularly long, he'd dreamt of her and awakened happy, only to be struck down by reality as if it were the flat of a sword.

Norman's new attempt at behaving as a caring brother was what finally got Jacob out of the house. Jacob pleaded for days, and after more than a week, they risked breaking the quarantine, seeing as he hadn't been exposed to anyone at the ball and had barely encountered anyone in the household for more than ten days. Norman whisked Jacob out to a waiting carriage with his trunk already strapped atop, and without so much as a proper farewell to his aunt and uncle, Jacob was free.

They did not return, as Jacob had assumed they would, to Audbury. Rather, Norman had business in London, and he'd let a flat until he could, in his words, "Find something more fitting a man of my station."

Jacob hadn't been to London for years and had only vague memories of the time he'd come along with his father on business. The city had certainly grown, expanding for miles more, and with all of the new buildings came more and more people, packed into tall, cramped spaces.

His sense of freedom, however, did not last long. They'd spent but one night in the flat—Jacob on the floor with a pillow and rug—when Norman sat him down at a table in the corner of the flat, insisting that he had something serious to discuss.

"It's time to begin planning your election campaign," he began. He opened a leather-bound notebook and uncapped a fountain pen.

"I will do no such thing," Jacob said firmly, despite his brother's sudden clenched jaw.

"You will not?" He sat back and regarded Jacob with hooded eyes. "And what do you plan to do instead? Live with me forever, paying for your clothing and shelter and food?"

"No, I—"

"I can help you become MP, and together we can create influence and power. I understand that you didn't want to before, but now . . ."

Jacob just shook his head. "Yes, my situation has changed, but my intent in that regard remains the same. I will *not* run for MP."

Norman put the cap back onto the pen, closed the notebook and set the pen atop it. "Very well. If you do not wish for my aid, then unfortunately, I cannot allow you to live here—or at Stonecroft Hall, either. Remember it will be let soon."

"Where am I to live, then? What am I to do?"

"That is not for me to determine. You wish to live in your own way? That is your decision to make." Norman stood and took the notebook and pen with him, tucking them under his arm. "You may stay here for another fortnight. After that, however, I will be moving into a permanent residence, and you will need to find your own." He consulted his pocket watch. "I'll be back for supper, if you change your mind."

Norman left the flat, and Jacob spent the next two weeks trying to find a place to work that would pay more than a pittance, and trying to find a place to stay that didn't require a rent so large that it might as well be a king's ransom.

Then the fortnight was past. Jacob had one last night available to him in Norman's flat, and come morning, they would leave the lodging house. Norman would move into a townhouse somewhere in or near London—he wouldn't say precisely—and Jacob would be left standing on the street with his trunk and nowhere to go. Norman was the only family Jacob had left, which meant that in truth he had no family at all.

So much for brotherly affection, he thought miserably as he trudged along a snowy street in the East End. At least his coat was relatively new, his boots were free of holes, and his belly, while not full, hadn't been empty for days. That was all more than could be said of many he encountered on the streets.

He hadn't found anyone willing to hire or house him. Unwilling to return to the flat and admit defeat to a gloating Norman, he wandered the streets well after dark.

Father hadn't intended any of this to happen—for Jacob to be left destitute after his death—but he was. He'd spent his only money on the expedited marriage license and the private stagecoach that was to bring Miriam and her father to Harton. Norman had cut off any further money, and Jacob had no way of knowing whether their father truly hadn't been able to leave him more, or whether Norman merely claimed as much. Jacob's accounts were empty, and though he'd written to his solicitor, he hadn't yet received any kind of explanation, and he wasn't let in to see the man, either.

Most businesses were locked up for the night, but Jacob came across several pubs that were open, with song and drink flowing. After passing a number of them, he came to The Red Lion and paused at the window. He watched the men inside, laughing and smiling with pints in their hands, their faces rosy—with warmth or drunkenness, he didn't know. Whatever the cause of their seeming happiness, he wanted a piece of it for himself. He wouldn't ever be truly happy again, but perhaps tonight he could drink his sorrows away and forget them for a brief spell.

The door jangled with bells as two men stumbled out. Jacob held the door for them, then entered himself. For the first time in his life, he intended to drink himself into oblivion, if that was possible to do with the few coins he still had in his pocket. With any luck, he'd have a few hours free of grief and guilt over the accident and losing Miriam, as well as a spell without having to worry over where he would sleep or how he would eat. How he'd survive the cold winter nights on the streets of London.

He'd never been much of a drinker, so getting utterly foxed didn't prove difficult. At one end of the pub, men took turns singing, often in groups, sometimes accompanied by a fiddle. Jacob remembered laughing so hard at some of them that he had tears streaming down his face. Were the songs that humorous, or was the alcohol so strong that he laughed at silly things? No matter. He'd gotten some relief.

As if he were looking at the world through another's eyes, he stood and went to the front of the room to take his turn—

an action very unlike him, but the alcohol must have removed his usual social judgment. There, standing up before the full room of mostly men, with a handful of rather scantily clad women, he joined two men in a drinking song, "Whiskey, You're the Devil."

When it was over, he laughed until he cried, and others in the room shouted, "More, more!"

For some reason Jacob would never be able to explain, he complied, not with a drinking song but with a tune of his own creation, something he'd hummed to himself during quarantine while thinking of Miriam and staring at the ceiling. And after reading plenty of Lord Byron's works. The poet's words returned now, fitting the tune as perfectly as it had when Jacob had quietly sung it to himself day after day:

And thou art dead, as young and fair
As aught of mortal birth;
And form so soft, and charms so rare,
Too soon return'd to Earth!

The riotous laughter died down, and all eyes in the room were trained on him. In the corner, an older woman sitting alone sniffed and wiped a tear, then gave him a nod, encouraging him to continue. He did, singing on and on, the words of Lord Byron reflecting on his young love, too soon dead, as his own Miriam was. He finished with the second-to-last stanza of the poem:

As once I wept, if I could weep,
My tears might well be shed,
To think I was not near to keep
One vigil o'er thy bed;
To gaze, how fondly! on thy face,

To fold thee in a faint embrace,
Uphold thy drooping head;
And show that love, however vain,
Nor thou nor I can feel again.

His voice grew quiet, and he stopped singing. The room was silent for several seconds. He felt his cheeks flush with embarrassment for injecting sadness into the fun evening. Yet as he moved to return to his seat, the audience applauded, long and loud. Jacob stood there in stunned silence, hardly believing it.

Many a time, Miriam had praised his singing, but he hadn't thought much of it; after all, she loved all of him. She probably would have complimented him if his singing sounded like an aging warbler in a tree. However, these strangers had tears flowing from their eyes, and not from laughter. He'd sung about love and death, about his grief and his loss. And they were applauding him. Several men thumped his back with congratulations as if he'd just won an award.

The moments after he finished singing were something he'd remember forever: a London pub filled with people of all backgrounds, their attention rapt, their faces filled with the very emotion he'd been feeling. Jacob, realizing he'd just bared his soul to strangers, awkwardly bowed a couple of times, then stumbled back to his table. At his chair, however, he thought better of sitting and instead walked—rather unsteadily—out the door and into the darkness of the newly fallen snow. He'd been plenty warmed by the Guinness; he needed to escape these prying eyes.

He'd walked a block when a man ran up from behind and stopped him. "You're the one who just sang in The Red Lion, aren't you?"

Jacob turned, glanced back toward the pub, and nodded.

His eyes were burning now, and the pain of losing Miriam threatened to overtake him in another wave. Strong drinks didn't take away the pain; they merely numbed it for a moment, only for it to rush back. "That was me."

"Where did you train?"

"Train? For what?" Jacob asked. "I attended school at Harrow."

"I meant your voice," the man said with a friendly smile. "I work with performers. Singers, mostly. Get them concerts around the country—London, Brighton, Edinburgh, Dublin. And outside the country too. I've had singers touring the Continent in Paris, Copenhagen, Rome. Even New York City." He reached into his breast pocket, withdrew a card, and held it out. Jacob took it with a suspicious look before reading the text on the card, which identified the man as Richard Wright.

"What has this to do with me?" Jacob asked.

"I would like you to consider a career in music. Have you truly never had singing instruction?"

"Never."

Richard shook his head in amazement. "I've never heard the like from someone not trained in a conservatory."

"That's very kind of you, but—" He stepped forward to move on, holding the card out.

Richard held his hands up, refusing the card—and walking alongside Jacob, too. Apparently he wasn't going to let this go. "Just consider it. You can find me at the address there. It's in Belgravia."

At that, Jacob's head came around, and his step came up short. "You live in Belgravia?" He was new to London, but even he was aware that only the rich and influential lived there.

His reaction brought a smile to the other man's face. "You could, too."

Jacob waved the card back in the direction of the pub. "If you're so well-to-do, why are you frequenting pubs in squalid neighborhoods like this?"

"In the hopes of finding someone like you." He pressed the card into Jacob's palm and waved, heading back toward the pub. "Call on me tomorrow at noon. I'll be waiting."

Ten

December 23, 1824
Bath

ONE YEAR. MIRIAM could scarcely believe that it hadn't been a decade or two, but the calendar said otherwise. Exactly one year ago today, she and her father had been on their way to Harton so she could marry Jacob—a journey that had set into motion events that had her crippled, in pain, and alone. She'd lost her father in the accident, and her grief was magnified by losing Jacob just as fully, if in a different way. How much easier would grieving have been if she'd been given a chance to be held in Jacob's embrace as she cried over her father's death?

The stairs outside her bedchamber creaked with Evie's steps—the caretaker whom Norman, true to his word, had hired. As Miriam could no longer navigate stairs, her bedchamber was on the ground floor of the townhouse, where others, no doubt, would have set up a dining room. One more part of her living situation different from most: Evie, the servant, lived upstairs in what was arguably the nicest room of the townhouse, with full use of the drawing room to herself. As servants' lives went, Evie had a good one.

She rapped on Miriam's door and called, "Good morning."

"Good morning, Evie," Miriam said, shifting in her bed as she could and wincing at the throbbing pain in her legs. Movement hurt dreadfully, but *not* moving made the joints and muscles stiffen up, which led to even worse complications. She and Evie were constantly trying to balance the benefit of stretches and attempts to strengthen her legs while ever mindful of not causing undue harm or unnecessary pain to her already serious injuries. Injuries she'd likely healed from as much as she ever would.

The bedchamber door opened, and Evie appeared with a tray. "I've your breakfast," she said, crossing to the bedside table, where she lay the tray, then put an infuser with fresh tea leaves into a cup. "Sleep well?" she asked, glancing at Miriam as she poured hot water over the infuser.

"As well as can be expected," Miriam said with a smile. She sat up—carefully—but she must have made a face, because Evie set the teapot back onto the tray and helped her into position. She added a pillow to help keep Miriam in a comfortable sitting position, then returned to her work at the tray.

Oh, how grateful Miriam was for Norman to have found a caretaker as kind and gentle as Evie. Truth be told, Miriam wouldn't have been surprised if he'd found the most bitter, disagreeable person possible, but Evie had become a friend in the months they'd been together. She was yet in her twenties, and Miriam both hoped and feared that Evie would herself find a husband. Miriam the friend wanted Evie to be happy, to have a family, or at least to have a life outside the walls of their townhouse, but Miriam the patient could not fathom a future without her.

Evie placed the tray onto Miriam's lap. Everything was arranged exactly so, and beautifully. She'd even included a small piece of a deep-purple shrub as decoration, cut from one of Miriam's favorite plants out front. "I've called for Dr. Swenson," she added, almost as an afterthought. "He'll visit this afternoon."

Miriam's brow rose in question. "Why is he coming today?" A plethora of possible reasons, all of them terrible, marched through her mind. "I'm feeling much better than I did even yesterday." She'd been a bit feverish over the weekend, and Dr. Swenson had been to visit a few times in the last week—something she never would have been able to afford in her past life and which she was grateful she could afford now, thanks to Norman. Though anything good coming from her agreement with that man was certainly tainted.

"No need to worry," Evie said with a smile. She'd been heading toward the door but turned and came back to the bedside. "I thought you'd like to attend a concert this week, but you've been unwell. Then, seeing as how it's been so cold and how the flu has been spreading in town, I wanted Dr. Swenson to come. Let him decide whether going would be wise."

A flutter of excitement went through Miriam, something all too rare of late. "Oh, I'd love to go to a concert. Though, is it snowy out?" Belvedere Street was terribly steep, and pushing Miriam in her wheeled chair down it—and then back up afterward—was hard enough for Evie in warm weather. Add snow or ice, and the trip could be downright treacherous.

"Assuming Dr. Swenson approves the outing, I'll check the roads before the concert or hire a buggy—and yes, one that can hold your chair."

"You really do think of everything, don't you?" Miriam said. "Thank you, Evie."

The latter pointed to the newspaper tucked into one edge of the tray, under a plate. "You'll find a piece about the concert in there. I circled it for you."

"You're a dear," Miriam said.

Evie slipped out of the room with a smile. When the door latched, Miriam ignored her food for the moment and pulled out the newspaper. There, as Evie had promised, was a small advertisement circled in ink about a concert to take place in Bath every night for a week. That night was the last performance. So good of Evie to try to find a way for Miriam to attend. She'd likely circled the advertisement days before but hadn't mentioned the concert until Miriam's health had improved.

But Miriam *would* get to the concert that night, even if it meant lying to Dr. Swenson about how she had yet to regain her full strength after her recent illness.

She read over the advertisement and learned that the concert had a small orchestra and several renowned singers, but the star of the show, whose name appeared in large print at the top of the piece, was a tenor soloist by the name of Davis Jacobson. The idea that she might be able to attend, and perhaps wear one of her pretty gowns, thrilled her in a way nothing had for months, for reasons she could not quite explain, even to herself. Perhaps it was simply that she and Evie had been stuck indoors for several weeks straight. Perhaps the young girl from the countryside, the one who'd grown up with her Sunday best as the nicest of her woolen dresses, anticipated dressing up.

Evie would likely spend more time than usual on Miriam's hair. Perhaps they could try one of the stylish decorative braids and curls about the face, which Miriam had always admired. Her eyes drifted upward from the newspaper toward her wardrobe, and for the first time in months, she thought of the gown she'd had made for herself last December, the one that she was supposed to wear to the wedding that never took place.

It wasn't her newest or finest dress, but the green velvet, the square neckline, and the flowing skirt had combined her favorite fashion ideas into one dress. Perhaps she could wear it tonight, if Dr. Swenson allowed her to go. Yes, she should wear it. Having been confined to a bed or a chair for months, she'd shrunk a bit, no longer having the muscle she once did, so the dress might be a bit large. No matter. She'd selected that color of green and that style because she loved them and because the green velvet brought out the same color in her eyes, which typically looked muddy brown.

Wearing her prettiest—if not her fanciest or most expensive—dress would make her feel pretty for the first time in, well, a year. Yes, she would wear that dress tonight, and perhaps, just perhaps, she'd once more feel a part of the land of the living.

Eleven

JACOB HADN'T BEEN back to Audbury, but it was time, despite Richard's protestations that the wintry country roads might make getting to that night's concert impossible. But he simply could not be so close to Audbury and *not* pay his respects to the graves of Miriam and Matthew Brown. He'd already performed in Bath several times, and tonight was to be the final concert before he and Richard returned to London for the Christmas holiday. Assuming, of course, that the more frequented roads would be passable.

"I haven't missed a single performance in a year," he'd told Richard after informing him of his intended day trip to Audbury.

"Yes, yes, I know, but—"

"I've been at your beck and call for months, living out of a trunk, moving from one place to another. I'm asking for just one day, and I'll be back in plenty of time."

Richard crossed his legs and sighed as if annoyed. "Listening to you, one could think that you hadn't been made into the most sought-after singer in England, that you hadn't sung before the wealthy or before royalty, that you hadn't performed in the Royal Pavilion in Brighton, the best theaters in London—"

"And Oxford, and a dozen others, I know." How could he explain? "This is simply something I must do. For Miriam."

Whether because Jacob's tone had shifted or his words had finally sunk in, Richard's demeanor changed. "Very well. But please be back at least two hours before the concert is to begin."

Jacob grinned. "I'll make it three." He stepped toward the door and put on his hat, then turned to look at Richard before stepping through. "Thank you. Truly. I'll see you tonight."

Rather than risk a carriage wheel getting stuck in mud, Jacob opted to hire a horse for the day. He hadn't been riding in months, of course, but he was certain that he'd have no trouble managing one. He might have an extremely tender backside come morning, but that potentiality was more than worth the sacrifice.

He rode for two hours until he reached Audbury proper, though it was even emptier of residents than it had been a year ago, as more and more failing sheep farmers moved away, off to cities where they could make a living. He'd been riding at a decent clip, not galloping but trotting most of the way, but when he came upon the Browns' cottage, now lying empty, weeds growing unchecked, chickens and a few unfamiliar cats seeming to have taken ownership of the place, he slowed. Seeing the house in disrepair made his heart ache. The more he looked, the more he found: broken windows, missing shingles on the roof that Miriam had hoped to repair, the front door hanging askew.

He looked away and rode on, wanting to remember the cottage as it had been in happier days: glowing golden orange from the lamp inside, flowers lining the walk, Miriam and her father inside, welcoming him. Things that would never again be.

At last he found himself at the graveyard adjacent to the small Audbury church. He tied the horse's lead around a tree branch and stepped onto the hallowed ground, unsure where to look for the headstone that Norman had sworn he'd paid for and had put in place to mark the Browns' final resting place. He found the grave in a shady corner. Lichen had already taken hold in spots, though the engraving was still as clear as it must have been when it was made.

Here lie Matthew and Miriam Brown, father and daughter who perished in an accident December 1823.

Jacob removed his hat and bowed his head, once more wishing he'd been able to say farewell to them or at least be present when they were buried here. He said a quiet prayer, then opened his eyes. He wasn't sure how he felt, but whatever he'd expected hadn't come. He'd hoped for peace, for this moment to be when he would be able to say the unspoken farewell, give Miriam to Mother Earth, and find some semblance of healing within his own soul. But none of those things happened. The soul wasn't so easily healed, then.

He bent down and used his gloved hand to brush away dirt and some of the lichen, making the stone as tidy as he could for the moment. "I'll be back," he whispered as much to himself as to Miriam.

Somehow, he'd need to return to find a way past this hurdle, this wall that kept him miserable. He'd spent the year in a darkness he wouldn't wish on anyone, and no amount of monetary or career success could shine a light into that darkness. Yet Miriam wouldn't want him to be like this, sorrowful and grieving, for the rest of his life. While he doubted he'd ever love another woman as he'd loved Miriam, he did want to honor her life by finding some measure of peace and healing.

Clearly, this was not to be that day. He brushed off the headstone a bit more, glad that Norman had kept his word on that point, at least; it was a beautiful marker made of limestone with streaks of varying colors that ranged from white to butter yellow, as if a speck of the sun were trying to shine upward from the columnar shape and light the world. The limestone looked very much like the entire city he'd been staying in for the last week; all of Bath was built from limestone from the same quarry. Though chimney smoke, street lamps, and dirty rainwater stained many, if not most, of the buildings to some degree, the underlying color still felt cheerful and affirming.

Norman had mentioned that the marker was of limestone, but until Jacob saw it with his own eyes, he couldn't have known how fittingly beautiful it was as a memorial to Miriam.

Jacob straightened and headed back to the horse, pausing to look about the village as best he could from that vantage. He could just make out the top of Stonecroft Cottage. It would never be Stonecroft Hall to him. He checked his pocket watch for the time, glad that he had an extra two hours more than he'd promised Richard to return. He mounted the horse and turned her around, heading back the way they'd come. Richard would be relieved to see Jacob return early.

As he left Audbury behind, Jacob didn't dread the night's concert as he had been. After nearly a week of performances, he'd grown weary of the town, of the sameness of the buildings and the sameness of the concert life. He wanted to plan something new to perform. He wanted a break from constant travel and stage appearances. He wanted sleep and rest and the opportunity to maybe enjoy some of the money he'd earned, provided such a time of relaxation didn't mean he'd find himself falling into despair again. Staying busy did have that rather helpful effect: when a man was too busy keeping track of concerts and schedules and rehearsals, he had little time for dark and dreary thoughts to slip in.

But now, he'd view tonight's concert as a way of saying goodbye to Miriam. Bath itself, with all of its limestone, now reminded him of Miriam. He'd dedicate the concert to her.

Twelve

As Jacob had predicted, his early return to Bath was a relief to Richard. After returning the horse to the stables he'd let it from and then going to the hotel they were staying at, he found Richard pacing the halls.

"There you are!"

"And I'm two hours early," Jacob pointed out.

"Yes, but tonight is your final performance, and we have much to discuss, practice to do . . ."

"Richard, I know precisely what to do tonight. Whoever you think may be in attendance, I will do my utmost to impress them." He always did his utmost; Richard should know that by now. "But if an additional rehearsal will put you at ease, I'm happy to do one."

"Good, good," Richard said, dabbing a handkerchief on his forehead. "Because there's a rumor that a duke is visiting Bath. That he was at *the* baths earlier today and dined in the Pump Room!"

A rumor. Those were dangerous, for when they referred to nobility especially, they were as likely to be true as false.

Jacob did his best to calm his manager, then found some supper with Richard in the hotel dining area before they headed to the theater for the concert: his last of the season, last of the year. He could hardly wait.

Backstage, he heard the crowd growing in size, the

rumbling sound of voices and footsteps increasing as their numbers did. As always, butterflies came to life in his middle, something that used to make him terribly nervous but that he'd managed to view, in recent months, as a sign of energy and excitement.

The concert itself was magnificent. The orchestra not only hit every note perfectly but played with such emotion and clarity that the accompaniment alone would have been enough to bring forth tears—and did, in some cases, before he sang. He looked out over the span of people gathered before him and wondered where they hailed from. How many were in Bath for the holidays? How many called this city home? How many, such as the duke and duchess—if the story was true—had come for a visit in hopes of benefiting from the restorative powers of the Roman baths?

The concert went extraordinarily well. As always, Jacob sang, the orchestra played some pieces alone, and a few smaller ensembles made up of orchestra members played as well. Sometimes Jacob told a story to lead into a particular song. When the concert was nearly over and he had one song left to sing, he addressed the audience directly.

"As I look out and see your smiling faces, I am grateful and humbled that you would spend your evening with me. This is my last concert of the year—"

The crowd moaned slightly at that, but he raised a hand and went on. "I am not retiring. I'm sure I'll return to Bath. But seeing as this is my last performance of this year, I wish to dedicate it to a very special young woman." He paused, feeling his eyes prick. He fought back tears; he couldn't very well honor Miriam's memory properly if he began crying. His singing would come out no better than a warble. He swallowed and continued. "As many of you know, I end each of my concerts with the same song, but I've never explained why."

Movement from the corner of his eye grabbed his attention, and he glanced into the stage wing. Richard was shaking his head and making an X motion with his arms. Richard always wanted to protect Jacob, had withheld as much personal information as he could from the public, including the newspapers, which was why Jacob had transposed his name to create his professional stage name: Jacob Davies had become Davis Jacobson.

He smiled at Richard in an effort to calm him. It wasn't as if Jacob was going to reveal personal information like Miriam's name, that they'd grown up in Audbury, or—especially—anything about the accident.

"I will end tonight's performance with the same song I have for a year, one which I created the music for and borrowed the lyrics from Lord Byron. This time, however, I am publicly dedicating this song to the woman who inspired it. A young woman who . . . who is no longer with us." His throat threatening to choke up, he let his gaze scan the audience from left to right, pausing for a moment to gather his composure. Then, there on the right, for a heart-stopping moment, he saw a woman who he could have sworn was Miriam—sitting not in a regular padded chair but in a wheeled one. He stared for the briefest of moments, but she quickly lowered her face, and he looked away, heart pounding uneasily.

His visit to Audbury and its graveyard must have awakened more in him than he'd realized. He cleared his throat in an attempt to loosen it. He looked at his boots for a moment, then lifted his face to the audience once more, but this time, he looked straight down the middle of the auditorium, barely over the attendees' heads.

"As I was saying, I dedicate this, my final performance of the year, to her. My love, who passed away one year ago." He gave a slight nod to the conductor—his cue to begin the music, a plaintive, melancholy, and utterly beautiful score that fit the melody he'd invented while lying in bed for those long days at Branbourne Manor.

"And thou art dead, as young and fair," he began, "As aught of mortal birth."

The audience hushed in a now-familiar way, silence rippling across the room until only the instruments and Jacob's voice could be heard. He kept his eyes straight forward, where shadows loomed, so he wouldn't look about the room. The limelights of the stage lit him so he was easier seen than he could see out, yet he had to fight the pull to look at the woman in the wheeled chair. His mind was so caught up in his visit to Audbury and the memories of that horrible day when he'd gone to the chapel, only to learn that his love had died, that afterward he had no memory of singing the next few lines. He must have, however, because the orchestra picked up after the verse, playing the interlude.

Jacob continued to sing. Every person's attention was locked on him. He felt that this was, quite likely, the best performance he'd ever given of this or any song. When at last he reached the final verse, he had to close his eyes to keep from looking at the woman who bore such a striking resemblance to his beloved Miriam. The emotion of the lyrics poured from him.

> *My tears might well be shed,*
> *To think I was not near to keep*
> *One vigil o'er thy bed;*
> *To gaze, how fondly! on thy face,*
> *To fold thee in a faint embrace,*
> *Uphold thy drooping head;*
> *And show that love, however vain,*
> *Nor thou nor I can feel again.*

The orchestra concluded the song with half a minute of a reprise, during which Jacob's self-restraint exhausted itself. He opened his eyes and could not help looking at the woman sitting near the aisle in her wheeled chair. Surely he'd imagined the resemblance, or so he'd assured himself until he looked on her again. If anything, she appeared *more* like Miriam than before—and she had tears streaming down her cheeks.

When she realized he was looking at her, she startled, then turned to her lady companion. After a quick, whispered interchange, the companion hurriedly stood and got behind the chair, and next thing he knew, the woman—a twin to his Miriam—was being wheeled away.

They stopped briefly for the friend—servant?—to place a wrap about the shoulders of her charge. A wrap of deep browns with swirls of blue and burgundy. He'd seen a wrap exactly like that before. He'd given its twin to Miriam on the night of their engagement.

Could a woman who looked just like Miriam also possess a wrap that looked precisely like the one she owned?

No. That was impossible. This had to be Miriam, or perhaps a hallucination. Either way, he had to find out. Catch the women before they were lost to him somewhere in the city's many buildings. Lost forever.

When the audience burst into applause, Jacob was only vaguely aware of it. Richard's motions from the wing reminded him to go through his routine of bowing for the audience, but he shortened it and left the stage abruptly. He had to chase after the woman in the wheeled chair. Had to find her, speak to her, learn the truth about what had happened a year ago. His heart told him she had just left the room.

That his heart hadn't needed to be broken.

That Miriam was alive.

Thirteen

EVIE PUSHED THE wheeled chair out of the theater, onto the cobbled street, and as quickly as she could onto the slightly more even sidewalk. She hurried past those out for an evening stroll, so much so that Miriam heard her breath huffing and noted the sound of her shoes slipping on the slushy ground. Bless the girl, she'd taken Miriam's plea to escape seriously.

"As soon as we're around the next corner, we can slow down," she told Evie over her shoulder.

"I'll go as fast as I can for as long as I can," she replied. She turned the corner and, true to her word, attempted to keep going at the same pace, but the incline of the street made maintaining the same speed impossible.

"Careful," Miriam said, as much for Evie's sake as her own. She'd had more than one nightmare of herself in her chair tumbling down Belvedere Street, Evie rolling down too, her skirts getting caught in the wheels, and the both of them landing in a heap at the bottom by Pulteney Bridge, Miriam dead and Evie a cripple.

"Perhaps we can slip into a doorway and hide in the shadows for a moment," Evie said, panting.

"Yes, let's," Miriam said.

Evie steered the chair around a corner townhouse that had a gate right at the corner and elaborate shrubbery and some statues on display. The size of it all provided good cover. With the chair turned to face the street and Evie still behind her, Miriam couldn't help but keep her eyes trained on the rounded corner wall, waiting with dread for what—or who— might come.

Emotion threatened to bubble up, but she tamped it down, resolving to be strong as steel to protect Jacob. How could she have known that Davis Jacobson was actually Jacob Davies, *her* Jacob? She hadn't any idea. She'd assumed he lived in Audbury at Stonecroft Cottage or in London—whether submitting to Norman or striking out on his own with some other venture, she hadn't known. But singing ... that had never occurred to her, though she'd long known he had the talent. She'd told him as much, but he'd never listened to her.

Or, apparently, he finally had.

Yet he believed her dead, and to keep his future from being dragged down like an anchor, he needed to continue to believe it. Moreover, if she were to have any kind of life, to not be on the streets begging for food or trying to find a hospital to take her in, she needed Norman's money. Not to mention that Evie needed her position as well. Too many lives and livelihoods were at stake.

As hard as it was to hear Jacob singing about her—and at the end, singing *to* her, she thought—about his loss and love, allowing him into her life would be the height of selfishness. As Norman, devil that he was, had said, if she loved Jacob, she had to remain dead to him.

Oh, what she wouldn't give for one more tender word, one more embrace, one last kiss. Her love for him flared within her, and with it came the most bitter ache, of knowing it was all for naught. She'd fought back the feelings for months, but now that she'd escaped the theater, she let them come to the surface, just a little. She'd been strong for so long.

She could let herself cry a bit. Silently. And only for a moment. But she let herself shed a few tears for Jacob and the life they could have had.

Heavy footsteps pounded in the distance, followed by a voice calling into the night. "Miriam! Miriam Brown! Where are you?"

She clamped her eyes shut, which squeezed out more tears, but she kept silent. She had to. For Jacob's sake.

Evie, however, leaned close and whispered, "Someone is calling for you?"

"Yes," she whispered back. Miriam hadn't explained the need to escape, just the urgency. The intensity of her request—and likely Miriam's look of sheer terror—had spurred Evie into action.

"Is he—a *bad* man?"

"The very opposite," Miriam said. *Because* Jacob was such a good man, *because* she loved him so dearly, she had to run away.

The footsteps and voice faded, though they didn't stop. Perhaps Jacob was down by the river now on the other side of town. "Let's go," she whispered.

Without another question, Evie obeyed, for which Miriam was grateful. They said nothing more as they slowly moved up the hill, past colorful doors to one of the many blue ones that marked their townhouse. Theirs was a bright blue. Cheerful, not dark, and not too pale either. She'd loved the color when she first laid eyes on it because it matched the blue accents of the silk wrap Jacob had given. The very wrap she wore now. Had he seen it? He must have.

Wait, where *was* her wrap? In their hurry, it must have fallen off, and in her panic, she hadn't noticed. She couldn't go out to look for it, and Evie certainly couldn't do so alone—a single woman out late at night? No, Miriam wouldn't so much as consider any chance of harming her friend's reputation. She'd simply pray that it would be found by someone trustworthy and that perhaps it had fallen off near the theater, where the finder would return it. A foolish hope, perhaps, but at the moment, it was her only hope of seeing Jacob's wrap again.

Evie set the brake on a back wheel and moved to unlock the door. After most excursions, she helped Miriam stand and very slowly take the step up required to get inside, where she could then reach her cane in its spot by the door and, leaning against Evie for much-needed support, slowly walk to her bed. Not tonight.

"Could you carry me inside?" she asked. Her legs were shaking too much from the shock of seeing Jacob again that she didn't trust them to support her any more than a mound of porridge could. Besides, being carried inside would be much faster, and if there had ever been a time that Miriam needed to move quickly, this was it.

Evie glanced at Miriam and seemed to understand her urgency. "Of course," she said. The door gave way to the key; she pushed it open, then returned to fetch Miriam, who was near to panicking over the possibility of being spotted in the street.

Jacob *could* be on the other side of town, but she knew him well enough to suspect that he'd run through every street in Bath in search of her—and the city wasn't terribly large. By now, he could easily be heading back northward, toward the abbey, and returning in their direction once more.

Drat the steepness of Belvedere Street; from the bottom, some half a mile away, one could look up and see their door. The cloak of night would help, but in the glow of street lamps, her chair would surely stand out in stark relief. If he reached the base of the street now . . .

"We must hurry," Miriam said, looking down the street, worried nearly to the point of tears.

Evie hurried back, then slipped one arm under Miriam's legs and the other below her arms, cradling her as she lifted her from the chair. With her charge in her arms, Evie's movements slowed down—wise, considering the chance of slipping on the wintry ground. In less than a minute, Miriam was placed upon her bed, where she let out a breath of relief.

From Miriam's vantage, she could see through her bedchamber door to the outside, where Evie was already leaning to the side to release the brake. She straightened and began to walk backward, careful to watch the wheels as she navigated them up and over the step inside, taking care to not scratch the door frame.

"Ho! You, there!" A man's voice carried through the door from the street—and *not* from a great distance. He was close. Too close.

Evie froze, as did Miriam. They stared at each other for a moment, during which Miriam silently pleaded with her caretaker to get inside and lock the door. Evie tried. Miriam could see that. But the man calling out had somehow arrived already—not from the bottom of the street, as she'd assumed someone might, but from the top, running so fast along the steep decline that he nearly flew past the door before he could stop. When he did, he bent over, breathing heavily, hands on his knees—and something in one of those hands. A flash of blue made Miriam catch her breath.

"Is that—is that my wrap?"

Evie had gotten the chair inside, and she had the door half closed. At Miriam's words, she looked over, confused—pausing only a moment, but long enough for the man outside to reach through the gap with his arm. He held onto the door and shoved his boot between the gap as well.

"Get out!" Evie tried to push the door closed, pressing on the man's arm. She was clearly terrified, and Miriam was anxious too, but she'd seen the wrap, and if this was a young man trying to return it . . .

"Ask if he has my wrap."

"Your—" Evie's eyes widened in understanding. "I didn't notice that it had fallen. I am so sorry, Miss Brown—"

"Evie." Miriam's firm voice stopped the effusion. "Don't call me that. And please, just ask him. See if it's mine. Maybe he'll withdraw."

With a nervous nod, Evie released some of the weight she'd been pressing against the door, resulting in the man outside letting out a sound of relief. "Thank you. Goodness, that hurt something fierce."

Jacob. It was Jacob. Miriam had no doubt at all. He knew she'd survived the accident. He'd seen her, followed her. What was she to do? Norman would withdraw his support—and his money was the only reason she had any kind of life at all. She would have to move to—somewhere. Ireland? Scotland?

"Give me that wrap," Evie demanded.

Outside, Jacob let out a breath of frustration. "Look. You can see it well enough, but I'm not giving it to you. I know it belongs to Miss Brown, and I demand to see her so I can return it myself."

Miriam felt as if her soul were being ripped down the middle, one side in agony over *not* seeing Jacob again, the other in agony over what seeing him again would mean for either of them. Oh, how she wanted to see him, hear his voice speaking to *her*, feel his embrace once more. And oh, how guilty she would feel for the rest of her life if she allowed it.

Evie held strong. "How do you know her name, and how can you possibly know whether it belongs to her?"

"You've essentially admitted that it's hers," Jacob said—

firmly, but kindly, as only he could. "And I know it's Miss Brown's because . . ." He paused for a moment, and when he spoke again, his voice wavered. "Because I gave it to her the day after I asked her to marry me."

Images from that morning flooded Miriam's mind, and she had to cover her mouth to be sure she couldn't make a sound when—not if—she cried.

For Evie's part, she stood stock-still, mouth agape, at Jacob's declaration. She looked at Miriam, who nodded miserably. "It's true." She'd kept her past shrouded from Evie, who knew Miriam only as the cripple Mr. Norman Davies hired her to care for. Evie dropped her hands from the door entirely. "This is your fiancé?" she asked. "How—why—does Mr. Davies know?"

She'd let down her defenses, which allowed Jacob to push through the doorway and enter the townhouse. "If you mean my brother, Norman, then yes, he knows."

Evie's face drained of color, making her look ghostlike against the light from a lamp that one of the servants had lit in their absence. "But we saw you singing. You're Mr. Jacobson. How can Mr. Davies be your brother? I don't . . ." Her hand went to her forehead, and Jacob stepped forward to support her should she faint. She took his arm, and they briefly disappeared from Miriam's view, but she could hear the creak of a step on the staircase and murmured voices. Evie was surely sitting there until she regained her composure.

Jacob's footfalls sounded as he returned from the staircase. At the entrance, he closed the front door and locked it, then cast a gaze at the wheeled chair before turning his full attention to Miriam. He stood so near, framed by her door, looking the same and yet older, different—possibly due to the elegant, undoubtedly expensive clothing.

He took a hesitant step across the threshold but kept his

distance, as if he didn't want to upset her or hurt her. As if Jacob could do any of those things. "You're—I—"

"I know." Miriam's voice cracked, and the tears began in earnest.

"Is your father . . . ?"

"He is gone, yes. Norman did not lie about that part."

"And you? How are you—" He held his hat in his hands, rotating it by the brim as he spoke—but suddenly he stopped. "Norman did all of this, didn't he?"

"He made sure I could live comfortably, but only if I did not ruin your life."

Jacob crossed the distance in several quick strides. "Miriam, how could you ever—"

"A politician needs—"

"I am not, nor ever will I be, a politician."

"But your life as a performer—Davis Jacobson's image must be—"

"Whatever I want it to be," Jacob said. He clearly was not about to let her explain away or rationalize anything. She was running out of reasons, and that fact both terrified her and made a dark corner of her heart spark with hope. He took her hand between both of his—so warm and strong and gentle. "I would give anything—anything—to be your husband. I would give up my life as a performer. It began as a way to not die on the streets alone from hunger and heartbreak."

"But I'm frail and weak, and I hardly walk at all. I may never be able to have children, and—"

This time he cut off her words by pressing a thumb to her lips, then stroking his thumb across them. She hadn't felt anything so welcome and comforting, so *loving*, since the accident.

"I love you, Miriam. I always have, and I always will. Fate broke us apart a year ago, but it has brought us back together again despite my brother's meddling. Marry me? Please? I don't need Norman's money, and neither do you anymore. I've earned enough this last year to not need to work at all for several years if I don't want to. We can finally be together. That is, if you still love me."

Warmth and happiness came over her that outshone the pain and dreariness of the last year by several orders of magnitude. "I'll never stop loving you, Jacob Davies. Ever."

He leaned in and, gently holding her face between his hands, kissed her as he might a fragile vase—until she drew him closer, demanding a kiss akin to the ones they'd once shared. She drank him in, every part of him, forgetting the expensive clothing and stage name. He pulled back ever so slightly, parting their lips by a whisper. "Will you marry me?"

She nodded, and tears of joy mingled with the ones she'd shed moments before from sadness. "Yes. Yes, yes, yes."

Jacob sat back, his eyes sparkling. "I can purchase a license that will allow us to marry as soon as we wish."

Miriam thought of the Christmas Eve wedding they were supposed to have. "As soon as tomorrow morning?"

If possible, his face brightened with even more happiness as he understood the suggestion. "I'll be there, my love."

"As will I. You have my promise."

Fourteen

MIRIAM AWOKE CHRISTMAS Eve morning to a chill in the air and the artwork of frost fairies' brushes on the windowpanes. A fire had already been lit in the grate, though the room had yet to warm fully. No matter; she was as warm as she needed to be today of all days; her joy filled her so completely that the aches in her legs and foot that came upon awaking every morning seemed dull and meaningless. She could endure any pain if it meant being with Jacob again—being with him and knowing that they would not be destitute. That he loved her despite her infirmities and was not marrying her out of pity. That becoming his wife would not, in fact, destroy his life as she'd been led to believe.

The change in Jacob's countenance was something she could not ignore. During the concert he'd been talented and powerful on the stage, but with a melancholy that cloaked him. Others might have seen that air as a mysterious thing, or an act he put on, but she'd known better then, and she knew even better now. For when he'd entered the townhouse after the concert, all of the heaviness and sadness dropped away like scales from the blind man's eyes. He was *her* Jacob, the man she'd come to love in the rolling hills of Audbury, tailored coat and silk cravat notwithstanding.

Today she would not wear anything nearly as grand as he possessed in his wardrobe, though she certainly had finer gowns than she'd ever possessed before, thanks to Norman's allowance. Today she had no desire whatsoever to wear any of those gowns—not the taffeta, the damask, or the lampas. Instead, she would wear the same gown she'd worn the night before to the concert, this time for its original purpose: for her to wear it as a bride, to speak her vows and be wed to the man who owned her heart fully and completely.

Jacob sent a buggy for her and Evie, wanting to ensure her safety en route despite the short distance. As Evie helped her inside, Miriam felt grateful that he hadn't sent anything larger that might have reminded her a bit too much of the stagecoach that had been part of their tragic past.

"The only bridge between here and the abbey is stone, with walls," she said, settling into her seat.

Evie gave her a strange look, and Miriam laughed, realizing she had yet to explain the entire story to her friend.

"We'll arrive safely," she said as an interim explanation. "And that's all that matters."

Minutes later, they were at Bath Abbey, with its soaring facade, arched windows, and immense carved door. Evie fetched the wheeled chair, and soon the pair were entering the abbey proper, with the door held open by a man who nodded and bowed as they went in. The grand interior, with a ceiling filled with what looked like patterns of stone fans, took Miriam's breath away. She clutched her cane more tightly on her lap, so as to not lose hold of it as Evie pushed her down the aisle. She was determined to stand while getting married, even if she couldn't quite manage walking down the long aisle.

As planned—twice now—Jacob stood at the end, waiting for his Christmas bride. On seeing her, his face lit up, and tears pricked her eyes. Evie pushed her closer, and when she was near him, Miriam realized that Jacob wasn't wearing a fancy brocade coat with a silk cravat as he had for the concert. No, he wore a navy coat that she recognized from Audbury—fine wool, but wool nonetheless. This was truly *her* Jacob, not wealthy and famous Davis Jacobson.

Evie set the brake and supported Miriam as she steadied the cane and eased herself into a standing position. Evie then opened a bag she'd carried on her arm, revealing a small bouquet of holly, laurel, and mistletoe. "A bride must have a bouquet."

"Thank you, sweet friend," Miriam said. She held the bouquet with one hand and balanced herself on the cane with her other.

Jacob stepped close and rested a hand on her lower back, offering additional protection. Despite the aches in both legs, she'd never been happier, and she was perfectly content to stand there in the abbey with Jacob for as long as she could.

The vicar began the ceremony, which was as beautiful as she could have hoped. They spoke their vows and exchanged rings Jacob had brought with him. At long last, they were pronounced husband and wife, and they shared their first wedded kiss.

They returned to the townhouse, where Jacob had arranged a fine meal. That night, after the servants had retired, before Mr. and Mrs. Davies went to bed, he locked what was now their bedchamber door and scooped her into his arms.

"Goodness!" Miriam said with laughing surprise.

"We haven't had a proper first dance," Jacob said. He kissed her soundly, then began swaying side to side and turning in slow circles, humming a tune as they "danced." Blissfully happy, Miriam rested her head against his shoulder, one hand pressed against his heart as if she needed to know that they were both indeed alive and experiencing the same joy.

And then Jacob began to sing, softly, in almost a whisper, for an audience of one.

O my Luve's like a red, red rose
That's newly sprung in June;
O my Luve's like the melodie
That's sweetly play'd in tune.

As fair art thou, my bonnie lass,
So deep in luve am I:
And I will luve thee still, my dear,
Till a' the seas gang dry:

Till a' the seas gang dry, my dear,
And the rocks melt wi' the sun:
I will luve thee still, my dear,
While the sands o' life shall run.

Miriam recognized the words as those of Robert Burns, but the love that sang them was all Jacob's, and when he finished, she kissed him and held him, returning the love that was entirely hers to give.

Annette Lyon is a *USA Today* bestselling author, a 6-time Best of State medalist for fiction in Utah, and a Whitney Award winner. She's had success as a professional editor and in newspaper, magazine, and technical writing, but her first love has always been fiction.

She's a cum laude graduate from BYU with a degree in English and is the author of over a dozen books, including the Whitney Award-winning *Band of Sisters*, a chocolate cookbook, and a grammar guide. She co-founded and was served as the original editor of the *Timeless Romance Anthology* series and continues to be a regular contributor to the collections.

She has received five publication awards from the League of Utah Writers, including the Silver Quill, and she's one of the four coauthors of the *Newport Ladies Book Club* series. Annette is represented by Heather Karpas at ICM Partners.

Find Annette online:
Blog: http://blog.AnnetteLyon.com
Twitter: @AnnetteLyon
Facebook: http://Facebook.com/AnnetteLyon
Instagram: https://www.instagram.com/annette.lyon/
Pinterest: http://Pinterest.com/AnnetteLyon
Newsletter: http://bit.ly/1n3I87y

A CHRISTMAS JOURNEY

-Jennifer Moore-

One

"TODAY, HE'LL COME," Lucy Breckenridge whispered to herself as she hurried down the stairs to breakfast. "It must be today."

The smell of Mrs. Fraser's tattie scones drifted through the house, filling Lucy with a warm nostalgia. For the last nine years, as war raged on the peninsula, she'd been shuffled from one relative to the next, only coming to her own home as a visitor for a few weeks when her father was on leave. But now she was home to stay, and with Napoleon finally defeated and banished to St. Helena, soldiers were returning home as well. And among them was Colonel William Breckenridge.

She smiled as she stepped into the entrance hall and glanced at the coat stand. She and Mrs. Fraser had pressed her father's winter coat and dusted his beaver-skin hat. He'd not need his regimentals now. There were no French to fight in North Yorkshire.

Lucy came into the kitchen and sat at the table. The three servants her father employed—Mrs. Fraser, the cook and housekeeper; Meg Riley, the maid; and Mr. Owens, man-of-all-work—were already seated, but they rose when she entered.

"Good morning, miss." Mrs. Fraser set a clean plate in front of Lucy and scooted the scones and butter near. She scooped a bowl of porridge and set it beside Lucy's plate, folding her arms and nodding in her practical way. Mrs. Fraser had maintained this same house since the time of Lucy's grandparents. She was tall and bony and seemed to wear a permanent frown. Lucy had been frightened of Mrs. Fraser when she was a small girl, but she'd learned that beneath her prickly exterior, the woman was softhearted and very loyal.

"Good morning." Lucy grinned. "I believe he will arrive today," she said.

The others nodded, and Lucy knew they were humoring her. She'd made the same announcement each morning since her father's letter had arrived weeks earlier and she'd returned to Pinnock Hill.

"I do hope so, miss," Meg said. She smiled, the expression looking particularly cheerful on her round, freckled face. The maid wore a white cap over her hair, but her red curls did not seem to know that they were supposed to remain beneath it. They poked out in every direction like springs.

"And whut tasks do ye 'ave fer us today, then, miss?" Mr. Owens grunted, wiping crumbs from his waistcoat.

Lucy thought through her extensive list of preparations. Mr. Owens had already dragged a large log to the stable to keep it dry until Christmas Eve. He'd washed all the windows, filled the wood box, cleaned the root cellar, repainted the wainscoting in the dining room, and repaired the wobbly stair rail.

"If you please," Lucy said, "the hedges beneath the north window need trimming."

"'Twill wait for spring, surely." The man glanced through the window at the newly fallen snow.

"Everything must be just right," Lucy said, not acknowledging his protest and smearing butter onto her scone.

"Very well, miss," he said. But she thought he grumbled something beneath his breath.

"I've finished dusting out all the hearths, like you asked," Meg said. "And polishing the silverware and beating the drapes and rugs. I rubbed down all the furniture with beeswax and put clean linens on the beds. And fresh towels in the washrooms."

"Thank you, Meg." Lucy gave a grateful smile. The girl had worked hard reopening the house—even though much of her work had been done in a heavy coat and scarf as the windows were thrown open and rooms aired out. But her efforts had paid off. Every room sparkled.

"And Mrs. Fraser, you—"

"Pudding was prepared weeks ago," the older woman interrupted, the slightest hint of irritation in her voice. "I ordered a Christmas goose from the butcher and found the scented soap the colonel fancies."

"Have we black currant preserves?" Lucy asked, glancing at the different types of jam before her. "Father loves black currant preserves on his toast."

Mrs. Fraser's brow ticked. "I will find some, miss."

Lucy knew she was being fastidious, but she'd not spent Christmas with her father since she was ten years old. And she was not going to let a single thing get in the way of their happy celebration. Everything must be perfect.

"Meg, I wondered if you might walk with me later this morning when the weather is warmer," Lucy said. "I hoped to search in the woods behind the parsonage for some ivy and a mistletoe."

"O' course, miss. There's always some Christmas greenery to be found." She winked. "If you know where to look."

Lucy nodded and took a bite of porridge. "Oh yes," she said, nearly forgetting to swallow in her excitement. "And we should stop in town for ribbon to decorate the mantel and Christmas table."

"Yes, miss."

When breakfast was finished, Lucy checked each room again. She did so in part to ensure that no detail had gone unnoticed but also for the sheer delight of knowing that she was here, in her real home. And she and her father would be a family again.

She hummed a Christmas tune as she arranged the inkpot and quills on her father's desk in the library, listening with one ear for the sound of a carriage. If her father came by stage and hired a coach in town, he should arrive this afternoon, but coach schedules were never definite, especially in the winter. She checked that the clock on the mantel was wound and smoothed the pleats in the drapes. Perhaps he'd purchased a new carriage, and he would arrive at any moment.

A book sat on a low table between the sofa and the library's hearth. *The Christmas Album.* After trying various spots throughout the house, Lucy had concluded that this was the proper location for it. A place of honor.

She pulled the book onto her lap and ran her hand gently over the worn leather cover. Colonel Breckenridge had given Lucy the book as a gift on the Christmas after her mother had died. In it, they'd recorded holiday memories together, documenting family traditions with Mother, lest they forget. The year following, they'd read the entries from the year before and added to it, remembering happy Christmas games and holiday visitors. Lucy had taken especial care to document their Christmas feast in pictures.

Over the next nine years, she and her father had continued to add to the book, though his contribution came through letters telling of the holiday traditions taking place where he and his troops were stationed.

Lucy turned through the Christmas album. She studied a handbill advertising *El Gordo* that she'd pasted to a page. She didn't understand the words on the paper, but her father had explained in his letter that even the Peninsular War didn't stop Cádiz from holding its annual Christmas lottery.

He'd sent drawings of Krampus, the imp from Austria who punished naughty children. He told of the candles and hymns at Midnight Mass in Portugal. One of her favorite drawings was of a Tannenbaum—a decorated evergreen tree brought into Bavarian homes on Christmas Eve.

Lucy noted how her entries were much duller, as she'd spent the holidays in the homes of different relatives. But true to her promise, she'd recorded the memories of the season with details and pictures to share with her father when they were together again on Christmas.

She placed the book reverently back on the table, a thrill of delight running through her as she pictured curling up on the sofa beside her father, perusing the pages in the warm glow of the firelight. In anticipation of a chilly evening, she'd folded her father's lap blanket over the arm of the sofa. It was just the right size to cover two laps. Perhaps she would ask Mrs. Fraser to prepare hot chocolate. And she would place a bowl of peppermints just within reach as the two reminisced and later added their memories of this year. She already had three party invitations from neighbors ready to paste inside after they attended the Christmastide gatherings.

Lucy gave a happy sigh. She stood and straightened the lap blanket, fluffed up the sofa cushions, and went to find Meg for their outing.

Hours later, Lucy rubbed her arms through her coat as she and Meg hurried up the lane toward home. The afternoon sun was dropping low. In spite of the cold air and the snow crunching beneath their feet, Lucy was pleased with what they'd accomplished.

"That was a successful trip," she said, smiling at the maid.

"That it was, miss." Meg shivered beneath her shawl. Her nose and cheeks were almost as red as her hair. "We found ribbon *and* black currant preserves. Won't Mrs. Fraser be happy not to have to go into town?"

"I imagine so," Lucy said, tucking her chin into her scarf as a cold wind blew. "When we return on Christmas Eve to gather holly, Mr. Owen will need a pole to retrieve the mistletoe." She grinned as a thought occurred to her. "And my father may choose to accompany us as well,"

"O' course he will, miss."

Shadows from trees and houses lengthened and darkened, stretching over the snowy ground.

"I wonder if my old sled is in the stable," Lucy said as the pair turned up the path toward her home. The windows glowed, a beacon of warmth, and they walked quicker. "Mr. Owens will—"

Lucy stopped. A carriage stood before the house.

Her heart jolted, and she gasped, grabbing on to Meg's arm. "He's come!" She dashed up the path and threw open the door, running inside. "Father!" Her voice echoed through the entryway.

An overcoat hung on the rack beside the door, and on the table beside it were a bicorn hat and a pair of gloves. Lucy ran into the drawing room, nearly bowling into Mrs. Fraser in the doorway. "Father, I'm here—"

A man in a regimental jacket rose when she entered.

Lucy rushed forward but caught herself only a moment before throwing herself into his arms. The man was not Colonel Breckenridge, but a much younger person. She stared at him for a moment, then looked around the room.

"Miss Lucy Breckenridge, I presume?" the man said, clasping his hands behind his back. He spoke with a trace of a Scottish brogue.

"Where is my father?" Lucy asked.

From behind her, Mrs. Fraser cleared her throat. "Miss, this is Captain Stewart."

Lucy recognized the gentle rebuke in the woman's voice. "I beg your pardon, Captain," she said, dipping in a curtsy. "How do you do?"

The sound of the front door closing indicated that Meg had come inside. Mrs. Fraser helped remove the heavy coat from Lucy's shoulders and unwound her scarf.

Captain Stewart stood straight, his manner confident. Even if he weren't wearing a red coat, she'd recognize him as a military man. He inclined his head. "A pleasure, Miss Breckenridge."

Lucy gave a smile that she knew must appear distracted. She pulled off her bonnet and handed it to the housekeeper. "Excuse me, Captain. I must see my father." Perhaps the colonel had gone to his bedchamber to freshen up after his journey. Or to the library. She turned and started from the room.

Mrs. Fraser caught her arm as she passed. "You need to talk to the captain, miss."

Lucy glanced up the stairs once more and let out a frustrated sigh before returning to the drawing room. She sat on a chair across from the sofa, forcing her shoulders to relax, and assumed a cordial expression. As the lady of the house, it was her duty to act the part of a gracious hostess—even when she didn't feel like one.

The captain sat as well, hands on his knees, his back ramrod straight and his expression serious. On the table in front of him was a cup of tea and a plate that held only scone crumbs.

"You served in Spain with my father, Captain Stewart?" Lucy asked in a polite voice.

"I did." The man's eyes were an interesting shade of blue, Lucy observed, thinking that at another time she might enjoy making the captain's acquaintance. He surely had interesting stories to tell about the peninsular campaigns. And her father must hold Captain Stewart in some esteem if he'd traveled with him all the way from London. Not to mention, the captain was quite handsome.

"I am grateful that you've accompanied him home," she said, listening for her father's footsteps on the stairs. "The journey would otherwise have been very dull for both of you."

Captain Stewart leaned forward the slightest bit. "Miss Breckenridge, I'm sorry, but your father isn't here."

Lucy pinched her lips together, confused. "You came ahead?"

Captain Stewart glanced at the housekeeper in the doorway and his brow furrowed. The expression made an uneasy tickle on the back of Lucy's neck.

"The colonel is still in London," Captain Stewart said. "He . . . couldn't get away."

"No," Lucy said in a firm voice, pushing away her unease. This captain was obviously mistaken. "That isn't right. He wrote to me from Calais a month ago. He is coming any day now."

The captain winced. "I am sorry, Miss Breckenridge. It is the truth. He regrets deeply that he won't make it home in time for Christmas."

Mrs. Fraser put a hand on Lucy's shoulder.

Lucy's throat got tight, and her eyes burned. Her thoughts felt jumbled as she tried to understand what he meant. "But he promised." Her voice came out sounding strangled. She swallowed, blinking hard and looking between the two of them. "Father always keeps his promises."

"The circumstances requiring him to remain are, unfortunately, out of his control," Captain Stewart said.

"He wishes he could be here, miss," Mrs. Fraser said in a gentle voice.

"Then why did he not write to me himself?" Lucy's disbelief was turning to anger. "Why did he send you, a stranger, to tell me the news?" This couldn't be so. He'd remained in France since the war ended six months earlier to station troops and see about the business of peace. The business of decommissioning military personnel and sending them home must surely be finished by now. And could the colonel not write further reports from home?

The captain's face softened. "Your father must have thought a letter too impersonal for such a message. He knew I would pass Pinnock Hill on my way to Edinburgh, and he asked me to pay a visit."

Lucy shook her head as the truth of the situation crashed down around her. She tried to maintain her composure, but her face would not stop jerking. Tears filled her eyes, spilling over to run down her cheeks.

Captain Stewart reached across the low table and offered her a handkerchief.

When Lucy opened her mouth to thank him, a sob tore free. She buried her face in the handkerchief, the pain of her disappointment outweighing the embarrassment of weeping in front of a stranger.

"There, there, miss." Mrs. Fraser patted her back.

Lucy couldn't respond. Her heart ached, and disappointment pressed down, making her feel like she couldn't breathe. What would happen to her now? She would likely have to leave Pinnock Hill and stay with another relative. The thought of saying goodbye to her home again was too much to endure. She just couldn't.

Mrs. Fraser continued to pat her shoulder. "Thank you for coming, Captain," she said.

"I'm sorry to be the cause of such distress," he said.

"Miss Breckenridge has suffered a great disappointment, but she will be well soon enough," the housekeeper said. "Have you far to travel tonight?"

"I planned to stay at the coaching inn in town," he replied. "The journey has been long for the horses, but we've made good time. If the weather continues to cooperate, I should be home tomorrow, a few days earlier than I'd planned."

An idea occurred to Lucy, stilling her tears. She wiped off her cheeks, sniffling as she contemplated. Yes, this was the answer.

"Are you all right, Miss Breckenridge?" Captain Stewart asked.

"I shall have to go to London," Lucy said. She folded his handkerchief and handed it back to him.

"I do not think that is a good idea." Captain Stewart looked up at Mrs. Fraser, as if hoping the older woman would agree with him. "Your father—"

"I understand he is busy," she said. "But even the War Office will be closed on Christmas Day. If Father cannot come here, then I will go to him." The idea was sounding better by the moment. She would have to act quickly, before her aunt learned her father wasn't returning. Aunt Prudence would never permit such a venture. Lucy just had to convince Mrs. Fraser, which she didn't think would be too difficult. If Meg accompanied her and Mr. Owens drove the carriage, how could the housekeeper argue?

"It is a very long journey, Miss Breckenridge." Captain Stewart took a drink of his tea. "And at this time of year, the condition of the roads is unpredictable. It can be treacherous."

"You just said that the weather cooperated, and the journey went faster than you'd predicted," Lucy pointed out.

She was becoming irritated with Captain Stewart. The man had known her for less than an hour, and he was already telling her what she could and could not do. It did not matter what he said, she thought. He had no business giving her orders. She was not one of his soldiers.

"I'm sure your father will be home by Epiphany," Captain Stewart said.

Why was he concerning himself like this? And Epiphany was the end of the holiday celebrations. If her father arrived in January, Lucy would have to wait nearly an entire year to spend Christmas with him. And that just wouldn't do.

"I believe the colonel mentioned you have an aunt in East Riding," Captain Stewart went on. "Perhaps you might join her for the holidays?"

That was the last straw. If her mind had not been completely made up before, the suggestion that she spend another Christmas with Aunt Prudence and her guestroom filled with porcelain dolls was the push she needed. She shivered just thinking of all the glassy eyes watching her as she slept.

"Yes, that is a very good idea," she said, speaking with false cheerfulness. "Christmas at Aunt Prudence's sounds splendid." She glanced up and met Mrs. Fraser's eye.

The woman's lips pursed. She knew Lucy was lying.

Lucy felt guilty about the deception, but she did not want to argue with the man, and there were plans to be made. She figured the trip would take three days, meaning she needed to depart tomorrow morning or she would be too late. But first, she needed Captain Stewart to leave.

"Thank you for your visit," Lucy said. "I appreciate you delivering the message, and I apologize for my reaction." She noticed her foot was tapping and stopped it.

Captain Stewart studied her, but after a moment his face relaxed. He smiled, looking relieved. "No apology necessary,

Miss Breckenridge. You were taken off guard and presented with unwelcome news. Entirely understandable." He glanced at his pocket watch and stood. "I should return to the inn. Mrs. Higgins was adamant that supper would be served exactly at six thirty."

Lucy stood as well. "You will not want to miss her fried sea bass. It is one of Father's favorites." She accompanied him to the entrance hall as Mrs. Fraser went to the kitchen to fetch the captain's driver. Lucy's mind was spinning with plans for her journey, but she pasted on a smile and handed the captain his hat.

"I am very glad to have met you, Miss Breckenridge." Captain Stewart buttoned his coat and pulled on his gloves. "Happy Christmas to you."

"Happy Christmas, Captain Stewart." Lucy waved and closed the door, pressing her back against it as she drew in a deep breath and firmed her resolve.

If Father cannot come home for Christmas, I will take Christmas to him.

Two

CAPTAIN JAMES STEWART woke the next morning, his belly still full of Miss Higgins's fried sea bass. He'd not left one scrap on the table—a habit of most soldiers who'd campaigned abroad for any length of time. Even though the war had ended and his next meal was guaranteed, hunger was not a sensation a man soon forgot.

He dressed and descended the stairs to the inn's dining rooms.

Private Matthews sat at a table near the hearth. *Nick* Matthews, James reminded himself. He crossed the room, making certain Matthews saw him before joining him at the table. James knew better than to startle a man who'd fought at Albuera and Badajoz. "Good morning, Matthews."

Matthews nodded but gave no verbal response. Not that James had expected him to. The man hadn't spoken in years—not since the battle that had killed both his brothers and very nearly himself.

James stretched his legs out beneath the table, accepting a mug of coffee from a server and ordering breakfast for the two of them. "Sleep well?"

Matthews gave another nod, but James had learned to discern the smallest fluctuations in his companion's seemingly expressionless face. His friend hadn't slept well.

Again, James wasn't surprised. He hadn't slept well

either—not for years. He wondered if one night he might actually dream of pleasant things and wake feeling rested instead of being jerked from sleep by nightmares of fear and battle and the screams that accompanied them. Would he ever close his eyes without remembering?

"We'll be in Edinburgh by nightfall. And from there, it's only a few miles farther." James spoke mostly to ease his own apprehensions. The family he was returning to wasn't the same as the one he'd left. Hardly surprising after nearly ten years.

James's parents were both dead, and his brother was the laird now, living in their ancestral home with a wife and family that James had never met. Of course they would welcome him home with open arms, but for reasons he could not fully understand, he dreaded returning.

James had changed as well. He was not the same lad of eighteen who'd gone away to see the world, become a hero, and defend the kingdom. How would he fit back into a life he could scarcely remember?

He glanced at his friend, feeling guilty. At least James had a home and a family to return to. Many men came back to nothing.

The server returned with their meals, setting down plates of beans, eggs, sausage, and toast before the two men. She darted a nervous glance at Matthews.

James recognized the young woman's unease. He'd observed the same reaction from nearly everyone who encountered the man's haunted eyes and expressionless face. A rush of defensiveness rose inside him. Matthews had saved his life. He was the reason James was sitting here in a pub in North Yorkshire instead of buried in an unmarked grave somewhere in the hills of Spain. James could only see the barest trace of the person he'd known before in Nick

Matthews's eyes. And it saddened him. Matthews was not the only man who came home from the war damaged, but he was the one James couldn't leave behind.

The man needed work, and James needed a manservant. The solution was simple enough. He hoped bringing Matthews home and settling him somewhere he could feel safe would give him a chance to heal.

Matthews took a bite of toast.

"This English toast has nothing on true Scottish tattie scones," James said. "No offense to Mrs. Higgins, but the cook at the colonel's house is far superior. Don't you agree?"

Matthews glanced at him, his gaze lasting a fraction of a second longer than usual.

"You still think I should have told Miss Breckenridge the truth," James said, understanding what his companion did not say.

Matthews went back to eating.

"I feel wrong about it too." James cut a bite of sausage. "But I promised the colonel."

Matthews glanced at him again.

"I know," James said. "You don't have to scold me." He scooped up a pile of beans and eggs with his toast and bit into it, chewing slowly. "Can you believe she actually threatened to travel to London to find him? That would have been a disaster." He cut more sausage. "Talked her out of it, luckily."

He scooped up some more beans. Miss Lucy Breckenridge had taken him quite by surprise the day before. She was nothing like he'd assumed from her small portrait on the colonel's desk. He shook his head. The portrait hadn't changed in the ten years James had known the man. James was foolish to believe the person depicted had not changed either, and yet encountering a young woman when he'd expected a girl had come as a complete shock to him.

Not only had she been ten years older than he'd pictured in his mind, but she was extremely pretty, possessing a bright energy and youthful innocence that he felt drawn to.

Remembering how she'd fallen to pieces upon learning that her father was not coming home brought a pang to his heart. But was his sorrow entirely for the young woman? Or was he jealous that the colonel was missed so desperately by his family?

He drummed his fingers on the table.

He'd not considered for a moment that his message would cause such devastation. He'd certainly not delivered it with the compassion it warranted. Was he truly so callous not to have foreseen her reception?

James had thought about the interaction with Miss Breckenridge late into the night. It had left him unsettled, but he could not put a finger on why. Did he simply feel remorse for making a lovely young woman weep? That did not fully explain it. Perhaps it had something to do with how quickly she'd agreed to his suggestion of staying with her aunt. She hadn't required much convincing to give up her plan to go to London. Had she misled him? Did she still intend to go? If the young woman was anything like her father, once she set her mind to something, turning her from the course would be practically impossible.

"Do you think I should return and apologize to Miss Breckenridge?" James asked Matthews. "I haven't made a girl cry like that since I pulled Millie Archibald's braids in the kirkyard when I was eight."

Matthews cocked his head.

"I'm not just coming up with an excuse to see her again, if that's what you're insinuating." James frowned. "And I have talked about *plenty* of other subjects since we left her house."

Matthews's face remained expressionless.

James tapped his foot on the floor, feeling a nervous energy that he knew he couldn't hide from his companion. He folded his arms, then unfolded them. "Very well, perhaps it is an excuse." He pushed back his chair and started toward the staircase with hasty steps. He called back over his shoulder, hiding his grin, "Prepare the carriage. I'll fetch our bags."

Ten hours later, James shoved open the carriage door and climbed out. He glanced at the sign hanging above the door—The Fox and Fern. This was the seventh coaching inn he'd stopped at in his search for Miss Lucy Breckenridge. This morning's excitement of paying a call on a lovely young woman was, by now, fully extinguished. He slammed the door behind him, shivering in the chill of the late afternoon. He'd forgotten how early evening fell in the winter in Northern Britain, but the cool air did little to temper his frustration.

What was the young lady thinking, rushing off to London on her own—or rather, as her housekeeper had informed him, with a maid and an elderly hired man? He shook his head at the foolishness of it all. He stomped toward the door, wishing he knew whether or not she had taken this route. The Great North Road was the fastest course to London. He estimated that one day's travel would bring them here to Lincolnshire, but his surety that Miss Breckenridge had come this way was dwindling.

"What am I doing, chasing after this young lady like a madman?" he muttered to himself. But he knew the answer. He must not allow Miss Breckenridge to go to London.

Matthews joined him, and the two stepped inside.

A wave of heat and the smell of baking met them as they crossed the threshold, making James's stomach growl. Though it was dark outside the windows, the dining room glowed. A few of the tables held trays of baked goods. They stepped up to the counter, seeing no one but hearing the happy chatter of voices and the clattering of dishes beyond in what he assumed was the kitchen.

James rapped on the counter with his knuckles. "Hollo there?" he called, hoping to be heard over the noise. When he received no answer, he stepped around the counter and pushed open the kitchen door.

A woman with a red face and a scarf around her hair hurried toward him. "Oh, sir. I'm sorry; I didn't hear you come in. How can I be of assistance?"

"I hoped you might—" James began, but his attention was drawn to the other side of the room where another woman was holding a bowl in one arm and a wooden stirring spoon in the other. "Miss Breckenridge?"

The young lady's face lit up in a smile. She set the cooking implements down on the table and came toward him, wiping her hands on an apron. "Captain Stewart! What a surprise." Her already rosy cheeks were rendered even pinker by the heat of the kitchen and sprinkled with flour. She looked even lovelier than when he'd met her before, and James reprimanded himself for the thought. The young lady was the daughter of his commanding officer, and besides, he was here to stop her, not admire her.

The older woman stepped back as Miss Breckenridge joined them.

"What are you doing here?" she asked, and then frowned, looking confused. "Did you come to find me?"

James gave a nod. "I did, Miss Breckenridge. I told you the road to London can be treacherous in the winter. You should return home before—"

"Oh, nonsense," she interrupted, swatting the air as if to hit his words away. "It has been simply delightful so far, hasn't it, Meg?" Miss Breckenridge turned toward another young woman with flaming red hair and freckles.

"Indeed it has, miss," the young woman, Meg, replied.

"Oh," Miss Breckenridge said, shaking her head. "Where are my manners? Miss Meg Riley, allow me to introduce Captain Stewart."

"How do you do, Captain?" The young woman dipped in a deep curtsy.

A boy squeezed between them and through the doorway, taking a tray of cakes out to the dining room.

"A pleasure, Miss Riley." James inclined his head, feeling foolish to be performing such pleasantries in the doorway of an inn's crowded kitchen.

"Miss Riley is my traveling companion," Miss Breckenridge explained.

"I see," James said, thinking the red-haired young woman could hardly be older than seventeen. He turned his shoulders, taking a step backward and motioning to his friend on the other side of the counter in the inn's dining room. "Ladies, may I introduce Private Nick Matthews."

The young ladies greeted Matthews cheerfully through the doorway, neither appearing at all bothered by the man's silence.

James relaxed, realizing his natural defensiveness of Matthews had made his muscles tense.

"Have you need of rooms for the night, Captain?" the woman with the scarf asked.

James blinked, caught off guard. He hadn't thought of what he'd do when he actually found Miss Breckenridge. He supposed he'd just planned to put her into a carriage and send her back north. "I . . ." He considered his next move. After waking every morning to the bugle's call, drilling and eating at precise times, having no strategy in place felt disconcerting to say the least.

"It's past dark, Captain," Miss Breckenridge said. "You cannot travel any farther tonight."

She was right, though he didn't appreciate the reminder. "Yes. I require two rooms if you please, madam."

"Crenshaw," she said, wiping her hands on the napkin and coming through the door to the dining room. "I'm Mrs. Crenshaw. My husband and I are the owners of The Fox and Fern." She started toward the staircase, motioning for him to follow. "I'll show you to your rooms. If your man will bring your bags, Mr. Crenshaw will see the horses tended to. Oh, and you'll be wanting supper."

An hour later, once James had washed up and eaten, he came back down the narrow staircase into the inn's dining room. A few girls were arranging little cakes onto platters on one of the tables, and on the other side of the room, a group of men sat near the hearth.

James was trying to decide whether to sit or to return to his room when the door to the kitchen opened and Miss Breckenridge stepped through, carrying a tray of cakes.

He took the tray from her, setting it on the table where she directed. "Miss Breckenridge, if you don't mind my asking, what are you doing?"

"Mrs. Crenshaw is making gingerbread cakes and biscuits for the mummers' play this evening," she said, as if that explained everything.

"And have you known Mrs. Crenshaw long?" he asked. Based on how comfortable Miss Breckenridge was helping in the woman's kitchen, the two must be old friends.

"Oh no." She smiled, brushing a lock of hair from her forehead with the back of her wrist. "We only arrived a few hours before you did. I've never been to Bradstock before, but it is a lovely village. Everyone has been so agreeable." She pushed open the kitchen door. "Come along; there is plenty of work to do."

Not knowing what else to do, he followed her back into the kitchen.

Seeing Matthews there, James froze, blinking and wondering if he was actually dreaming. The man was in his shirtsleeves with an apron tied around his waist, scooping spoonfuls of batter into pans with Miss Riley.

The red-haired young lady was chatting happily, and though Matthews didn't talk back, a shadow of a smile played over his face.

James leaned back on the counter, hardly noticing when Miss Breckenridge handed him a dish towel and a wet pan. He stared at his friend, seeing a hint of the man he'd known years ago, and something constricted inside his chest.

He wiped the towel absently over the pan as he tried to make sense of the odd moment. Perhaps coming after the colonel's daughter was not a waste of time after all.

Three

THE FINAL GINGERBREAD cakes were baked, biscuits sprinkled with sugar, and dishes cleaned and dried. At last, the time had come for the mummers' play.

Lucy put on warm stockings and her heaviest coat. She wrapped a scarf around her neck and pulled on mittens as she exited her room. The idea of attending an outdoor play in the darkness thrilled her to no end.

Meg waited in the inn's upstairs hall. When she saw Lucy, she flapped her hand, waving her forward. "Come along, miss. We don't want to be late."

Lucy didn't need to be told twice.

With quick steps, the pair descended the narrow staircase and hurried outside, crossing the road and joining a small crowd that was gathering at the village green.

Torches and lanterns illuminated a circle of light, creating a stage on the frozen grass in which the actors strolled about, telling jokes and singing songs to welcome the audience. The brightness of the firelight made the night outside the circle seem even darker, which made the entire event seem all the more exciting. Lucy and Meg found a spot in the crowd where they had a good view of the performers.

"I've not seen Mr. Owens since we arrived," Lucy said, glancing at the unfamiliar faces around them and wondering if he might be among them. "Do you think he's sleeping?"

Meg smirked. "I'd guess he's enjoying himself at a pub, now that he's away from Mrs. Fraser's watchful eye. Grows tired o' being scolded when he'd just like a drink."

One of the actors, a tall man dressed in a costume representing a suit of armor, stood in the center of the stage and, with a loud voice, welcomed the audience to the performance.

"It would be a pity if he were to miss the play," Lucy whispered.

Meg didn't respond. She was scanning the crowd. After a moment, she started. "Oh, look. There is Mr. Matthews and Captain Stewart. Perhaps we should invite them to come watch with us."

The men apparently had the same thought. Seeing them, Captain Stewart waved, and the two moved through the crowd to join the women.

The actors in their comical costumes began introducing themselves, using clever rhymes that elicited laughs from the crowd. Parents lifted small children onto shoulders, and other children pushed their way to the front of the audience for a better view.

Lucy motioned for a group of children to stand in front of her, and she stepped back to let them squeeze past. When she did, she stepped directly onto Captain Stewart's foot, throwing her off-balance.

He caught her elbow, steadying her. "Careful, Miss Breckenridge."

"I'm so sorry." She looked down at his foot, and then up at him, grimacing.

"I hardly noticed it," he said, though she was certain he was not telling the truth. She had stepped down hard, and he'd likely have a bruise in the shape of her boot heel tomorrow.

She turned back around to watch.

Two of the actors fought with swords, and the audience pressed closer, excited by the action taking place before them. A group of men who smelled very much like they had been joining Mr. Owens at the pub jostled one another to Lucy's right, growing louder as the fighting continued on stage.

One of the men shoved another, making him stumble toward Lucy.

Captain Stewart took her by the arms, moving her away from the men and settling her directly in front of him.

Lucy's heart beat fast. The crowd was rowdier than she'd expected. Men and women yelled and cheered at the performance, and the actors seemed to be encouraging it. She'd not expected a Christmas play to be such a rambunctious event. She glanced back, but Captain Stewart did not seem nervous at all, apparently perfectly happy to watch the play over her head.

Looking to the side, she saw that Meg had taken Mr. Matthews's arm and stood close to him to avoid the press of the crowd. Lucy studied the pair for a moment in the torchlight. Mr. Matthews stood quietly, watching the play with his sad eyes. When Meg said something, he glanced at her and appeared to want to smile, though the expression didn't quite manifest. Mr. Matthews did seem more at peace when he was with Meg. That wasn't difficult to understand at all. Meg was kind and warm, and her smile was pure joy.

Hearing a loud cheer, Lucy turned back to the performance. The knight had slain his enemy. The vanquished man lay on the ground with a wooden sword poking up from between his arm and torso.

The crowd grew louder, yelling at the stage, and Captain Stewart put a protective hand on Lucy's arm. The simple gesture made her feel safe, even though she suspected it was done out of a desire to keep her from being bumped and stepping on his foot again.

The rowdy group called out, boisterous, and she moved closer to the captain, his chest warming her back comfortably.

On the stage, a doctor came forward with a magical potion, and the crowd cheered when he brought the knight's dead opponent back to life. The play continued, and the crowd seemed to calm somewhat, but Lucy didn't move away, and Captain Stewart didn't take his hand from her arm.

She'd felt resentful and a bit angry when the captain had come to Bradstock after her and insisted that she should return home, but right now she was immensely grateful that he was here. His calm confidence set her at ease. She knew he wouldn't let any harm come to her.

She sighed, feeling a tinge of disappointment. All of Captain Stewart's behavior toward her, from the delivery of his message the day before to the way he protected her from the crowd now, was done out of duty and respect for her father, his commander. And she would do well to remember it. But a part of her—a foolish, romantic part—wished his actions were directed by desires of his own.

Hours later, Lucy sat alone in The Fox and Fern's dining room. She turned to a blank page in the Christmas album and wrote about the mummers' play, telling of the humorous costumes and the cakes and wassail they'd enjoyed after. She attempted to draw a picture of Father Christmas with his red beard and green robe lined with fur. His appearance had been the climax of the performance, eliciting cheers from old and young as he led the crowd back to The Fox and Fern for Mrs. Crenshaw's sweet treats.

Hearing a footstep on the stairs, she looked up.

Captain Stewart came down the steps and sat beside her.

He rested one arm on the table. "Miss Breckenridge, you're very early for breakfast."

"I didn't want to wake up Meg," she explained, nodding toward the lantern.

He glanced at the album. "Surely this can wait until morning. You must be tired after traveling all day and celebrating late into the night."

In spite of herself, she yawned. She was tired, but she wanted the album to be perfect—and up-to-date—when she presented it to her father. "I could say the same to you, Captain," she said. "Shouldn't you be sleeping?"

He rubbed his eyes and shrugged. "I suppose I should." He tilted his head to the side to get a better view of the page she was drawing on. "What is so important that it keeps you up into the wee hours of the morning?"

For an instant, Lucy was tempted to hide the book. The album belonged to herself and her father alone, and sharing it with an outsider felt like letting a stranger into a private conversation. But she decided that he meant no harm, and besides, she hoped he would stay longer and talk with her.

"It is a Christmas album," she said. "It is how Father and I share our Christmases, even when we aren't together."

"May I?"

Lucy pushed the book toward him and put her quill in the inkpot. Captain Stewart turned through the pages slowly, studying the entries.

"I'm bringing it to Father," she explained. "We will read it together and add to it this year, to remember our Christmas in London."

The edges of his eyes tightened, but he didn't say anything, turning another page.

Lucy did not understand what bothered him about her taking the journey. But she wasn't going to miss the opportunity to see her father just because a person she'd only met the day before told her to.

Captain Stewart studied an invitation to a Christmas dance that she'd glued to one of the pages. She'd attended with the family of a second cousin three years earlier when she'd spent Christmas with them in Northallerton.

"Father's letters are much more interesting than my own entries," she said, feeling as though the silence had become too uncomfortable. "He spent one December in Calcutta." She scooted her chair closer so she sat directly beside him, and then turned the pages to a particular letter with an illustration. "The English officers threw a grand Christmas party, riding down the river in a barge lit with colored lanterns." Lucy smoothed down her father's drawing of the boat on a tree-lined river.

Captain Stewart stopped at the lottery handbill, running his finger over the cartoon in the corner. "I remember this," he said softly. He looked at her entry on the facing page where she described church with Aunt Prudence followed by a Christmas dinner at the parsonage. Lucy had drawn the parson's wife's spiced apple centerpiece.

"You have had a variety in your celebrations as well," he said.

Lucy frowned. His words left her feeling completely misunderstood. "In all the time Father has been gone, I've not celebrated Christmas at all. Not truly. I've been an addition to other people's celebrations, but none were my own." She turned the pages back to the last entry, indicating the blank page beside it. "This year was to be different." She let her fingers trail over the page. "Father and I were going to have Christmas together in our own house like a regular family. Neither of us would be a guest or a visitor or a stranger." She felt a lump in her throat at the reminder of her disappointment. "We'd have roast goose and dumplings and black currant jam on our bread just like we used to, because they are *our* favorite foods, not somebody else's. We would play the games we love, sing the songs we choose... and we could even have a dog."

"A dog?" Captain Stewart's brow furrowed, and he gave her a confused look. "What has a dog to do with Christmas?"

"We had a dog before Father went away," Lucy told him, embarrassed to feel tears coming to her eyes. "A black terrier named Donald." She swallowed and blinked quickly. "But one cannot have a dog when she is moving from one relation's house to the next every few months. In my own home, I can have a dog."

"I suppose that's what we all want," he said. His voice sounded softer than it had before. "A home and a family"—he glanced at her—"and a dog."

Lucy felt silly for sharing something so personal. She could blame her outspokenness on the late hour. She *was* very tired.

"Do you have family in Edinburgh?" she asked, wanting to deflect the attention from herself.

"Aye. A large one."

"Then why are you here and not with them? I'd think you'd want to be home after being away for so long."

"I should," he said. "But home isn't really home anymore, if that makes any sense."

Lucy shook her head. It made no sense at all.

"I left home when I was eleven to attend school," Captain Stewart said. "I returned on some holidays, but not every one. Edinburgh is a long way from London." He clasped his hands together on the table. "I attended Sandhurst and left directly to fight in Naples." He let out a sigh. "The house—it hasn't really been my home in nearly twenty years. It belongs to my brother now. And his family." He kept his gaze on the

Christmas album. "He is pleased that I am returning, and he will be happy to have me stay. But I'd be a visitor there, and..." He shrugged and gave a small smile. "I couldn't have a dog."

"I'm sorry, Captain Stewart," Lucy said in a low voice. Her hand twitched, and for a second she imagined reaching to touch him.

"I think you are one of the few people who understands, Miss Breckenridge."

She looked up, and his gaze captured hers. His head tipped the slightest bit as he studied her. Lucy's pulse quickened, and her cheeks flushed. She pulled her eyes away and made herself busy wiping ink off her quill.

"You could be in Edinburgh by Christmas morning," she said. "Or do you still think to stop me from going to London?"

"I have no intention of stopping you, Miss Breckenridge."

She nodded, satisfied that he'd at last seen reason.

"On the contrary. I plan to join you."

Four

THE NEXT MORNING, or rather a few hours later, James dressed and came downstairs before the sun rose. Miss Breckenridge had said she'd meet him in the inn's dining room for breakfast, but the young lady had evaded him once, and he'd be a fool if he let her get away from him again. He did not care to spend the entire day searching through coaching houses in Cambridgeshire and Rutland.

Miss Breckenridge hadn't seemed pleased by his intention to accompany her to London—which, truth be told, wounded his pride. Instead, she'd acted suspicious, as if he would somehow sabotage the journey or even kidnap her and return her to Pinnock Hill.

Both thoughts had occurred to him yesterday—however briefly as his frustration with the situation had compounded with each coaching inn he'd stopped at—but last night, his motives had taken a complete reversal. Christmas with her father meant more to Miss Breckenridge than James could have imagined. Probably more than even the colonel knew. She'd built up her expectation into something that would never possibly be realized, no matter how desperately she wanted it.

Seeing how she'd treasured her Christmas book—how she'd painstakingly documented the holiday for thirteen years—had touched a place deeply buried in his heart. And it hurt. He knew exactly how it was to feel lonely, to miss family, and the thought of the young girl alone, shuffled from relative to relative... without even a blasted dog. It was the last straw. He would make certain that she had Christmas with her father. Even though... His stomach felt sick as he came again to the point, the reason Christmas as she'd imagined with her father wasn't possible.

The truth would hurt her, but she'd discover it eventually. And he didn't want her to confront it alone.

Besides, he was disobeying a direct order. He needed to face the colonel and accept the blame for his actions in person.

Perhaps he would think of something on the way—something to make the truth more bearable to a young lady who ached for her father. If nothing else, James would find a village with another mummers' play. Or a church choir concert. Or a group of carolers singing house to house and drinking wassail. He'd find something to distract Miss Breckenridge, something she could write about in her book.

As he contemplated, customers filled up the dining room. Many were travelers, some soldiers on their journey home. Others were villagers whom he recognized from the night before.

Matthews joined him at the table.

"Sleep well?" James acknowledged his friend with the same greeting he'd said each morning since leaving France.

Matthews's mouth pulled to the side.

James stared. The expression was nearly a smirk, and the closest to an actual smile that James had seen on his friend in over a year. If Matthews had jumped on the table and begun juggling hams, James would not have been more surprised.

"Well then," he said, lifting his brows. "I'm glad to hear it." He was tempted to ask if a particular red-haired young lady's company at the play last night had anything to do with his friend waking well rested and cheerful, but he did not want to pry.

A few moments later, Miss Breckenridge and Miss Riley entered the dining room. They waved to an older man sitting at a table on the far side of the room, motioning for him to join them as they sat at the table with James and Matthews.

Miss Breckenridge introduced the older man as Mr. Owens.

Mr. Owens regarded the men through squinty eyes, as if trying to take their measure. But before he could do more than give a suspicious greeting, Mrs. Crenshaw came to the table and inquired after their accommodations. Once she was assured that they'd all spent a comfortable night, she left to fetch breakfast.

"Now that you've had a chance to consider, Captain Stewart," Miss Breckenridge began, "do you still intend to come with us to London?"

"We do indeed." James nodded. "And it would be expedient, not to mention much more enjoyable, for both of our parties to travel together."

Mr. Owens frowned. "Isn't room for two more in th' carriage."

"That is true," Miss Breckenridge said. "Especially with extra luggage."

"We will all fit easily in my carriage," James said. "And the driver's bench has room for two. I'd wager Mr. Matthews wouldn't be opposed to some company. Or to driving in shifts."

"I'd like that," Mr. Owens said, nodding and rubbing his chin. "Could use a few more hours o' sleep, to tell th' truth."

Miss Breckenridge fixed James with a scrutinizing stare. "I'm not certain I care for that proposal, Captain. I do not fully understand your reasoning for wishing to travel with us to

London when yesterday you were so against the idea. How am I to trust that you will take us where we wish to go?"

"I will you give you my word, Miss Breckenridge, to deliver you safely to your father in London. Will that do?"

She considered for a moment and looked at his friend. "Have I your word as well, Mr. Matthews?"

Matthews dipped his chin the slightest bit.

Apparently, it was enough to convince the young lady. She nodded. "Very well."

Mrs. Crenshaw returned and delivered plates of food. She set a tray of leftover gingerbread cakes in the center of the table. They thanked her and began to eat.

"Captain," Miss Breckenridge said. "I still do not understand why you've come in the first place. Why did you follow me from Pinnock Hill? And why do you insist on traveling back to London?"

James chewed a bite of egg before answering. "It is because of my message that you're here," he said. "I told the truth when I said the road is dangerous—highwaymen, fallen trees, damaged bridges . . . I feel responsible, as a close friend of your father's, to ensure your safety." The answer wasn't complete, but the reasoning was true enough.

Miss Breckenridge glanced at Miss Riley and Mr. Owens, and seeing approval in their faces, she turned back to James and nodded. "Very well, sir. Your action is unnecessary, but appreciated."

An hour later, their meal was complete, luggage loaded, and the five companions rode in Captain Stewart's carriage south on the Great North Road toward London. Miss Breckenridge sat beside Miss Riley, and James was on the bench facing them. Mr. Owens and Matthews rode in the driver's seat.

Miss Breckenridge yawned, settling back and looking out

through the window. Dark circles stood out beneath her eyes—evidence of her lack of sleep the night before.

"You should rest, miss," Miss Riley said, shifting the blanket they shared more fully onto her mistress's lap.

"Thank you, Meg." Miss Breckenridge spoke in a tired voice. She glanced at James. "Perhaps in a little while." She went back to looking out the window, yawning again.

Her blinks were slow. James guessed she would be asleep any moment. "Miss Riley, tell me about yourself," he said. "Do you come from Pinnock Hill?"

"I do, Captain." Her round cheeks lifted when she smiled. "Born an' raised. My father keeps a farm on the east side o' town."

"And have you brothers and sisters?" he asked.

"Oh yes. There are nine o' us in all. Five girls and four boys. I am the eldest save one brother."

James smiled. "I come from a large family myself. I, however, am the youngest."

"A pity you'll miss Yuletide with your family," Meg said. "If they're anything like mine, it's a grand celebration to be sure. Feasts, games, visitors . . ."

Miss Breckenridge sat up. Her brows pulled together, and she frowned. "I didn't know you would be missing your family's Christmas celebration. Why didn't you tell me, Meg?"

Miss Riley shrugged. "You needed a companion for your journey, miss."

Miss Breckenridge took the young lady's hand. "How selfish of me," she said. "I didn't even consider it. I was so focused on seeing my father. I am so very sorry."

"I'm havin' a lovely time, miss. Never been to London. Farthest away I've ever been from Pinnock Hill is to North Milford when my cousin had her baby." She put her other hand on Miss Breckenridge's and squeezed. "Don't worry yourself, miss. I'm happy to be here."

Miss Breckenridge sat back in the seat, frowning as she watched through the window. She didn't look convinced by her friend's words.

After a few hours, the group stopped at a spot where the road was wide and overlooked a valley of rolling hills, taking the opportunity to water the horses, stretch their legs, and eat the picnic lunch that Mrs. Crenshaw had packed.

Matthews and Miss Riley sat on a fallen log, eating and enjoying the view.

Mr. Owens finished his lunch quickly and led the horses to a brook to drink.

Miss Breckenridge walked along the edge of the road. She held her coat tight around her and kept her head down, braced against the cold wind.

James joined her. "Bitter wind, isn't it?"

She nodded, looking distracted.

"Is everything all right, Miss Breckenridge?" he asked.

"I should send Meg and Mr. Owens home to Pinnock Hill." She looked down the road toward London. "But I cannot travel alone with two men. And I must go to my father." She stopped, glancing in both directions. "I can't stop now, but it was narrow-minded of me to bring her. I didn't even consider . . ."

James motioned toward the log where Miss Riley ate her lunch with Matthews. The two sat very close together. "I do not think Miss Riley considers the journey a disappointment."

Miss Breckenridge gave a small smile, her head tipping as she regarded the pair. "Perhaps not. But I should make it up to her all the same. I am so ashamed that it did not occur to me that there are other families who wish to celebrate together aside from just mine."

James led her back toward the carriage. "Love does that to us, Miss Breckenridge. It makes us behave in ways we never would have otherwise. Love can make the most logical person irrational."

"But I love Meg as well," she said.

"I know you do. That is why you are bothered at the thought that she might be unhappy."

He stopped and turned so that only Miss Breckenridge could see his wink, then looked back toward the others. "Miss Riley," he said in a louder voice. "I wonder if Matthews might want some company on the driver's bench for a time. Mr. Owens could use a rest."

Miss Riley blushed. "Oh, yes. I would be happy to." She glanced at Matthews. "If you would like."

Matthews's cheeks seemed a bit pink as well. He gave a nod.

Miss Breckenridge waited until the pair weren't looking and gave James a wink in return, her brows lifting and her face lighting in a conspiratorial smile.

When they started off again, Mr. Owens lay across one of the carriage benches, snoring softly.

James sat on the other beside Miss Breckenridge.

"Why doesn't Mr. Matthews speak?" she asked, motioning with her chin toward the window that separated the driver from the inside of the carriage. "Was he injured?" She looked curious, but there was also compassion in her face.

"He was, but not in the way you might think." James tapped his forehead. "Matthews's pain is here."

"Do you know why?" she asked.

"Aye." He let out a sigh. "Albuera." The word hung in the air, the sound of it making his heart beat faster and his palms sweat. He could taste the musket powder in the air, feel the mud slip beneath his boots, hear the screams as the Polish cavalry charged through the hail and rain. James swallowed hard, pushing it all away and focusing on the young lady before him.

"What happened?" she asked in a softer voice.

"Both of Matthews's brothers were killed," James said. "His younger brothers. Cut down in a bayonet charge right in front of him."

"Oh." She put her hand to her mouth, and her gaze darted toward the window again. "How awful. That poor man."

"It is a heavy thing. Feeling responsibility for the life of others." James knew completely how it was to see men who'd trusted him to lead killed in a battle. "He'd promised to keep them safe."

"He blames himself." Miss Breckenridge's voice was tight. "It is as you said, 'Love can make the most logical person irrational.'"

James nodded. "I believe all of his emotions are trapped inside him—the good and the bad—and he's holding them tightly, afraid that if he allows any of them free . . ."

"They will all come out," she finished. "And he couldn't bear to feel them." She shook her head. "Such a tragedy. I am very sad for him."

"He is not the only soldier to return damaged," James said. "All manage their trauma differently. Some turn to drink, some become wanderers unable to adjust to society, some simply end it all. I don't believe it is possible to come back from war unchanged in some way."

"And how do you manage?" Miss Breckenridge turned her knees to the side, facing him as well as she could while sitting beside him on the bench. She studied his face.

James swallowed. "I push the thoughts away when they come. Avoid allowing myself to think of them."

"Is it effective?"

"It's become easier over time. Until I sleep," he admitted. "It is impossible to control the memories then."

"It must be exhausting," she said.

He opened his mouth to reply but stopped when Miss Breckenridge slipped her hand into his. The gesture stilled his thoughts. It was such a simple thing, so tender and filled with compassion. She did not claim to understand or offer advice for healing, as others had done, but simply indicated that she cared. His throat grew tight, and his eyes burned.

Miss Breckenridge scooted back around to face forward but did not release her hold on his hand. She leaned her head on his shoulder.

James rubbed his eyes, glad she wasn't watching as he fought against the emotions. The feel of her leaning against him was more comforting than a thousand reassuring words. After a moment, he laid his head back on the seat. He closed his eyes. And slept.

Five

THE CARRIAGE WENT over a bump, shaking Lucy awake. She lifted her head from Captain Stewart's shoulder, color filling her cheeks as she realized she'd slept leaning against him. Glancing across the carriage, she was glad to see that Mr. Owens was still sleeping. Perhaps he hadn't noticed.

Captain Stewart's head rested against the back of the seat, and his eyes were closed. She listened to him breathing for a moment. His breaths were deep and steady, and she decided that she'd not woken him when she moved.

She shifted carefully, stretching out the kinks in her neck and looked through the window, contemplating their earlier conversation.

The things Captain Stewart had told her about Mr. Matthews had left her heart heavy. She worried for him. Could he ever heal from something so dreadful? And what of the others who'd endured such trauma? The captain had said that nobody returns from war unchanged. Did he speak of himself as well? And what did that mean for Lucy's father? Did he bear scars as well? How would she help him?

Looking forward, she could see the carriage approached a town. A rather large one, she guessed, based on the church steeple that rose above the rooftops.

Mr. Matthews's eyes still seemed sad, but Lucy thought

she'd caught a glimpse of a smile at times. Was his friendship with Meg making a difference? Could he heal? Lucy hoped so.

Thinking of Meg reminded her of the other matter that had been weighing on her thoughts. Her maid had agreed to the journey without hesitation, but why hadn't Lucy stopped to think? She'd been so wrapped up in making arrangements for her father's return that she'd not even given a thought to what the young woman's Christmas might entail, what she would be missing. The realization made Lucy's throat thick with shame. She swallowed hard and glanced at Captain Stewart.

He was awake, his head still resting on the seat, watching her.

Lucy gave a smile, feeling heat burning her cheeks at the memory of holding his hand and falling asleep against him. She couldn't believe she'd acted so brazenly.

The captain smiled in return, making her blush grow hotter.

She turned to look back through the window, her thoughts still running over their conversation. She wished she could make Christmas special for her companions instead of only herself, but doing anything about it felt impossible while she was so far from home.

As she considered, the carriage passed a ladies' clothing emporium. Hats, hosiery, parasols, and gloves were on display in the window.

"Oh," Lucy said to Captain Stewart. "I should like to visit that shop, if you don't mind."

He leaned over the sleeping Mr. Owens and rapped on the driver's window, giving Mr. Matthews instructions to halt the carriage. Mr. Owens woke, grumbling. Mr. Matthews opened the carriage door, helping Lucy to alight. She thanked him.

"Shall I come with you?" Meg asked from her spot on the driver's bench.

"No thank you," Lucy said.

Captain Stewart stepped out of the carriage, rubbing the small of his back and leaning from side to side to stretch. "I'll accompany you if you like, Miss Breckenridge."

"Thank you." Lucy smiled at Meg, hoping the young woman wasn't disappointed at not being invited to come as well, but it would defeat the purpose. "I will be just a moment." She pulled her coat tighter against the chill and walked with the captain to the shop.

He held the door, and Lucy entered ahead of him, taking in the cluttered room. A counter holding baskets of ribbons, buttons, gloves, hats, and stockings was directly in front of them with rolls of fabric and a large gilded mirror nailed to the wall behind. Hats and bonnets hung from hooks on one side of the room, and on the other were shelves of stockings, slippers, nightclothes, and underclothing. Scarves and capes dangled from the ceiling and coat stands near the door.

Captain Stewart's brows rose when he entered.

Lucy wondered if he'd ever been inside a ladies' clothing shop before.

Two women were at the far end of the counter. The one wearing a shopkeeper's apron held up a short corset beneath the large bosom of the older lady as they discussed the proper measurements.

"I want to find a Christmas gift for Meg," she said before the captain could make an excuse to leave. "Will you help me?"

"I do not think I am the person to advise on such a matter." He ducked his head, sweeping the tassels of a hanging shawl out of his way.

She wasn't surprised. Her father would not have lasted longer than a few moments in a shop like this.

Seeing her frown, Captain Stewart gave a good-natured smile and an exaggerated sigh. "Very well, Miss Breckenridge. What sort of gift did you have in mind?"

"Something special." She glanced through a basket of gloves. "Something that she wouldn't purchase for herself."

He fingered the edges of a lacy mobcap. "She seems to enjoy sitting on the cold bench with Matthews. Perhaps something to keep her warm?"

Lucy smiled, excited by the idea. "Yes. A cape or a muff—"

"Good afternoon." The shopkeeper approached, standing on the other side of the counter. She was an older woman. Lucy estimated she was in her late forties, tall and slender with a long nose and enormous eyes. "I'm Miss Pembroke; can I be of assistance?"

"How do you do?" Lucy nodded at the woman. "If you please, I am looking for—"

"Something to wear to the dance this evening, I'd wager," the woman interrupted with an exasperated puff of her cheeks. "That is all anyone has wanted this week." She started to fold a silk chemise on the counter, shaking her head. "I keep telling my customers, it is not a formal affair, but of course at Christmastime, everyone likes to dress a bit fancier."

"There is to be a dance this evening?" Lucy asked. Her plan of giving Meg a special Christmas was getting better and better.

"You must be visiting our town," Miss Pembroke said, glancing at Captain Stewart and giving a coquettish smile. "Quentlin Ferry's Christmas Assembly is famous throughout the county. It's held each year at the reception hall over the Goosefeather Inn. A small gathering, but my sister, Mrs. Gregory—she's the proprietor of the Goosefeather—she makes it quite a splendid affair." She laid a hand on the captain's arm and fluttered her lashes. "I do hope you can attend."

"It sounds very . . . agreeable," Captain Stewart said. He cleared his throat and took a step back.

Lucy met his gaze in the mirror, trying to keep a composed expression. The man's discomfort was palpable. His brow ticked, but that was the only change in his expression. It was enough to make Lucy cough to hide a giggle.

She turned toward him, angling herself so Miss Pembroke couldn't see her face past her bonnet's brim. "How far are we from London, Captain? Will we still arrive in time if we stay in Quentlin Ferry tonight for the dance?"

Captain Stewart studied her, all traces of humor gone from his face. "We may have an extra hour or so of travel time to make up tomorrow, but a Christmas dance is unquestionably worth it."

His tone was sober and his voice low. Lucy felt her blush return, and a flutter started in her belly.

"Oh, I am simply delighted," Miss Pembroke said, pressing her palm to her breastbone.

That evening, in their rooms at the Goosefeather Inn, Lucy helped Meg dress for the dance. They pulled up her hair into a fashionable twist and arranged a few red curls around her face and shoulders. Meg wore a deep blue shawl over her gown with a matching feathered comb, both of which Lucy had purchased that afternoon.

Lucy straightened the shawl, letting it drape gracefully over her friend's arms. "There. You shall turn every gentleman's head tonight."

Meg studied herself in the mirror, turning her head from side to side to see her coiffure from every angle. "I feel very elegant, miss." She lifted her chin and inclined her head, practicing a gracious greeting

"I'm glad of it," Lucy said, smiling.

"Do you think . . ." Meg glanced at Lucy and bit her lip. "Might Mr. Matthews ask me for a dance?"

"How could he not?" Lucy answered. She prayed that the man would do so. It would mean so much to Meg.

Meg turned back toward the mirror. She gave a practice curtsy, then shifted her feet, lowered her shoulders, and did it again.

When Meg dipped down, Lucy studied her own new accessory in the mirror, a pearled bandeau with silk flowers that Meg had woven through her tresses. She felt nervous as well. Had Captain Stewart felt obligated to attend the dance in Quentlin Ferry because of her? He'd acted as if he were happy about the prospect, but how could she be certain? Would he ask her to dance? The thought made her hands tremble. She balled them into fists, holding them tight, then opened them and let out a slow breath.

Music started, the sound coming from the reception room above them.

Meg gasped, looking upward. "Oh, it is time."

Lucy held out her elbow, putting on a cheerful face in spite of her nervousness. "Shall we?"

The two linked arms, sharing an excited smile, and made their way to the upper floor of the inn.

The reception room was extremely crowded, with tables of refreshments at one end of the long room and a quartet at the other. In the center, couples danced a cotillion.

Lucy and Meg kept their arms linked together, both for moral support and to avoid being separated in the crowd of strangers. They walked along the edge of the reception hall, out of the way of the dancers, scooting between couples flirting, old ladies gossiping, and friends enjoying a holiday visit.

"I can't believe so many people fit in this one room," Lucy said, feeling a drip of sweat roll down her back. "Surely they will open a window soon." She unfolded the fan hanging on her wrist and waved it in front of her face.

They moved past a group of older gentlemen. Ahead, near a table holding a punch bowl, an officer and a soldier came into view, looking resplendent in scarlet regimental jackets and freshly shined boots.

Beside her, Meg drew in a quick breath and squeezed her arm.

Lucy's stomach flipped over.

Captain Stewart met Lucy's gaze, holding it steadily as he came toward her. His eyes were softer than she'd seen before. His smile was warm. When he reached them, he took Lucy's hand, lifting it as he bowed. "Good evening, Miss Breckenridge."

Lucy dipped in a curtsy. "Good evening, Captain." Her fingers tingled in her gloves.

His eyes held hers a moment longer, before he released her hand and turned to take Meg's. "Miss Riley."

Meg curtsied as well.

"You ladies look especially lovely this evening. Do they not, Matthews?"

Mr. Matthews nodded and bowed. His eyes lingered on Meg, and her cheeks flamed red.

"Miss Riley," Matthews said in a voice that was hardly more than a whisper. He took her hand.

Captain Stewart's eyes widened.

Meg's blush deepened.

Lucy's smile grew.

Mr. Matthews placed Meg's hand on his arm. He inclined his head, excusing them, and led her away through the crowd.

Captain Stewart watched the pair go.

"Meg looks happy, doesn't she?" Lucy said. "And perhaps Mr. Matthews's condition is improving."

"Perhaps," he said. His voice was thoughtful as his gaze followed the couple. His brows drew together.

"You're concerned about him," Lucy said. She fanned herself with more force, feeling defensive of her friend.

"I am."

"You can trust Meg," she said. "She will not cause him distress. She cares about him."

Captain Stewart turned back toward Lucy. His brow was still wrinkled. "I do trust her. But I worry about Matthews. I've not heard him speak in years, and I . . . I just hope he can manage the changes happening in his life."

"His eyes look much less sad than when we first met him," Lucy pointed out. "Perhaps he is healing."

He nodded. His face relaxed slowly, and he tilted his head, his eyes softening. He smiled. "Miss Breckenridge, have I told you how utterly enchanting you look this evening?"

She looked down to hide the flush that his words created, brushing her hands over her skirts. "It is just an evening dress—I didn't pack a ball gown."

"I wasn't speaking about your dress." He took her hand in his, studying her face. "It is your eyes, I think. Or perhaps your smile."

"Thank you, sir. You look very handsome tonight as well."

"Would you join me in a dance?" he asked, motioning with a tilt of his head toward the center of the room. The music had changed, and couples were taking their positions for a quadrille.

Lucy nodded and allowed herself to be led to the dance floor.

Captain Stewart, as it turned out, was an exceptional

dancer. Lucy began to wonder if there was anything the man could not do. His posture was straight, his motions sure as he moved through the steps. And when it was the turn of the other couple in their set, his eyes found hers, holding that same soft expression that made her chest feel light and her knees soft.

Lucy saw Meg and Mr. Matthews dancing on the other side of the room, and she could not help but be pleased at the happy expression on her friend's face. She believed that Mr. Matthews was healing and thought Captain Stewart's worries misplaced.

Their turn came again, and Lucy and the captain took hands, stepping along with the music. Lucy had performed the quadrille numerous times over the years, but the dance had never felt so magical. Each touch of the captain's hand sent warm shivers up her arm, and each smile made her heart expand and its beat intensify to the point of a dull ache. He reached behind her, clasping her hand as they spun, and his gaze locked on to hers, making her feel as if the rest of the world had disappeared, leaving only the two of them. When they drew apart, Lucy's feet moved on their own, stepping back into her position. Captain Stewart's eyes stayed on her, and the others around them were reduced to blurry images.

When they left the dance floor at last, Captain Stewart brought her to the edge of the room, giving a formal bow.

Lucy opened her fan again, waving it beneath her chin to create a breeze. But this time, she could not fully blame the crowded room for causing her to become overheated. She glanced up at the captain, enjoying the rush of nerves and the jump in her chest when he looked back.

"Perhaps a cool drink?" The captain indicated the table with the punch bowl. He ladled punch into a cup, which Lucy gratefully accepted.

"You are a fine dancer, Captain," she said, feeling as

though she should make some conversation to shake off her fanciful thoughts.

He opened his mouth to reply, but before he had a chance, a voice called his name. They turned to find Miss Pembroke bustling through the crowd toward them. She was accompanied by a lanky gentleman with protruding cheekbones who seemed near her age.

"Oh, Captain Stewart, you did come after all," Miss Pembroke said when she reached them.

Lucy's eyes went wide at the sight of the woman's dress, which was extremely revealing, low in the front and even lower in the back, showing quite a bit of her spine and shoulders. The style was quite shocking, especially for a woman of her age.

Lucy took a sip of the fruity drink.

"Miss Pembroke." Captain Stewart bowed. "How nice to see you again."

"And Miss Breckenridge, your bandeau is just the thing to spruce up a plain dress."

The woman's expression contained no malice, and Lucy decided that Miss Pembroke had intended to pay a compliment. "Thank you. Your gown is lovely, Miss Pembroke," she said. "Very fashionable."

Miss Pembroke closed her eyes, giving a slow nod as a gracious acceptance. She held her hand to the side, pointing with her palm up at the man beside her. "Might I introduce my brother, Miss Breckenridge?"

"Oh yes."

"Thomas Pembroke, allow me to present Miss Breckenridge and Captain Stewart."

The two exchanged greetings with the slender man. Now that Lucy looked closer, she could see the family resemblance in Mr. Pembroke's wide eyes, though his nose was not as long.

"I was just telling Thomas how pleasant it was to meet you this afternoon, Captain Stewart," Miss Pembroke said. "It's not often that I have a military officer in my shop."

"I say," Mr. Pembroke cut in. "What type of punch is that?"

"Ratafia," Captain Stewart said. "It is very good. Shall I pour you some?"

"Yes, indeed." Mr. Pembroke smacked his lips. "I do enjoy a good ratafia now and then."

"And would you care for punch as well?" Captain Stewart asked Miss Pembroke.

"Oh, no thank you," she said. "I am rather chilly this evening."

Captain Stewart took Lucy's empty cup, set it on the table, and poured Mr. Pembroke's punch.

"Oh." Miss Pembroke put her hand behind her ear. "I believe the orchestra is playing a Scotch reel. It is my favorite dance, and you know I am quite adept at the steps. I imagine you are as well, Captain?" She stared at him with a wide-eyed, expectant expression.

His brow ticked, but that was the only indication that he found her behavior surprising. "Miss Pembroke, I would be remiss if I passed up the opportunity to dance the Scotch reel with an accomplished dancer such as yourself." He offered his hand.

Miss Pembroke smiled widely as she took it and stepped quickly to the dance floor, pulling Captain Stewart along with her.

Lucy smiled, pleased that Captain Stewart was so polite to Miss Pembroke, even when the woman was so peculiar. How he treated people said a lot about the man's character. He certainly had treated her well, and he took care of Mr. Matthews like a brother. Her chest warmed as she watched him take his place on the dance floor.

Mr. Pembroke set his cup on the table and wiped his sleeve over his lips. "Might you wish to dance, Miss Breckenreid?"

She smiled, following Captain Stewart's example of politeness, even though the man had called her by the wrong name. "Certainly."

When the Scotch reel ended, Mr. Pembroke returned Lucy to the side of the room and introduced her to an elderly gentleman, a Mr. Wilkinson who, he explained, was his uncle. While Lucy danced with Mr. Wilkinson, she scanned the room for her friends, seeing Meg and Mr. Matthews near the punch table and Captain Stewart visiting with Miss Pembroke and a group of women. Miss Pembroke rested a hand on his arm.

At last, the dance with Mr. Wilkinson ended, and he returned her to the side of the room.

Captain Stewart caught Lucy's eye. He excused himself from the group of women and offered to dance with her once more. She happily accepted.

Lucy took her place facing Captain Stewart, noticing how straight he stood. He cut an impressive figure, tall and broad shouldered. She, of course, had noticed that he was handsome before, but tonight, something about him seemed different. Perhaps it was the candlelight shining in his eyes and gleaming on his dark curls. Or maybe it was the soft smile that made her heart race whenever he caught her gaze.

Captain Stewart took her hand and released it as they passed, moving among the other dancers. When they came together again, his touch sent her stomach rolling, and a realization struck Lucy with a jolt. She was falling in love with Captain Stewart. The thought was so surprising that she hesitated, making one of the other men stumble to keep from colliding with her.

When she turned back to face Captain Stewart, her cheeks felt hot, and she found it nearly impossible to look him in the eye. Could it be true? Her thoughts were fuzzy as she considered how this could have possibly happened. And what did it mean?

The dance continued, but instead of feeling magical, the music sounded loud and the room was too crowded. Everything moved too quickly, and people were too close. Lucy took deep breaths. When the music stopped at last, Captain Stewart put an arm around her, leading her from the floor. "Are you all right, Miss Breckenridge? You're flushed." He looked worried, which made her heart race even more.

She nodded, feeling foolish for her reaction. "I'm just overheated, I think."

"It is very hot in here." He unfolded her fan, putting it into her hand. "Shall I bring more punch? Or we can go outside for some air."

"I'll be fine," she said, her embarrassment making her even hotter. She waved the fan in front of herself. "Perhaps if I just stand near the window for a moment."

They moved to the wall where one of the windows was cracked open, and Lucy stood in the cool breeze. She needed to get control of her emotions and stop romanticizing. Captain Stewart was a gentleman who treated everyone with kindness. It was time to stop seeing in his attentions more than what was there.

He pulled off a glove and touched the back of his fingers to her forehead. "You feel warm. Are you certain you're all right?"

Lucy nodded. "Yes. I'm so sorry." The breeze was helping.

"Do not apologize." He left and returned with another cup of punch, instructing her to drink the entire thing.

She did, glad for something to do besides blush and act ridiculous.

"There now." Captain Stewart took the cup when she finished. "I believe your coloring has nearly returned to normal."

"I feel much better. Thank you."

"I'm glad of it," he said, balancing the cup on the windowsill.

From the corner of her eye, Lucy saw Miss Pembroke walking past. The older woman moved slowly, eyes downcast, not appearing to notice them.

"I think Miss Pembroke is hoping for another dance," Lucy said.

He glanced at the woman. "I did intend to dance again, but I hoped you would be my partner. Once you're recovered."

"A third dance?" If her skin were not already red, she would have blushed at his implication. "Captain, that is unseemly."

He shrugged, giving a teasing smile. "Are you worried about gossip? Your reputation?" He leaned closer and put his hand to the side of his mouth as if sharing a secret. "Nobody knows us here, Miss Breckenridge. We can dance as often as we like."

"Captain! Miss!" Meg rushed up to them, her eyes wide. She looked to be on the edge of panic.

"What is it, Meg?" Lucy took her friend's hand, her brows drawing together. "What has happened?"

"It's Mr. Matthews." Meg's lip quivered, and tears spilled from her eyes. "He's run away!"

Six

JAMES'S STOMACH PLUMMETED at Miss Riley's words, and in spite of them, he looked around the room for his friend, hoping to see him among the crowd.

"Oh, Meg." Miss Breckenridge put an arm around the young lady's shoulders. "Come, let's find somewhere quiet, and you must tell us what happened."

James agreed. He produced a handkerchief for the weeping Miss Riley and escorted the women from the ballroom.

As they walked, he watched Miss Breckenridge closely, hoping that she had indeed recovered from her spell. Seeing her flushed and shaky had been unsettling, and he worried that in her desire to help her friend, she would neglect her own health. What if she'd contracted a fever? He rubbed his eyes, his concern for the young lady and Matthews making his muscles tense.

They descended the staircase and came to the inn's dining area. The room was nearly empty, with only a few patrons here and there enjoying a drink. James searched the faces, but he was disappointed again when Matthews was not one of them. Where had he gone?

The three sat at an empty table, and seeing them, Mr. Owens came from another table to join them.

Miss Breckenridge scooted her chair close to Miss Riley's

and took the young lady's hand. "Now tell us what happened, Meg."

Miss Riley glanced at the others through her teary eyes. "Everything seemed to be going so well," she said, wiping her nose with the handkerchief. "Mr. Matthews and I danced and ate refreshments. He appeared to be happy. I didn't mean . . ." She shook her head, sobbing.

James tapped his fingers on the table, forcing himself to be calm.

Miss Breckenridge must have seen his impatience because she gave Miss Riley's shoulder a gentle shake. "If we are to help Mr. Matthews, we need to know what happened." Her voice had a calm firmness to it.

Miss Riley nodded, gathering in a deep breath. "We went for a walk. The assembly room was so warm, and—"

"And where did you go?" James asked.

"We stopped near the churchyard." She fidgeted with the handkerchief. "At the wall."

"Go on," Miss Breckenridge urged. "What happened next?"

Miss Riley glanced at the men, then back down at her handkerchief. "Mr. Matthews . . . he— Well, he and I . . . we kissed." She looked up at Miss Breckenridge, apparently too embarrassed to meet the eye of either of the men. "Then he just left."

"Oh my," Miss Breckenridge said. She looked at James, confusion and worry playing over her features

"Did he say anything?" James asked Miss Riley.

"He said he was sorry," Miss Riley whispered. Her chin trembled.

"Which way did he go?" Mr. Owens asked.

Miss Riley sobbed again, pressing the handkerchief to her face. "Toward the bridge."

James's mouth went dry. He jumped to his feet and started for the door.

"Wait, Captain," Miss Breckenridge said. "We're coming with you."

"Absolutely not."

The young lady didn't pay any attention. "Fetch our coats, Meg."

Mr. Owens hurried out the door, but James stopped. "Miss Breckenridge, there is no time to spare."

"You intend to go toward the bridge," she said. "We will search in the other direction."

"It is too dangerous for young ladies in the darkness." His words did not hold the unequivocal tone he'd intended. She was right. More searchers gave a better chance of finding Matthews. He frowned. "Do not go past the town limits," he said. "And stay with Miss Riley."

Miss Breckenridge gave his arm a push. "Go, Captain. Your friend needs you."

James felt a swell of gratitude. He hesitated one instant longer, trying to find the right words to express his appreciation, and to admonish her to be safe, but she gave another push, and he spun, rushing out the door into the cold night.

The high street curved past shops and houses and the stone wall of the churchyard. James squinted through the darkness. The moonlight was dim, and he cursed himself for not bringing a lantern. There were too many shadows and darkened pathways. Matthews could be anywhere, and James had no idea of his mental state. His stomach felt ill as he thought of what the man might do in a deep melancholy.

He came to the arched bridge and took a deep breath before looking over the edge. The banks were steep, shadowing the water beneath. "Matthews!" James yelled. He slipped down the muddy slope to get a better view. Beneath the bridge, he could scarcely make out anything in the darkness. He climbed back up, crossing the bridge and sliding down the slope on the other side. He could see no better on this side.

A cold feeling of despair wrapped around his lungs, squeezing. He felt helpless. And with every minute that passed, he worried it was one more minute he'd been too late to find his friend.

He climbed back up the riverbank, slipping in the mud as he did. When he came to the top, he considered walking farther along the road. He looked up and down the river in both directions, wishing he knew which way to choose. If he selected one, was he getting farther away from his friend or closer? He finally decided to follow the water's current and tromped through the reeds and tall grass until the brambles became too thick to move through. Even the moonlight couldn't pierce the shadow of the trees, and if not for the sound of the water, he would have lost his way in the darkness.

He turned around and followed the river back to the bridge, trying to judge how long it had been since he'd left the inn. An hour at least. With each step, he felt heavier. How had things gone so wrong? A week ago, his plans had been so simple: deliver a message to the colonel's daughter and bring Matthews home to a place he could feel safe.

Somehow, he'd botched everything. He peered over the bridge again and sighed. He was wasting time trying to see anything in the darkness. He started back to the town, holding on to the shred of hope that Matthews had returned to the inn. Or perhaps the ladies had found him. But James did not feel confident with either scenario. Matthews was his responsibility. And he'd let his friend down.

When he returned to the inn's eating area, he found Miss Breckenridge there, speaking to one of the servers.

Seeing James, she broke off her conversation, hurrying toward him. Her mouth was tight. "You had no luck either?"

He shook his head.

"Meg and I walked up the high street to the edge of town and returned," she said, rubbing her arms. "We looked down side roads and between houses, but it was just too dark. I'm so sorry, Captain." She glanced at his trousers and boots, and following her gaze, he saw that he was covered in mud. "You searched by the river?"

James nodded, pulling off his soiled gloves and moving to stand by the hearth. "I'm going back," he said, rubbing his hands together before the fire, "with a lantern." Images of his friend in the dark, cold waters came into his thoughts, but he pushed them away, hoping desperately that the man was somewhere safe.

"I'm going with you," Miss Breckenridge said. "I put Meg to bed, and a drink is being delivered to her room to help her sleep. She was very upset."

"Out of the question," James said. The very idea of Miss Breckenridge climbing around the muddy riverbank in the dark was preposterous. And if they discovered Matthews while she was there . . . He shook his head. "I'm going alone."

Miss Breckenridge's eyes narrowed. "Captain, I am perfectly—"

Her words cut off when the door opened and Mr. Owens entered. Mr. Matthews followed behind him.

"Oh!" She put her hands over her mouth, gasping.

Relief flooded through James, making his muscles feel weak.

Miss Breckenridge rushed to the door. "Mr. Matthews, come in." She took his hand and led him toward the hearth. "Your skin is like ice. Sit here by the fire. And you as well, Mr. Owens."

The men did as they were told.

Matthews leaned forward in his chair, staring at his hands.

"I am so glad you're safe, Mr. Matthews," she said. "We were so worried."

"Didn't mean to make you worry," the man muttered in a quiet voice. He didn't look up.

Mr. Owens patted Matthews's shoulder.

Miss Breckenridge glanced at James, her eyes still worried. "I'll fetch you men something warm to drink," she said.

He gave a grateful nod, and she left to find a server.

James sat at the table next to his friend. "You all right?" he asked.

Matthews nodded. "Mr. Owens and I talked."

James looked up at the older man. "How did you find him?"

Mr. Owens shrugged. "Just 'ad a feeling. Thought he'd just keep walking. 'S whut I'd have done. Found him on the road, halfway to the next town." He patted Matthews's shoulder again, resting his hand on the back of the younger man's chair. "Know what the lad's going through. Wasn't myself for a good while after Guilford Courthouse."

James nodded, recognizing the name of one of the bloodiest battles in the war for the American colonies. He was immensely grateful for the old man's wisdom.

Miss Breckenridge set three mugs on the table.

Mr. Owens took a sniff and scowled at the drink but gulped it down anyway.

James took a sip and let the warmth from the buttered toddy spread through him. He'd never have ordered the drink himself—especially in a public place—but found it soothing. And he enjoyed the feeling of being taken care of by the young woman.

Miss Breckenridge sat at the table with them. "Do you feel better now?" she asked in a soft voice.

For an instant, James thought the question was directed at him, and he felt a bit of disappointment when he realized she was talking to Matthews.

"I just... shut myself away for so long after..." Matthews began, then swallowed hard. His voice was so soft that James had to strain to hear it over the crackle of the fire. "So much easier than feeling the pain." Matthews glanced up at Miss Breckenridge.

She nodded and gave a compassionate smile.

"Then Miss Riley and I... It all came back, all that pain."

Mr. Owens put the drink into Matthews's hand, motioning for him to drink. "Have to let yourself mourn, lad. Let yourself hurt for whut you've lost. Or you'll never move past it."

Matthews drew in a jagged breath and nodded, taking a sip of the toddy. "So much easier to hide from it," he whispered.

"I'm sorry, Mr. Matthews," Miss Riley said. She stepped to the table, moving so quietly that none of them noticed her until she spoke. "I didn't mean to upset you tonight."

Matthews looked up, and James saw that his eyes were red. He'd wept, which, according to Mr. Owens, was a good thing.

"I'm damaged, miss," he said, dropping his chin to his chest.

"Damaged, but not worthless," Mr. Owens said. "You'll just have to be patient with 'im, Meg. He'll be all right. But healing takes time. And there will be setbacks." He turned to Matthews. "You're a new person living a new life. Might take some work to find where you fit in it. Do ya understand?"

Matthews nodded.

Miss Breckenridge wiped her eyes. When she saw James looking at her, she gave him a sad smile.

"Mr. Matthews," Miss Riley said after a long moment.

He lifted his head, looking up at her with nervous eyes.

"If there's room for a friend in your new life, perhaps it might be me?" She bit her lip, eyes wide and hopeful.

Matthews bent his head back down, rubbing his eyes, and nodded. "I'd like that very much, miss." He spoke in a creaky voice.

James and Miss Breckenridge left the table quietly and moved to the other side of the room. He wanted to give the couple privacy but remained close enough to keep an eye on his friend.

Mr. Owens watched Matthews for a moment before he departed as well. The man seemed hesitant to leave, and James didn't blame him.

Miss Riley moved to sit beside Matthews.

Miss Breckenridge yawned. Her hair, which had been arranged so carefully earlier tonight, hung messily around her face, and the hem of her dress was dirty. She looked exhausted.

"Shall I order you a drink, Miss Breckenridge?" James asked. "A toddy?"

She shook her head. "No thank you. It will make me too sleepy."

"You should sleep," he said. "I will see Miss Riley safely to her room."

"Perhaps in a bit," she said. She looked pensive, running her finger along the wood grain of the tabletop. "You were worried for Mr. Matthews, weren't you?"

James nodded, the feeling still too raw for him to speak about it easily.

"You thought you might not find him, or if you did, it would be too late." She spoke slowly, in a quiet tone as if still considering the thoughts she was putting into words. "That is why you did not want me to accompany you to the river."

James nodded again.

"You are a good man to care so much for your friend," Miss Breckenridge said. "He is fortunate to have you."

"Matthews saved my life," James said in a low voice. "Such an action is not something one soon forgets or takes lightly."

Miss Breckenridge studied him for a moment, then glanced across the room to where Miss Riley sat quietly beside the discouraged young man. "Then I owe him my gratitude as well," she said. Her cheeks turned pink, and she stood.

James stood with her.

"Please tell Meg to wake me when she comes to bed," she said.

"I will." He studied her, feeling as if he should say something significant. Tonight had felt different—dancing with her, worrying about her, and then later, worrying with her. Something had changed between them, but did he dare put into words the transformation that was taking place in his heart? Not yet—not when he didn't fully understand it himself.

A sick feeling roiled around inside. He still hadn't told the young lady about her father. But would the truth be too much for her after the strain of this evening? Or was he finding another excuse to avoid a conversation he knew would cause her pain? In the end, he decided that more than anything she needed sleep. They had another day's journey tomorrow. He would surely find the opportunity to talk to her then.

"Good night, Miss Breckenridge."

Seven

LUCY FELT FRUSTRATED when the carriage at last got underway the next morning. The drink she'd ordered for Meg had made her groggy, and she didn't wake until much later than Lucy would have liked.

The gentlemen moved slowly as well, and by the time they'd all loaded their luggage and eaten breakfast, the hour was nearly ten.

Captain Stewart and Mr. Owens rode inside the carriage with Lucy. The two men had been much more amiable toward one another after their shared experience the evening before. They shared a new respect, evident in their friendly banter through breakfast.

Meg had chosen to ride with Mr. Matthews and sat up on the driver's bench beside him, wearing her new fur-lined gloves. The two had seemed happy this morning, and Lucy was glad that no tension remained.

She settled back onto the carriage seat beside Captain Stewart and pulled the blanket onto her lap, careful not to wrinkle her skirts. She was disappointed that her best dress was dirtied in the search for Mr. Matthews last evening, but her father would not think any less of her if she wore another. She felt tired and nervous and so anxious all at the same time. How pleased he would be when she arrived this afternoon. She looked up through the window and saw the sky was clear.

Hopefully it remained so, and they would enjoy dry roads and a quick journey.

Resting her head back against the bench, she closed her eyes, imagining Christmas with her father, and the familiar thrill moved through her. How surprised he would be to see her. They would attend church services in the morning, and of course arrangements would be made to include her fellow travelers in their Christmas dinner. But once the others had all gone home, she and her father would tell stories and look through the Christmas album with a blanket on their laps and watch the fire burn low, just as they used to. She tucked back her heels, feeling the lump of the Christmas album in her bag beneath her bench. She had updated it this morning as she waited in the dining room for the others.

"Mr. Owens," Captain Stewart said. "I must thank you again for your assistance last night with Matthews. If not for your intuition—I don't believe my friend would be here with us today."

"Any soldier would ha' done the same," the older man replied. "Fine young man, that one. Reminds me of myself once upon a time."

"I'm grateful for your words and your understanding," Captain Stewart said. "They gave him hope."

Lucy listened with her eyes closed. She didn't want to interrupt the conversation or make the men feel as if they needed to include her in it.

"Taken him under your wing, haven't ya, sir?" Mr. Owens said. "How is it that a captain with hundreds in his command has such an interest in this one private?"

"He saved my life," Captain Stewart said simply, in the same tone he'd used the night before.

"Do you want to tell me about it?"

Captain Stewart didn't answer right away, and Lucy got

the impression he was checking to see if she were sleeping. She kept her eyes closed, breathing steadily. She knew he wouldn't tell the story if he knew she was listening. A prickle of resentment tightened her skin. He was protecting her, but she wished he understood that she was not as fragile as he believed.

"I haven't told anyone," Captain Stewart said at last. "Not since making my report that day to my commander."

"'S good for you to talk about it," Mr. Owens said. "Most men want to forget completely. But the wars changed us, made us who we are now, and pushing the memories away just leads to confusion later. Best to face it and see it for what it is."

"That is very wise," Captain Stewart said. "I don't think I've ever heard it put that way before, but I believe you're right. If only it weren't so blasted difficult."

"Aye, it can be that," Mr. Owens said. "Matthews told me the pair of you fought at Albuera. 'S that where it happened?"

"No, it was before that," the captain said.

Lucy strained her ears to hear his low voice over the noise of the carriage wheels and the horses' hooves.

"It wasn't during a battle," Captain Stewart continued. "Private Matthews and I were part of a reconnaissance team, reconnoitering in the Sierra Morena mountains." He puffed out a heavy breath. "We were ambushed by a band of French deserters. When they saw they'd captured an officer—"

"They meant to make an example of you," Mr. Owens finished.

The captain was quiet for a moment, and Lucy was tempted to peek, but she didn't dare risk it.

"They held my men at gunpoint and forced me to kneel." Captain Stewart's voice was raspy.

Lucy's heart was pounding, and she was certain the men could hear it. She fought to keep her breathing steady.

"Matthews broke away from his captor and somehow dodged a musket shot. He tackled the man whose sword swung for my neck. It glanced off my shoulder, but I walked away with just a scar."

"Brave lad," Mr. Owens said.

"He was a leader," Captain Stewart said. "Even though his rank was low. He'd have made an excellent officer. Men listened to him, trusted him. The man freed me and our entire team without any of us receiving more than a few scrapes."

Mr. Owens started to tell about his experiences fighting in America, but Lucy didn't listen. She couldn't get the image of Captain Stewart kneeling while a blade swung toward him. Her hands shook. These men had seen terrible things, experienced horrors. If only she could think of something to bring joy to their lives. She thought again of the Christmas dinner with her father and promised herself she would make it special for all of her friends. They deserved it.

It was late in the afternoon when Lucy saw a road sign for the town of Stanley. She had never heard of the place.

"Stanley." She pointed out the window. "Surely that is near London."

Captain Stewart glanced at the sign. He grimaced. "I'm sorry, Miss Breckenridge. It will be dark within the hour and we've still fifteen miles to go." He shook his head. "We won't make it to London tonight."

"Sorry 'bout that, miss," Mr. Owens said.

Lucy tried to swallow her disappointment as they stopped at a coaching inn. They had come so far and were only a few hours away. So close. She put on a smile. At least she would see her father tomorrow on Christmas Day.

She and Captain Stewart went inside with Meg while the

other men tended to the horses. While he made arrangements for their lodgings, the women spoke to the wife of the inn's owner, Mrs. Whitaker. The woman was plump and cheerful with graying hair beneath her mobcap. She seemed to be a motherly sort of person, and Lucy liked her immediately.

"Oh, how lovely to have guests at Christmas," Mrs. Whitaker said. When she smiled, wrinkles fanned out from the edges of her eyes. She settled them near the hearth and brought mugs of hot wassail. She chatted for a moment, telling them about the inn and asking about their journey. "I do hope you are hungry this evening," she told them. "I always prepare a lovely meal on Christmas Eve. We've a few folks in town who come for supper every year."

Lucy smiled. She thanked the woman for her hospitality. An idea was forming, and she thought about it as she drank her wassail, considering the details and what it would take to make it happen.

A few moments later, Captain Stewart joined them, carrying a mug of his own. He sat at the table and took a drink. "I can't remember the last time I had wassail," he said. "It's surprising how something as simple as a drink can bring back so many memories."

"Isn't it?" Meg asked. "The smell of sugarplums reminds me of visiting my grandmother," she said, looking toward a bowl of the delicacies on the inn's counter.

"Mr. Whitaker told me there's to be a nativity play this evening at the church in the next town," Captain Stewart said. "Shall we attend? The event will be a nice addition to your book, Miss Breckenridge."

Lucy's excitement grew, and she gave a cheeky smile. "If you don't mind, I have a different plan for tonight."

That evening, Lucy came into the private dining room just as Mrs. Whitaker was putting the finishing touches on the decorations.

"Oh, it is simply splendid." She clapped her hands together as she took in the trailing ivy over the tablecloth and the bouquets of holly. Mrs. Whitaker had even decorated the mantel of the small fireplace with ribbons and garlands and hung a pine wreath on the chimney stones. It had turned out better than Lucy had imagined.

"Just ring when you're ready for dinner to be served." Mrs. Whitaker wiped her hands on her apron, pointing to the bellpull in the corner with her chin. "And I do hope you have a lovely celebration, dear."

Lucy thanked the woman as she left. She studied the table settings. Instead of the fine china or porcelain, Mrs. Whitaker had set the table with the inn's sturdy pewter. The dishes had been polished to a shine, and there was even a sprig of holly and berries tucked into the napkin rings. It all looked perfect.

The others arrived a few moments later, and Lucy greeted them each at the door, inviting them to sit. She took her place at the head of the table, standing behind her chair, and motioned for the gentleman to remain seated.

"I am so glad to have you all here tonight." Lucy moved her gaze over each of the four faces, smiling at her friends. "Every year, I've attended holiday celebrations as a guest, but this year, I am hosting the first of what I hope to be an annual Christmas party."

The others clapped, and Lucy felt a warm glow inside at their encouragement. "I cannot imagine a finer group to celebrate with." She swallowed. "Each of you has sacrificed to come on this journey. You've put aside your own holiday plans to give me a special Christmas with my father. And I must tell you all how grateful I am. You have all become dear to me over the past days . . ." Her voice grew raspy, and she cleared her throat against the emotion clogging it. She reminded herself this was a celebration. "Since I have never celebrated Christmas at home, I have no traditions of my own. And I would like to start one tonight."

The others watched her expectantly, and she smiled, secretly thrilled with her idea, and prayed they all enjoyed it as much as she hoped they would.

"After our meal, I want each of you to share a holiday tradition with our company—whether it is a game you love to play or a story your aunt tells each year, whatever is important to you—and we will make it part of our celebration. The tradition I am sharing is a delicious Christmas Eve dinner with friends. I do hope you enjoy it."

She stepped back, giving a tug on the bellpull. "Without further ado . . . let us eat."

The company applauded the speech.

Lucy blushed. She returned to the table and sat in her seat, lifting her pewter goblet into the air. "Happy Christmas to you, my friends."

The others raised their goblets, repeating the Christmas wish, and the door opened, letting in the servers with their meal.

Dinner was every bit as delicious as Mrs. Whitaker had led them to believe. The servers brought course after course of chestnut soup, roast partridge, meat pies, potatoes and vegetables in a rich butter sauce, pastries, and finally, they finished with an exquisite figgy pudding. The conversation was pleasant and her friends cheerful as they shared memories of Christmases past. Lucy paid particular attention to the stories, noting things she could incorporate into her future celebrations.

Once they'd eaten their fill and the last dish was taken

away, the party dispersed to give everyone a chance to prepare for their contribution. Lucy sat back, her stomach full and her heart happy. She could not wait to see what her friends came up with.

The first to return was Mr. Owens. He carried a large bundle hidden beneath a towel, and when he entered the room, he stashed it away in a corner, then hung a tea kettle on a hook above the fire in the hearth.

Lucy's brows rose, but he just gave an enigmatic smile and took his seat at the table.

The others brought items as well, each keeping them hidden away and looking excited at the prospect of the secrets that would be revealed.

Once they had all returned to their seats, Mr. Owens stood. "Suppose I might as well go first," he said, "'fore my pot boils over." He brought the bundle from the corner and removed the towel to reveal a large silver bowl.

"Rum punch has become a bit o' a tradition during the holidays." As he spoke, he took the items out of the bowl and set them on the table. A lemon, some kitchen implements and mugs, a jar of what appeared to be sugar, and two liquor bottles.

"Don't have a story to go with it. Just like the stuff," Mr. Owens said. He dumped sugar into the bowl and used the towel to remove the teakettle from the fire, pouring hot water over the sugar. He sliced the rind off the lemon with deft fingers, tossing it into the bowl, and strained the lemon juice from the pulp. "And I make a fine batch, if I do say so myself." Popping the corks from the bottles, he poured brandy and rum, stirring it all together until he was satisfied. He dipped a mug into the punch and took a sip, letting out a sigh and smiling. "That's the ticket." He ladled punch into the other mugs and passed them around the table.

Lucy took a sip of the sweet drink. "It's delicious."

Captain Stewart drank deeply and raised his mug. "Hear! Hear!"

The others joined him, drinking and toasting Mr. Owens, his health, and his rum punch. Even Mr. Matthews made a toast. And nobody gave a second glance when Mr. Owens refilled his mug for a third time.

"A fine presentation," Meg said. "And now who will go next?"

"Would you like to, Meg?" Lucy asked.

The red-haired young lady's face lit up, her eyes bright with excitement. She brought out her bundle from beneath her chair.

"I come from a family with lots o' children," she said, setting a metal platter on the table. "Our tradition is to play games together on Christmas Eve." She set a bag of flour beside the platter. "This is my favorite one."

She poured the flour onto the platter slowly, making a high peak in the center.

"Bullet pudding," Captain Stewart said. "I've not played since I was a child."

Mr. Matthews smiled.

Lucy was delighted.

The men pulled the chairs away from the table to allow the group to stand in a cluster around the platter.

"Mrs. Whitaker didn't have a bullet," Meg said, taking a marble from the bag on her wrist and holding it up between two fingers. "But she found this." She set the marble on the top of the flour mountain, then picked up a butter knife, offering it to the group. "Who will go first?"

"Oldest takes the first turn," Mr. Owens said. He set his mug on the table and took the knife. "'Twas my family's rule." He sliced it through the flour, then handed it to Lucy.

Captain Stewart cut into the white mountain, making a small avalanche of flour slide down one side, but the marble did not move. He gave the knife to Matthews.

He cut closer to the center, but the marble stayed atop the flour peak.

Meg had a turn, then they passed the knife around again.

When Mr. Matthews slid the knife into the flour, the marble rolled, sinking down and disappearing into the white mound.

Meg clapped her hands, and Lucy giggled. They all watched expectantly. Would he do it?

Mr. Matthews did not hesitate. He plunged his face into the flour, using his mouth to search for the marble. Flour went everywhere, and the sight of the man rooting through the white mess made Lucy laugh so hard that her sides hurt. Meg pressed her hands to her mouth, shaking with laughter.

"Don't inhale, lad," Mr. Owens said between guffaws.

Captain Stewart let out a hearty chuckle.

When Mr. Matthews finally raised his head and spit out the marble into his hand, they all laughed again. Flour covered his face and dusted his hair. He snorted, blasting a cloud of flour into the air, and Meg had to sit to contain her giggles.

Mr. Owens raised his mug. "Huzzah!"

Captain Stewart offered his handkerchief, and Mr. Matthews grinned as he brushed off his face and shook the white powder from his hair.

"That was excellent, Miss Riley," Captain Stewart said in a breathless voice. "I've not laughed so hard since . . . Well, it has been a long time." He patted Mr. Matthews's chest, making another white cloud and causing Mr. Matthews to cough.

Meg wiped her eyes and brushed the flour from Mr. Matthews's shoulders when he sat back into his chair. She smiled at him, her eyes shining. "That was very diverting," she said.

He smiled back, flour creasing in the lines around his mouth.

"You were very sporting, Mr. Matthews," Lucy said. "So you may choose who goes next."

The man looked at Captain Stewart, then back at Lucy. "I'll go next, if I may," he spoke in a quiet voice.

The captain nodded.

"Of course," Lucy said.

Mr. Matthews cleared his throat, looking nervous. He took the bundle from beneath his chair. "My mum always read to us the Christmas story." When he unwrapped the towel, he held a Bible. "I hope none of you object?"

"That's a lovely idea," Meg said.

Captain Stewart nodded, his eyes looking thoughtful. "My ma did the same."

Mr. Matthews turned the pages until he found what he was looking for. He took a breath, glanced at the others, and then began to read.

The words were familiar, but tonight the story felt particularly poignant to Lucy. Perhaps it was knowing the struggles of the man who read them. Or maybe it was the affection she felt toward her friends sharing this special night. Whatever the reason, hearing the story of Mary and Joseph and their baby born in a stable touched her heart, and she dabbed at her eyes.

When Mr. Matthews finished the account and closed the book, a reverent silence settled in the room.

Captain Stewart stood after a moment, moving quietly to the corner near the hearth and unwrapping the bundle he'd put there. He took out an old guitar, bringing it back to his chair and sitting with it on his lap. He plucked the strings and turned the knobs to tune it.

"Would ha' taken you for a bagpipe player," Mr. Owens said.

Captain Stewart gave a good-natured smile. "I dragged this instrument all over the continent over the past years," he said. "Music's the one thing that remained constant on Christmas." He glanced at his friend, raising his brows and smirking. "Matthews may have hoped I'd left it in France."

"The songs kept up morale, Captain," Mr. Matthews said. "Don't know what we'd have done on those cold nights otherwise."

Captain Stewart strummed the strings, and the hushed room seemed to grow more still. He settled into a tune, playing the familiar melody of a Christmas carol, and started to sing.

Lucy leaned forward as the low tone of his voice filled the room. The captain sang beautifully, the melody sounding effortless and strong as his fingers moved over the strings. Meg clasped her hands together in front of her chest, and Mr. Owens nodded his head. Mr. Matthews watched with a contented smile.

Captain Stewart was an accomplished musician, his voice strong and deep. Seeing how surely he played and how confidently he sang, Lucy could imagine how his music had soothed worried and frightened men. She hoped her father had taken comfort from the captain's music when he'd been lonely.

Captain Stewart's eyes met hers, and she realized she was leaning forward, lips parted as she stared. She sat up, feeling foolish.

He winked, but the signal wasn't impudent. Rather, she understood it as a friendly token. The silly gesture was the captain's way of acknowledging her and sending a message that was only meant for Lucy to see. Her cheeks grew hot, a reaction she was coming to both expect and resent, as it revealed more than she wanted the others to know.

Captain Stewart finished his song and began a new one, "God Rest Ye Merry, Gentlemen." The tune was livelier, and he played with more joviality, bringing a cheerful feeling to the group. After a few lines, Mr. Matthews joined in, his voice blending nicely with Captain Stewart's.

Seeing the captain's encouraging nod, Lucy and Meg sang as well.

Mr. Owens seemed contented to listen with eyes closed, his finger waving as if conducting the music.

The company moved from song to song, some cheerful and others reverent. Meg and Mr. Matthews sang a duet to "I Saw Three Ships," and even Mr. Owens joined in when Captain Stewart played "Here We Come A-Wassailing."

The night grew late, and once the singing was over, the party came to an end. Lucy stood beside the dining room door, bidding each guest a warm farewell as they departed for their rooms.

Meg embraced Lucy. "Miss, tonight was wonderful. Thank you."

Mr. Matthews held her hand and thanked her in his soft voice.

The pair left together, walking arm in arm.

Captain Stewart returned the chairs to the table, pushing them back into place.

Mr. Owens came to the door with the large punch bowl and a mug. "Best party I ever attended, Miss Breckenridge," he said. "Happy Christmas to you."

Lucy turned back toward the table, thinking she should clean up the flour instead of leaving the mess for Mrs. Whitaker.

Captain Stewart stood in front of her. His eyes had the

same soft look they'd held at the dance in Quentlin Ferry, and seeing it made Lucy's stomach flip over itself again, like it had forgotten how to stay still.

"Did you enjoy the party, Captain?" she asked, wanting to dispel the silence.

"More than I can say."

"I did as well," she said. "I am so pleased with how everything turned out. Your music was just the thing. Thank you."

Captain Stewart pursed his lips, pulling them to the side and tapping his chin, looking thoughtful. "You know, there is one Christmas tradition we forgot—one I am particularly fond of."

"Oh?" Lucy said, wishing he'd told her earlier. "What is that?"

He took her arms, pulling her to a spot beneath the doorway, and then he looked upward.

Lucy followed his gaze. A kissing bough made of mistletoe hung on a red ribbon from the doorframe. How had she not seen it earlier? Her skin flushed hot, and her heartbeat raced.

Captain Stewart watched her, studying her face as his hand slipped beneath her ear and behind her neck. His thumb brushed her jaw. The other hand moved around behind her waist, pulling her closer.

Lucy touched her fingers to his arms, hesitating to rest her hands fully against him. Her insides shook.

The captain's chin tilted toward her, his eyes looking hopeful, and Lucy's nervousness stilled. She wanted this, and that realization didn't frighten her. It made her brave.

When she moved her hands to his shoulders, his arms tightened around her, pulling her against him. Lucy closed her eyes, rising up on her toes, and then his lips were on hers, warm and gentle, his curls brushing over her fingers.

He held her tightly, his lips tasting like punch and his

whiskers scratching her cheek, and she let herself be swept away.

In just a moment, it was over. He stepped back, and her arms dropped. She felt the loss of his heat immediately.

Captain Stewart took both of her hands, studying her face. Although his smile held the slightest tease, his eyes were earnest. "I'm glad we did not neglect that tradition."

"As am I." Lucy tried to smile in return, but she did not recover as quickly as she pretended. Her knees were weak, her lips tingled, and she ached to be held again in his embrace.

Once the table was cleaned and the borrowed items returned to Mrs. Whitaker, Captain Stewart walked with her back to her bedchamber. He kissed her again before he bid her good night, and Lucy's worries about waiting a few more hours before arriving in London flew from her head completely.

Eight

JAMES PACED BACK and forth across the sitting room between his bedchamber and Matthews's. Tonight had been the most pleasant in memory, and not only because he'd kissed a lovely young lady—though that did contribute enormously to his contentment. He smiled, allowing the memory of Miss Breckenridge's warm lips to fill his mind. He'd enjoyed himself immensely at the Christmas celebration. The gathering of friends had felt more like a family than any he'd experienced in years.

And that only made what he had to do harder.

He rubbed his eyes. Why hadn't he just told Miss Breckenridge the truth about her father? Over the past days, he'd had countless chances. And yet when the opportunities presented themselves, he just couldn't bring himself to do it.

He supposed his intentions were honorable at first. He'd made a promise to the colonel. And he'd intended to obey orders. But his reasoning had changed as he got to know Miss Breckenridge. He'd become protective of the young lady. He'd not wanted to see her hurt. And the truth was definitely going to hurt.

James could make all the excuses he wished, claim that he'd not wanted to upset her, not wanted to ruin her Christmas party, but he knew deep inside that his motivation was much more selfish. He'd wanted the time spent with Miss

Breckenridge to be happy, wanted her to smile and to enjoy herself in his company, and he felt ashamed for it.

He took a candle and walked along the inn's darkened hall toward the ladies' rooms. He must do it. There was no getting around it. And he'd put it off long enough. Miss Breckenridge deserved to know. He couldn't allow her to go into this blind. She needed to be prepared.

Seeing the light still glowed under her door, he knocked softly.

Miss Breckenridge opened the door, just a crack. "Captain!" She smiled happily, but seeing his face, the cheerful expression faded and her brows drew together. "Is something wrong? What has happened?"

"I need to speak to you."

"Now?" she asked, her eyes widening in worry. "Can it not wait for the morning?"

"It can't."

"One moment." She closed the door, and he heard rustling beyond. When she reopened, she held a wrap around herself, clutched in front of her breastbone with one hand. Her hair was loose and hung down over her shoulders in shiny waves. Around her face, a few locks were wrapped in curling papers.

She looked charming and naive. And so vulnerable. The rum punch felt sour in James's stomach. How could he do this to her?

Miss Breckenridge motioned to the small table in the room. Atop it were an inkpot, quill, and her Christmas book. He must have caught her as she was working. "Would you care to sit? I was just finishing my entry about tonight's party. Father will be happy to hear about it, I think."

He winced as he took a seat across from her.

"Miss Breckenridge." He let out a breath. "Your father did not stay in London for military duties."

She tipped her head, confused.

"He is a patient at the hospital in Chelsea."

Her face went pale. "What do you mean? He sent a letter from Calais just a few weeks ago. He wasn't injured. He . . ." Her voice trailed off.

"Colonel Breckenridge suffered an attack of apoplexy on the boat from France. His mental capacity is extremely limited."

She put a hand over her mouth. "What do you mean, limited?" She whispered the words, her breath coming in quick bursts between her fingers.

"There are times when he is aware, and he recognizes people and speaks intelligently as he used to. But a moment later, he will be confused and frightened. He's wandered off through the streets in his nightclothes. And his memory . . . it is faulty. He forgets people he's known for years."

"But surely he'll remember me?"

"I don't know, Miss Breckenridge."

She rubbed her forehead. "But why . . . why am I just hearing of this now? Why did nobody tell me?" Her voice shook. "There must be a doctor who . . ."

"Your father didn't want you to know. He doesn't want you to see him like this. He insisted. I believe he thinks this is only temporary."

"Is it temporary?"

"The doctors do not believe so."

She sat back in the chair, tears spilling over her cheeks and splashing onto her wrap.

"I'm sorry, Miss Breckenridge." James offered his handkerchief.

She reached for it but stopped, pulling her hand back. Her eyes narrowed. "Why didn't he want me to come to him? Did he think I would not understand? That I would be repelled to see him in his current state?"

"I believe that is the case," James said. "He feels humiliated. Embarrassed by his spells of dementia."

"But he's my father. Of course I wouldn't..." She focused her teary gaze on James. "And you. Why did you not tell me? We've traveled together for three days, and you did not once find the occasion to mention what I would face when I found my father? Did you think it would be better if I were surprised by it?"

"I'm sorry, Miss Breckenridge. Your father gave strict orders that you were not to know the extent of his condition. He—"

"That is hardly an adequate reason." She stood, folding her arms in front of her. "You kept this from me, listened to me chatter on about Christmas with my father and all of our happy memories . . . and all along, you knew? And you said nothing." Her voice was getting higher.

"I'm sorry."

"And you . . . We . . ." Her cheeks flamed red, and he knew she was thinking of their kiss. "You deceived me."

"I truly thought to protect you."

She leveled her gaze, her eyes becoming frighteningly serious. "I am a grown woman, sir. I do not need to be told that a journey to London is too dangerous or that I cannot walk along a street at night. I do not need you to wait until you think I am asleep before telling a story about Spain. I do not need you and my father claiming to protect me when in truth, neither of you trusts me."

She slammed closed the Christmas album and strode toward her sleeping chamber.

"Miss Breckenridge—" James took a step toward her.

She turned, holding up a hand to stop him from speaking. "I am stronger than either of you thinks. And I am weary of being underestimated." She whirled and went into the room, closing the door quietly.

Based on the anger in her face, James suspected that she'd have liked to slam it but didn't want to wake Meg.

He let out a heavy breath. That had gone poorly. He knew she'd be worried, expected the tears, even imagined she'd feel betrayed, but her words had cut straight through him. He *had* underestimated her. Miss Breckenridge was determined and capable, as she'd proven again and again over their short acquaintance. And James had continued to treat her as someone needing to be watched over. The realization made him uncomfortable.

He cleaned off the quill and capped the inkpot.

James wanted to show Miss Breckenridge that he had faith in her, that he trusted her decisions and knew she was strong. But after tonight, he feared she wouldn't listen to anything he had to say.

The next morning, the group met in the inn's dining room.

When they finished eating, Matthews and Owens went to prepare the carriage, and Miss Riley left to finish packing. Miss Breckenridge remained sitting at the table. She'd been quiet throughout breakfast, and when Miss Riley showed concern, she'd apologized, claiming to be simply tired from the night before. She picked at her food, her gaze unfocused.

Once they were alone, James moved to the chair beside her. "Miss Breckenridge—" he began.

She shook her head, stopping his words. "I'm sorry, Captain. I'm not inclined to conversation this morning."

Before long, the carriage was ready and the luggage loaded.

Mr. Owens stumbled inside and fell asleep across the bench before they were even underway. Apparently, he'd enjoyed the remainder of the rum punch.

Miss Riley rode inside with Miss Breckenridge, likely at her request, and so James, knowing that he would only make the young lady uncomfortable, climbed up to ride with Matthews on the driver's bench.

Matthews flicked the reins, and they were off, leaving Stanley behind.

James gave a heavy sigh, rubbing his eyes.

"Told her, didn't you, sir?" Matthews said.

He nodded.

"She didn't take it well?"

James shook his head.

"Didn't imagine she would."

James allowed himself a smile at the reversal in their roles—Matthews carrying the conversation and he the silent one—and spent the remainder of the journey pondering how he could possibly make things right with Miss Breckenridge.

Nine

Lucy went up the steps of the Royal Hospital and walked between the stately columns flanking the entrance. The Christmas album was clutched to her chest. Her movements felt slow, like she was pushing through water, and instead of the excitement she'd expected, a heaviness hung over her.

James held open the door, and she kept her eyes forward as she stepped past him. She couldn't bring herself to look at him. Not only because she was angry, but because she was so hurt, and her pride didn't want him to see how betrayed she felt.

Deep inside, she understood why he'd done what he did. She thought perhaps she may have done the same in his position. But knowing it didn't stop the pain.

A young man approached, coming down a long hall. He was short with round cheeks and wore a waistcoat tight around his waist, but no jacket. His sleeves were rolled to the elbow. "Captain Stewart. I didn't expect to see you again so soon, sir. Have you come to visit the colonel?" He glanced at Lucy.

"I have," the captain said. "Miss Breckenridge, this is Mr. Alfred Pennington, surgeon's assistant. And here is Miss Breckenridge, the colonel's daughter."

"How do you do?" Lucy said.

He bowed his head. "A pleasure, miss."

"Mr. Pennington is one of your father's primary caregivers," Captain Stewart said.

"Then I am very grateful to you, sir."

They started down the hall. Doors branched off at intervals, and Lucy glimpsed rows of beds in the wards. The hospital was crowded and loud with moans of pain and coughing. The thought of her father living in such a place for nearly a month was almost more than she could bear.

"How is the colonel?" Captain Stewart asked.

"He's . . . he's not having a good day," Mr. Pennington said. They stopped outside a doorway, and he glanced back at Lucy. "Dr. Warren is considering moving him to the asylum ward." He spoke in a lowered voice but not so low that Lucy couldn't hear.

The blood pounded in her ears, and she held the Christmas album tightly to her chest. This all must be a dream. It couldn't be true.

"Come along, then, miss, if you please." Mr. Pennington pointed toward the doorway. "Your father's bed is this way." An anguished scream came from within.

Lucy clasped on to Captain Stewart's hand, terrified of what she'd find beyond the doorway. "Captain, you'll stay with me?"

"I will." He wrapped his fingers around her hand, and she felt immediately safer. Perhaps she did need some protection after all.

Captain Stewart led her down the ward between the rows of patients.

Lucy tried not to stare at the men in the beds. Some wept or cried out in pain. Others were wrapped in bandages. A few coughed or made other unhealthy noises. None of the men had visitors, and she was sad that they were spending Christmas Day alone.

My father doesn't belong here, she said over and over to herself. *He can't.*

The captain stopped at the foot of a bed at the very end of the ward with a wall on one side and a space of a few empty beds around. "Good morning, Colonel."

Shaking, Lucy peeked around him.

She scarcely recognized the man in the bed. He bore a resemblance to her imposing father. But he looked so much older. His eyes were sunken and his skin a sickly color. His hair was almost completely gray. He was propped up with pillows. "Captain," he barked in a commanding voice. "There you are at last. Where have you been?"

"How are you feeling, sir?"

"Never mind that. Have Blücher's reinforcements arrived?"

The colonel glanced at Lucy, then back to Captain Stewart. "Someone tell me what the devil is going on. Does Hougoumont still stand? Where are those Prussians?"

Lucy took a step closer.

Colonel Breckenridge's gaze snapped to her. He studied her, and after a long moment, his eyes focused. "Lucy?"

"It's me, Father." Her voice cracked, but she stood straight.

Colonel Breckenridge held out his hands. "Oh, my little Lucy. How you've grown." His face relaxed into the smile of the man she knew. "I've missed you, my darling."

Lucy's fear vanished. She gave the book to Captain Stewart and rushed forward to embrace her father. Tears burst from her eyes, and sobs erupted.

Her father held her as she wept. He patted her back. "There, there, little Lucy."

She pulled back, sitting on the edge of the bed and wiping her eyes with her fingers. "I'm here now, Father. Everything will be all right."

The colonel looked around the room, his expression confused. "Are we at home?"

"No, we're in the military hospital in London. You've been ill, Father."

He scowled, blinking, and then turned his gaze to Captain Stewart. "Captain, you were to deliver a message to Lucy."

"Yes, sir." Captain Stewart stood straight, at attention, holding the Christmas album at his side. "I did deliver it, sir."

"Then why is she here?" He motioned to Lucy. "I expressly ordered you to tell her—"

"I decided to come, Father." Lucy resented the men discussing her as if she weren't in the room. "Captain Stewart came along to make certain I was safe."

Her father's scowl didn't go away.

"I traveled with Mr. Owens," Lucy said. "And the new maid, Meg."

"Owens . . ." Her father nodded, looking away as if pondering." A good soldier. Fought in America under Cornwallis." He looked up, his face surprised, as if seeing the captain for the first time. "Captain Stewart, there you are. Have Blücher's reinforcements arrived?"

"Today is Christmas, Father," Lucy said.

"Oh, it's Christmas." The colonel blinked, looking around the hospital ward. "Are we at home?"

"We're at the hospital in London, Father." Lucy kept her voice cheerful as her worry over her father's mental state grew. "But I brought our Christmas album." She pulled a chair beside the bed so they could both see and opened the book on her father's lap.

Captain Stewart cleared his throat, capturing her attention. "Will you be all right if I leave? I'll be back soon." His words were little more than a whisper.

Lucy nodded. The captain needed to make lodging arrangements for the others in the party.

"Mr. Pennington will be nearby should you need him," he whispered.

She nodded her thanks and settled in to turn the pages and reminisce with her father. "Do you remember this?" she asked. "I was in a nativity play at the church."

"You were so angry that the part of Mary was taken." Her father chuckled, sounding more like his old self.

"I had to be a shepherd," she said, her tone full of mock indignation.

He chuckled again, turning the page to Lucy's childish drawing of a holly garland. "Your mother did love to decorate on Christmas Eve."

"I hardly remember," Lucy admitted. "I'm so glad for this book."

"My memory's a bit spotty at the moment as well," he said.

Lucy squeezed his hand, hoping to reassure him. She turned another page. "This is a drawing you sent from India."

Her father squinted, running his finger over the image as if trying to remember.

She turned the pages, skipping quickly over those that frustrated him and reminiscing about the ones he recognized. She told him about her Christmas journey, describing the mummers' play in Bradstock and the dance in Quentlin Ferry. She told him about Meg and Mr. Matthews and about the Christmas Eve celebration in Stanley.

After a while, her father grew calm, lying back on the pillows. Eventually, he slept.

Lucy stayed beside him, holding his hand and resting her cheek on her other palm.

A gentle hand touched her shoulder, and she lifted her

head. She hadn't realized she'd fallen asleep. It was Captain Stewart. She stood and stepped away from her father's bedside where they could speak without waking him.

"How is he?" Captain Stewart asked.

Lucy was grateful that the man felt such concern for her father. "He's sleeping now. He seemed to remember for a little while, but he got confused and rather agitated. I just . . . How do I help him?"

"I don't know," Captain Stewart said. "But if anyone can figure it out, it's Miss Lucy Breckenridge." He smiled warmly. "Your father needs someone who is gentle and understanding. And you are just the person for the job. He's lucky you're his daughter."

She felt warm at the compliment. "Captain, I'm sorry I was angry last night. I acted very rudely."

"I had no right to keep something like this from you." He took her hand, and the gesture felt natural.

"I know why you did it." She squeezed his fingers.

"If you have a moment," the captain said, "I'd hoped to speak with you." He offered his arm.

Lucy glanced toward her father.

"We'll return before he wakes."

She nodded, taking his arm and walking with him out of the ward to the long hall. "Where did you go? Did you get the others settled?"

"Yes," he said. "I found lodgings close by. And I did a bit of shopping as well." "Oh?"

He gave a secretive smile but didn't explain more. They reached the hospital entrance, and he held the door open, gesturing for her to precede him.

Lucy stepped outside, and her shoulders relaxed. London's air was cold, and it was far from fresh, but it was much better than the hospital's smell of sickness and medicine. She could not let her father stay in that place.

They descended the stairs and strolled along the walkway in front of the hospital. When they came to a bench near the road, Captain Stewart motioned for her to sit. He sat beside her, pulled a wrapped parcel from inside his coat, and presented it to her.

"What is this?" she asked.

"A Christmas gift, of course."

She pulled off the wrapping, revealing a leather-bound album filled with blank pages.

"To record your own Christmases," he said. "The ones you celebrate just how you wish for you and your father." He took her hand. "And hopefully . . . I might be included as well?"

She looked up at him. What was he trying to say? Did he want to be invited to her future Christmas parties? Or could his words mean more? Seeing the look in his eyes, her nerves started to tingle.

"I know we've been acquainted for only a short time," he said. "But knowing you longer will not change how I feel." He rested his arm on the back of the bench and turned fully toward her. "I am in love with you, Miss Lucy Breckenridge. And nothing would make me happier than if you will consent to be my wife."

Lucy looked into the captain's eyes, seeing in them hope and such adoration that it took her breath away. She smiled, feeling as if the world was filled with joy. Her heart expanded until she thought it might burst. But a realization came down cold and dismal, like a pile of snow falling from a branch, squashing the few seconds of bliss. "I can't." She swallowed past the lump in her throat and looked down at the book in her lap. "I'm so sorry, Captain. My father needs me. I can't leave him."

Captain Stewart touched beneath her chin, lifting her

face. "I would never ask that of you. If you are agreeable to it, we can live together at Pinnock Hill." His hand settled on her shoulder. "I know you are fully capable of caring for him. And you have an able housekeeper to assist. Matthews and I know the colonel well. We can help." He lifted her hand to his lips. "Please say you will."

Her heart expanded again, and this time there was nothing to keep it from growing until it ached with utter happiness. "I would like that very much, Captain."

"James," he said. "You should call me James." He slid his hand behind her neck, pulling her gently forward. When their lips met, Lucy's fears were gone. She felt calm and cared for, and she knew that with James by her side, she could face anything. She poured her heart into the kiss, wanting him to feel the same, to understand that she trusted him and that, in his arms, she knew she was safe.

The sounds of cheering made her pull away. Mr. Owens, Meg, and Mr. Matthews applauded from the carriage that stood at the side of the road. Lucy blushed from the top of her head to the tips of her toes.

Captain Stewart stood, grinning. "There is one more thing." He went to the carriage and came back with a bundle of fur tied with a red ribbon.

"A puppy!" Lucy clapped her hands. "Oh, he is perfect."

She pulled the puppy into her arms, burying her face in its fur. The puppy licked her face and gave a wide puppy yawn. Lucy thought she couldn't be happier. She remembered his words days earlier. *I suppose that's what we all want, a home and a family and a dog.* James offered her all three.

"Thank you, Cap—James. I absolutely love him."

He watched her with the soft look that made her insides melt. "You love *him*?" He gave a teasing smile. "I rather hoped I might warrant a similar honor."

Lucy stood, holding the puppy close against her chest. "I do love you, Captain James Stewart. Almost more than my heart can bear."

He wrapped his arms around both Lucy and the puppy, leaning close to whisper, "Happy Christmas, Lucy. And we will have many more to come. I promise."

Jennifer Moore is a passionate reader and writer of all things romance due to the need to balance the rest of her world that includes a perpetually traveling husband and four active sons, who create heaps of laundry that is anything but romantic. She suffers from an unhealthy addiction to 18th- and 19th-century military history and literature. Jennifer has a B.A. in linguistics from the University of Utah and is a Guitar Hero champion. She lives in northern Utah with her family, but most of the time wishes she was on board a frigate during the Age of Sail.

You can learn more about her at: AuthorJMoore.com

www.ingramcontent.com/pod-product-compliance
Lightning Source LLC
LaVergne TN
LVHW021800060526
838201LV00058B/3176